# the
# **REAL**
## *thing*

# MORE BOOKS BY MELISSA FOSTER

## LOVE IN BLOOM ROMANCE SERIES

### SNOW SISTERS

*Sisters in Love*
*Sisters in Bloom*
*Sisters in White*

### THE BRADENS

*Lovers at Heart*
*Destined for Love*
*Friendship on Fire*
*Sea of Love*
*Bursting with Love*
*Hearts at Play*
*Taken by Love*
*Fated for Love*
*Romancing My Love*
*Flirting with Love*
*Dreaming of Love*
*Crashing into Love*
*Healed by Love*
*Surrender My Love*
*River of Love*
*Crushing on Love*
*Whisper of Love*
*Thrill of Love*

### BRADEN NOVELLAS

*Promise My Love*

*Our New Love*
*Daring Her Love*
*Story of Love*

### THE REMINGTONS

*Game of Love*
*Stroke of Love*
*Flames of Love*
*Slope of Love*
*Read, Write, Love*
*Touched by Love*

### SEASIDE SUMMERS

*Seaside Dreams*
*Seaside Hearts*
*Seaside Sunsets*
*Seaside Secrets*
*Seaside Nights*
*Seaside Embrace*
*Seaside Lovers*
*Seaside Whispers*

### THE RYDERS

*Seized by Love*
*Claimed by Love*
*Chased by Love*
*Rescued by Love*
*Swept into Love*

# PRAISE FOR MELISSA FOSTER

"You can always rely on Melissa Foster to deliver a story that's fresh, emotional, and entertaining. Make sure you have all night, because once you start you won't want to stop reading. Every book's a winner!"
—Brenda Novak, *New York Times* bestselling author

"What sets Melissa Foster apart are her compelling characters who you care about . . . desperately. I dare you to read the first chapter and not be hooked."
—M. J. Rose, *New York Times* bestselling author

"With her wonderful characters and resonating emotions, Melissa Foster is a must-read author!"
—Julie Kenner, *New York Times* bestselling author

"Melissa Foster is synonymous with sexy, swoony, heartfelt romance!"
—Lauren Blakely, *New York Times* bestselling author

"I'm highly addicted to her stories and still want to kick my own behind for taking so long to finally read her."
—The Power of Three Readers

"The author's writing was amazing, and to be completely honest here, to get me to read a subgenre I would not normally touch with a barge pole shows that her writing can make even the pickiest reader fall in love with her books—you just have to give them a chance."
—Cara's Book Boudoir

"Melissa creates quite a palette of feelings for the reader to experience all through the novel."
—Cruising Susan

# SEXY STAND-ALONE ROMANCE

*Tru Blue*
*Truly, Madly, Whiskey*

# BILLIONAIRES AFTER DARK SERIES

Wild Boys After Dark

*Logan*
*Heath*
*Jackson*
*Cooper*

Bad Boys After Dark

*Mick*
*Dylan*
*Carson*
*Brett*

# HARBORSIDE NIGHTS SERIES

Includes characters from Love in Bloom Series

*Catching Cassidy*
*Discovering Delilah*
*Tempting Tristan*

# STAND-ALONE NOVELS

*Chasing Amanda* (mystery/suspense)
*Come Back to Me* (mystery/suspense)
*Have No Shame* (historical fiction/romance)
*Love, Lies & Mystery* (three-book bundle)
*Megan's Way* (literary fiction)
*Traces of Kara* (psychological thriller)
*Where Petals Fall* (suspense)

# the
# REAL
## thing

# MELISSA
# FOSTER

Montlake
Romance

Published by Montlake Romance, Seattle

www.apub.com

Amazon, the Amazon logo, and Montlake Romance are trademarks of Amazon.com, Inc., or its affiliates.

ISBN-13: 9781542045810
ISBN-10: 1542045819

Cover design by Letitia Hasser

Printed in the United States of America

*For my readers.*

# CHAPTER ONE

WILLOW DALTON SPED into the parking lot of Landry's Resort with six minutes to spare, telling herself it didn't matter if she was late. She'd just turn up the charm, hand Patrick Carter one of her famous Sweetie Pie Bakery's Loverboys—a delicious and colorful cross between an éclair and a cupcake—and he'd remember why he'd sought her out to cater desserts for the Lake George Boating Club's annual meeting in the first place.

At least she hoped he would.

She couldn't afford to blow this job. It was her ticket to expanding her bakery's catering business from her small hometown of Sweetwater, New York, to the outlying areas. Lake George was almost two hours away, but catering jobs like this could double her income. She dreamed of not only expanding the catering side of her business but at some point making Sweetie Pie Bakery into more of a café and bookstore. The job also paid twice as much as her bakery would have earned over the weekend, and she needed every penny, since one of her ovens was on its last leg.

Stuffing her keys in her purse, she took a quick peek in the rearview mirror. *Ugh.* Her blond hair was tousled, and the lipstick she'd put on so carefully this morning had been talked off as she'd hurried customers out the door so she could close up shop and get on the road. With no time to primp, she scooted out of the car, noticing a smudge of black near the hem of her dress. Her company van had gotten a flat, and she must have brushed against the tire. She'd been forced to drive Chloe, the refurbished '66 VW Beetle her father had given her when she'd graduated from high school.

She swiped at the stain, and the residue spread. *Frigging perfect.*

She blew a lock of hair from in front of her eyes with a practiced upward tilt of her lower lip and a quick, hard breath and reached into the backseat for the box of Loverboys she'd brought for Mr. Carter. Her stomach lurched at the sight of blue frosting and gobs of thick custard clinging to the seat and floor.

"No, no, no." She snatched the box from the floor, acutely aware of the seconds ticking by. The pastries tumbled out in jagged chunks and a shower of crumbs. Groaning, she plunked the box down on the backseat, closed her eyes, and inhaled a deep, calming breath. *You've got this, Willow.*

Her inner realist laughed at her.

Even though her inner realist had gotten her through too many challenges to count, right now she hated that bitch. Willow lifted her chin, squared her shoulders, and smoothed her dress. *To hell with inner calm.* She needed a box of cupcakes and a stiff drink. Or maybe a man. A man covered in frosting *and* a stiff drink just might take the edge off. She hurried toward the resort to prove just how awesome she was.

She pushed the fancy glass doors open, silently practicing her greeting, and took her place in line at the registration desk, glad for a moment to breathe. The resort reeked of money, from the rich hardwood floors to the elaborate two-story arched windows along the back wall overlooking the water. Leather sofas and intricately carved armchairs created a nook opposite the reception desk. If only she could take a minute to sit in one of the plush seats and calm down. She fidgeted with the knot on the belt tied around the waist of her simple lavender dress. Maybe she should have taken her sister Bridgette's advice and worn a fancier outfit. She was a world away from Sweetwater, where she wore heels only under duress.

*Just another hurdle. I've got this.*

"Willow."

She whipped her head to the side at the sound of Zane Walker's deep voice, shocked to see his piercing dark eyes gazing hungrily down at her. Zane was her older brother's best friend turned A-list actor, and he had a sluttier reputation than a prostitute.

He was also the guy who'd taken her virginity. Okay, he hadn't *taken* it.

She had *given* it to him.

Or rather, to save her the embarrassment of being an inexperienced virgin, he'd done her the *favor* of being her first before she'd gone away to college. She'd wanted her first time to be with someone she cared about. Her legs buckled with the memory of their one perfect night down by the creek, and her heart sank as she recalled how she'd broken her own carefully thought-out rules and had gone off to college with romanticized ideas in her head about them. What followed had been painful and embarrassing.

This was not good. Not good at all. She couldn't afford to get any more flustered. Forcing her eyes away from the sexy scruff she definitely *did not* want to touch, she snapped, "What are you doing here?"

He wrapped his hand around her arm with a devilish grin on his perfectly plump lips and pulled her from the line. His dark hair had just-rolled-out-of-bed sexiness going on, and over a gray T-shirt he wore the leather jacket she'd given him for Christmas two years ago. She and Zane had a complicated relationship that *didn't* include sex beyond their one night more than a decade ago—a complicated relationship that had been put on hold for several months after Willow's heartbreaking realization during her first semester of college. But that didn't stop him from propositioning her over text as often as he was bored. If she had a penny for every time a text rolled in at 3:00 a.m. that read something like, *Filming at [wherever]; come see me*, she'd be rich. She always sent her standard reply—*Not a chance*. Although he never let it go at that. He wanted to know what she was doing that could possibly be better than a night with him. She often wondered what he thought of her honest answers, which varied from watching her favorite movie—*The Notebook*—to thinking up new recipes.

"Let go. I have a meeting, and I'm already late. Why are you here? Are you filming?" She wrenched her arm free, looking around for his ever-present entourage of beautiful women and photographers. All the women in Sweetwater had their panties in a bunch over his newest movie, which was being filmed there next week. Soon, their quiet little town would turn into a bustling Zane Hotter-Than-Hell Walker slutfest.

"Chill out, Willow," he said, way too calmly.

"Chill out?" She rolled her eyes. "I'm seriously late for a huge meeting. I can't play your games, Zane."

She stormed back to her place in line, and he dragged her away again.

"Zane! What is wrong with you? Stop it."

"Wills, listen to me." He lowered his chin, narrowed his eyes, and flashed another wicked smile. His signature look.

Hell if it didn't make her insides melt every damn time. Zane was messing with her again. It was his *thing*. He screwed with women without an ounce of regret, and according to the tabloids, he did it often.

She exhaled loudly, shaking her head, and laughed, because on top of the flirtatious texts, they'd maintained a quirky friendship. "You are quite possibly the biggest pain in the ass I have ever met, and if I lose this job, I swear you're going to pay me for it." She looked over her shoulder at the line, which was moving quickly.

"I already am," he said in a low voice.

"Zane, I'm serious. I've got—" She glanced at the line again and then processed what he'd said. "Wait. What?"

"Can we talk outside? You're a little high-strung today."

"A little *high-strung*?" She hurried to keep up as he dragged her out the front doors and down the steps. "Zane. Stop!"

He tugged her to the grass beside the resort. For a brief second, the unusually cool summer breeze, the smell of the water, and the gorgeous man standing before her, looking at her like he wasn't messing with her at all but had come there to see her, left her flustered. This was why she usually tried to keep her distance. The man bathed in testosterone and reeked of sex appeal, making it hard to stay annoyed at him, and the last thing she needed was to get caught up again in some sort of one-sided love affair.

"Wills, there is no job."

She stepped closer. "What did you just say? I swear, Zane, if this is one of your games, I will maim you for life."

He moved his hands in front of the enticing package between his legs. She knew just how talented that part of his body was. *Ugh.* She could *not* go there.

"Promise you won't kick me?"

"That depends." She crossed her arms and glared at him.

He held up his hands in surrender, and a veil of tenderness started in his eyes and slid all the way down to the innocent smile forming on his lips. It was too easy to become transfixed by his ability to morph into anything he wanted her to see in the blink of an eye.

"This is where I proposed to you," he said sincerely. "More specifically, right over there in that gazebo by the water."

"I don't know what kind of drugs you've gotten into, but I'm out of here. I don't have time for this." She turned to leave.

"I need you, Wills. This time for real."

ZANE WAS GOING straight to hell for even thinking about putting Willow in this position. But he needed her. And she was storming away, her long blond waves bouncing against her back with every irritated step. Her rounded hips swayed with determination and confidence no actress could come close to. She even made that simple belted dress look sexy as sin, as if it were a designer piece made just for her. She'd probably gotten it on sale at Misty's, the local dress shop in their home-town. Willow was the real deal. A smart, funny, no-bullshit, no-frills woman with real curves to prove it. She lived in cutoffs and jeans and ate cupcakes and éclairs like models downed weight-loss pills. And she was the only woman on earth Zane trusted—or wanted—enough to ask for help.

*Goddamn it.* Why had he thought this was going to be easy? Willow was never easy. Even all those years ago, when he'd gone back to Sweetwater for a visit and she'd asked him to help her lose her virginity, she'd been controlling. He'd been sure she was fucking with him or that it was some kind of test. Her older brother, Ben Dalton, was his best friend. He'd spent more time at their house than he had at his own, and he'd had a major crush on Willow for years. She had practically begged him to help her, saying she'd thought it all out and she didn't want to go to college as an inexperienced virgin. She had a list of rules and had planned every detail. Where, when, how—all the way up to when he was supposed to let her walk home alone so she could *process* what they'd done, and then they'd move on like nothing had happened. It was a good plan. A reasonable plan, considering what was at stake. And God knew he'd tried to abide by her rules. But she'd felt too good, been too sweet and trusting, not to get completely swept up in her.

"Please, Wills," he called after her.

Willow stopped abruptly. Her head tipped forward, her shoulders dropping a smidge as she turned, her hair curtaining one eye. "Zane, just tell me what you've done."

He went to her and reached for her hand, feeling shittier than he'd thought he would. "There is no baking gig. I set all this up to get you here." Anger flared in her eyes. He continued explaining as fast as he could. "Wills, there's this focus group for my new film, and they're worried my reputation will hurt the movie. That fans won't buy me as a romantic hero."

She scoffed. "Smart fans."

"Come on. I need your help."

"What am I supposed to do? Write a letter to the public telling them Zane Walker isn't a self-centered playboy? Sorry, not your girl."

She took a step away, and he hauled her against him. Her hands landed on his chest, which felt *amazing*, and even with darts shooting from her jade-green eyes with deathly precision, she was still the most beautiful, alluring woman he'd ever known.

"No," she seethed. "Whatever it is. *No.*"

"Come on. Just hear me out."

Her lips formed a tight line.

"I need a . . ." He could hardly believe what he was about to say. "A fake fiancée."

"A *fake fiancée*? What does that mean?"

"We'll pretend to be engaged so everyone thinks I'm a stand-up guy."

A disgusted look washed over her face. "No."

"You owe me, Wills." *Oh shit. Why did I say that?*

Her jaw dropped open. "Hell no, you did *not* just say that." She thrust a finger into his chest. "First off, it wasn't a *hardship* for you to"—she lowered her voice and poked him in the chest again—"sleep with me. Second, you've turned into an arrogant, self-centered player. And third!" She poked him harder. "I have a *life.*"

She stormed toward the parking lot with Zane on her heels.

"I'm sorry. I didn't mean it like that. I know you have a life. It was anything *but* a hardship. But you're the only one who can do this."

"No." She dug her keys from her purse. "You know how much money I've already lost in inventory and sales for this supposed event?" She spun around, nearly knocking him over. "Who did you get to play the part of Patrick Carter? How many people know I was supposed to be your . . . *God.* I can't even say it. You're such a jerk."

"Patch." Patch Carver was Zane's personal assistant. Willow had met him a few years ago when they'd passed through Sweetwater after filming. "He's the only one who knows what the plan is."

"Patch? I'm going to slaughter that tattooed ass—"

"It's my fault," he interrupted. "I told him I'd fire him if he didn't do it. He fought me for a week before finally agreeing."

"Well, he just moved right out of being a solid, reliable glazed doughnut and into being bread pudding." She spoke in a mocking voice. "Cut me up and cover me with goo. I'll be whatever you want me to be. Weak. Pathetic . . ."

"What are you talking about?"

"Nothing," she grumbled, and stopped beside her car.

"You brought Chloe?" He knew she didn't like to put extra miles on Chloe. When her father had given her the car, she'd said she loved it too much to take it to college, where *anything could happen to it.*

"Yes, I brought Chloe. My van had a flat, and I *thought* I had a big meeting that would finally put Sweetie Pie Bakery on the map."

Her eyes rolled over his face, and guilt sliced into him. He put his hand on the car door so she couldn't open it. "Wait. I can help you get Sweetie Pie on the map, and you can help me win over the public."

"Uh-huh. How? Cater our *fake* wedding?" She shook her head. "Go get some Hollywood actress to play your part. Can't you just ask your costar? Remi Divine? Costars hook up all the time, from what I hear. I've got to go."

He tugged her against him again, knowing he shouldn't. Knowing she might knee him in the junk. But he was desperate, and he *loved* the way she felt. "I don't want to ask Remi Divine. I want *you*. I'll make sure you cater the set."

Her brows knitted, as if she was considering it.

"Think about it, Willow. You'll be *my* fiancée. You and your bakery's name will be all over the tabloids. You'll gain more exposure than you can handle."

"As your *fake* fiancée," she said skeptically.

"Yes." He tightened his hold on her. *"Please."*

She huffed, but her gaze softened. "Zane, nobody who knows me will believe this."

He wrapped one arm around her waist, holding her close as his other hand slid beneath her hair, and he kneaded the back of her shoulder the way he knew she loved. "I've got this, Wills. I'd never leave you hanging, feeling unprepared, like you didn't know what your next move should be." He felt the tension drain from her body, and just as quickly, as if she'd noticed her guard slipping, she stepped back, putting distance between them again.

"I can't just leave my bakery closed this weekend. I don't make millions on movies, Zane. I need my income."

"Patch already wired the money you thought you were earning for the event into your account."

She shook her head.

He stepped close again. "Don't look at me like I've crossed some imaginary line. We're *very* good at crossing lines, remember?" That earned him the sweet, feathery laugh he loved so much, and he knew he almost had her. "Cross this line with me, Willow."

"I'm supposed to just give up my life for you to save your rep? For how long?"

"Until the week after we're done shooting in Sweetwater. Then we can stage a breakup, and I'll drag my broken heart back to California to finish filming. The tabloids will cover it, and you can go back to your life. Only better, because everyone will know who you are."

"This is crazy. What about my family?"

"We've been secretly meeting for months. We didn't want to tell them because we weren't sure it would last."

"You've actually put thought into this. Or *Patch* did."

"Give me some credit. I've got our whole backstory figured out. All we need is this weekend together." He brushed his scruff along her cheek and whispered, "Please? For old times' sake?"

"God, I hate you right now." She huffed out another, slightly less frustrated breath. "I have to be back tomorrow night to get ready for Louie's birthday party on Sunday." Louie was her sister Bridgette's almost five-year-old son.

"Done. We'll go back tomorrow."

Confusion riddled her brow. "You're coming with me?"

"Of course. We're engaged, remember?"

"I don't know, Zane. You're asking a lot of me." She crossed her arms again.

"I know I am. But, Wills, who do you text when you need advice from someone other than family? Who do you text when you have a bad breakup or want to bitch about needing a foot rub after a particularly long week?"

Their lives were threaded with texts giving each other as much support as they did torment. Over the years she'd turned to him for advice about everything, from risking her savings to open her bakery to things that annoyed the shit out of him, like which slinky dress she should wear on dates. He always chose the one that covered the most skin. Their relationship had been strained for months after they'd slept together, but he'd never been able to stay away from Willow. She was his voice of reason, his sounding board, his friend, despite the annoyance shooting from her eyes at the moment.

"I have no ring," she snapped. "You're a rich actor. I would need a ring to pull this off."

He reached into his jacket pocket, pulled out a Tiffany's jewelry box, and flipped the top open. Willow's jaw dropped again, and then her luscious lips curved into a smile.

"A princess cut?" she said breathlessly. "Aw, Zane. You do have a heart. You remembered I loved them?"

*Princess cut?* "Uh, yeah. Of course."

Her mouth formed a pin-straight line again. "Patch got this, didn't he?"

He shrugged. "I was filming."

"Jesus, Zane." She pushed away.

"Give me a break, Willow. I'm here, aren't I? I didn't send Patch. It's a rented ring, anyway. It's not like I sent him out to get you a *real* engagement ring."

She eyed the diamond.

"It's a real diamond. You know what I mean." Willow had a generous soul, and as he watched her mulling over his situation, he saw her resolve softening. He remembered how conflicted he'd been about giving in to her request all those years ago, and he remembered why he'd done it. He closed the distance between them, making a concerted effort not to *act*, not to be the cocky guy his fans knew him to be, but to find the person he'd been all those years ago. If he could show her *that* Zane, the Zane she'd trusted, then she'd remember, too.

"Wills, there was a time when I was the only person you trusted to do you a favor. I'm asking the same of you."

She looked at him for a long moment.

"Please? I need you, Willow."

"God, Zane." The defeated whisper cut him to his core. "You'll make sure I cater during some of the filming?" she asked skeptically.

"Yes." *Please do this for me, Wills.*

"And it's only for—"

"Two weeks. A week when we go back to Sweetwater to get everyone used to the idea, then a week of filming. After that you can publicly break up with me and we'll each go back to our lives. But you can't tell anyone this is a fake arrangement."

"I must be crazy, but . . . *fine*. But you're helping me clean out Chloe."

He hauled her into his arms again. "Of course. Anything. Thank you so much. You're the best. For a minute there I thought you'd turn me down."

"Who was your fallback girl? Your backup plan?" She set her hand on her hip, glaring at him again.

"You didn't have a backup plan that summer. I didn't think I needed one now." He draped an arm around her waist. "Let's get your stuff and put it in our room, and I'll fill you in on our whirlwind relationship."

"*Our* room? No. No way."

He leaned in closer and lowered his voice. "We're engaged. Engaged couples share rooms. Besides, you've got nothing I haven't seen before." He dropped his hand and patted her ass.

She grabbed his crotch and squeezed.

"Ow. *Fuck*, Willow."

She eased her grip, but the narrowing of her eyes told him she thought she was making the rules again. "This is *pretend*, remember? Keep your hands off me and I will allow your man parts to go unharmed."

Sweet, curvy, sass-mouthed Willow was sexy as hell. But pissed-off, demanding, in-control Willow? *Hot. As. Fuck.*

She tore her hand away with a disgusted look on her face. "Oh my God! I cannot believe that got you hard."

He chuckled, unable to stop the grin tugging at his lips, and pulled her against his side. "There's something about a hot blonde with her hand on my dick." She rolled her eyes and he said, "There's something about *you*, Wills. There always has been."

"Yeah." She laughed. "I'm the only woman on earth who *doesn't* want you. Deal with it."

*Oh, I plan on it.*

# CHAPTER TWO

"YOU'RE SLEEPING ON the couch," Willow said for the fifth time in as many minutes as she and Zane left their suite. He was busy texting, and she wasn't sure he was even listening anymore. He used to be such a great listener. When they were younger, he'd never acted like he was above her, despite the fact that he was the star quarterback, lead pitcher, and eventually the prom king, and she was two years behind and as awkward as a foal on new legs.

"Are you listening to me?" she asked as they walked down the hall.

"Yes. I just got confirmation. You're catering breakfasts for the set. Cool?"

"Yes, perfect. But did you hear what I said?"

She had almost backed out of their deal twice since she'd accepted. First when she'd seen the king-size bed, which really drove home their situation, and again when Zane had whipped off his shirt to change and her sex-starved body had buzzed to life. She was still a little nervous about the whole thing, mostly due to that second issue, but she felt a certain obligation to help him. Regardless of how arrogant he was, she'd never forget how tender he'd been with her when she'd given her almost-eighteen-year-old self over to him, *and* he was a true friend, even if they had a weird friendship. The truth was, even if he hadn't done her that favor before college, she would have agreed to his plan. She liked him despite his insatiable appetite for women. He was everything she loved in a person and more. He was confident and funny, direct and thoughtful, and honest when it counted. *Painfully* honest. The exposure for Sweetie Pie Bakery was just the icing on the fake-fiancée cake. What a difference national exposure could make.

Zane shoved his phone in his pocket. "Yes. *Sleeping on the couch.* Got it. But you can't blame a guy for trying."

She laid her best damn-right-I-can stare on him and pushed the button for the elevator.

"Fine. I'll behave. Jesus, Wills, you're never this uptight when I visit."

"You mean that five minutes twice a year?" Willow remembered how happy he'd been when he'd finally left town to pursue his dream of being an actor. He'd been bursting at the seams for a *bigger* life. But her "five minutes" comment wasn't really fair. He never missed Ben's birthday, and he almost always made it back for a few days over the holidays, even though his parents had moved to Florida right after he'd graduated from high school and left town. He'd been back a few other times when he was filming nearby. Even though she rarely saw him, their texts—and the fact that he was her first real love, even if he didn't know it—had kept him in the forefront of her mind. Unfortunately, it also kept her heartbreak pretty close to the surface, no matter how deep she tried to bury it.

The elevator arrived, and they stepped inside. Zane brushed his hard chest against her as he pushed the button, and her temperature spiked. She felt her cheeks burn, and he smirked. *Asshat.*

"I hear they have great couples' massages." He waggled his brows.

"No."

"Come on, Wills. We're supposed to be a couple."

"A *fake* couple." She stared at the lights counting down the floors to avoid his convincing gaze.

Zane stepped in front of her, blocking her view of the numbers. If *alpha male* had a scent, it would smell like Zane Walker, rugged and musky, with an underlying hint of *come-hither* and a dash of panty-melting lust.

"We need everyone to buy this," he said smoothly. "That means doing things couples would do."

"Like you know the first thing about that?" She didn't know why she was being so snarky. It wasn't like he knew how hurt she'd been all those years ago when she'd romanticized their tryst—breaking her own stupid rules—and he'd gone on living his life. Plus, he hadn't exactly forced her to agree to take part in this ruse.

His lips tipped up in a sinful grin. "I know all the best parts, and you know the rest. We're a team. So when I do this"—he ran his hand lightly up her arm, squeezing her shoulder just hard enough to send shivers down her spine—"that's *exactly* the reaction they need to see."

She shifted her gaze away, pissed off at her stupid female hormones. Lifting her chin, she said, "We don't have time for massages. I told you, we're cleaning Chloe. It's your fault she's a mess in the first place."

Little did he know she'd named the ruined pastries after him. She often likened people to the pastries they reminded her of, or the ones they ate. Even though she rued the aftermath of their tryst, the pastries were as sumptuous and surprising as Zane had been that night. They were the perfect mix of pleasurable, memorable, and guilt inducing. *Loverboys.* The name perfectly suited both the pastries and the player Zane had become.

"Right, the pastries," he said. "I can get the car detailed while we go enjoy ourselves. Why waste our time?"

"I'm not letting a stranger touch my car when we're perfectly capable of cleaning it. Besides, you are *not* going to have someone else do your dirty work."

When they were kids, he and Ben used to wash the neighbors' cars, mow lawns, help with gardens. They did anything they could to earn a few bucks. But she knew there were times Zane hadn't charged some of the families because they didn't have much money, or for other similar reasons. She wondered what happened inside a person's head to flick the switch from taking pride in doing things himself to hiring out. What else did he hire out?

*Probably every single thing besides acting, friendship, and sex.*

The elevator doors opened, and he gave a leggy blonde who was waiting for the elevator a long, hungry once-over.

"Are you kidding me?" Willow pushed past him and stormed toward the concierge.

"What?"

She glared at him. "*Fiancés* don't leer at other women. This is not going to work, Zane. You don't have it in you." She turned away, surprised when he approached the concierge and requested cleaning supplies.

He stood with his back to her, running a hand through his hair. It was a nervous habit he'd had since he was a kid. He turned with a serious expression pulling his brows into a deep V. "You're right. I'm sorry. I'll do better."

"Right." *Not in this lifetime.*

"I'm an actor, Willow. I've been doing this shit forever. There's no role I can't nail."

One of the hotel staff brought the cleaning supplies, and Zane took them from her and stepped closer to Willow. His gaze softened, and he gently stroked her arm. "That was rude and tacky, and I'm truly sorry. I respect you, Wills, and the last thing I want to do is to make you feel uncomfortable. Give me another chance, and I promise you won't be disappointed."

She'd expected him to smirk or to make a sexual remark, but the sincerity in his voice and the way he was looking at her, like he felt guilty and hopeful at once, made her feel bad for reacting so sharply. Being in a relationship was new for him, too, even if it was fake.

"It's okay." They headed out of the resort. As they crossed the parking lot, his eyes were downcast, and he wore a pained expression. Silently chiding herself for being a bitch, she said, "I'm sorry for overreacting."

He met her gaze and tilted his head like a puppy waiting for a snack, melting her resolve a little more. And then those utterly kissable lips quirked up, and he said, "Told you I could nail it."

"*Ugh!* You really *are* a jerk, you know that?" She stalked away.

"I think you mean a *kick-ass* actor," he called after her.

IT WAS ALMOST as fun to see Willow's reactions in person as it was to check out her sweet curves as she bent down to retrieve her keys, which she'd dropped as she lectured him about what an ass he was being. She was the only woman who could keep up with his remarks. Her reactions were funny over text, but they had an even more powerful effect in person.

"I still can't believe you drove Chloe," he said as she opened the door to her VW Beetle.

She tore a few paper towels from the roll and handed the rest to him. "I *thought* I had an important meeting to attend. Don't just stand there. You're helping me. This is *your* fault."

"Helping you do what, exactly?"

She waved toward the backseat, and he peered in through the window.

"Christ, Wills. What'd you do, have a food fight in the backseat?"

She ducked into the car, and he couldn't help but take another long gawk at her perfect rear end. And it *was* perfect. Heart shaped and firm yet squeezable, unlike most of the rail-thin women he knew.

"Yeah, that's exactly what I did while I was driving a million miles per hour to get here on time. I thought, 'Oh, what the hell. Let me ruin my most loved possession in the whole world.'"

*Whoosh*—another gust of guilt blew through him.

She glanced over her shoulder with an annoyed expression. "Stop looking at my butt and get in here."

"Sorry," he mumbled, and climbed into the back from the passenger's side. "Jesus, it looks like someone jizzed all over your seat."

"Do you ever *not* think of sex?"

He flashed a deadpan look, which she ignored. He reached over the mangled box and grabbed her hand. "Wills, seriously, I'm sorry. I know how much this car means to you." The sadness in her eyes got to him. "On the plus side . . ." He dipped his finger into what looked like custard and sucked it off. "You're still a hell of a baker."

She laughed. "Did you have any doubt?"

"No, but really . . ." He scooped some of the blue frosting that was smeared over the inside of the box onto his finger and held it out toward her. "Taste."

Rolling her eyes, she grabbed the spray cleaner from behind her and applied it to the carpet. She glanced at the sweet treat on his finger, then went to work scrubbing the offending stain. The buttons on her dress stretched to their limits over her full breasts, revealing a large amount of smooth, tanned cleavage. Her breasts swayed with her effort, and he forced his gaze up to her face, which was equally gorgeous. Even as a teenager she'd hated being so well endowed, and she'd gone to great lengths to hide her assets. Although like today, nothing could hide those beauties. They were as appealing as the rest of her.

"Come on, Wills. You know it's your favorite." He wiggled his finger, and when she didn't take the bait, he climbed across the seat, his broad shoulders knocking against the seats, earning one of her killer smiles. Man, he'd missed seeing her smile. He'd even missed those damn eye rolls she was passing out like candy. He reached around her shoulder, drawing her closer. Her eyes darkened, and his pulse kicked up. She smelled just like she had as a teenager, like her mother's homemade lilac lotion. The familiar scent brought a rush of memories, rendering him momentarily numb. He could still feel her silky skin beneath him, the frantic beat of her heart against his chest as he pushed inside her, and he remembered the fear and trust he'd seen warring in her eyes. Swallowing hard against the memories, he could do little more than watch as she lowered her mouth over his finger and sucked the icing off.

*Fuuuck.*

Licking her lips with a seductive glint in her eyes, she said, "Mm. You're right, Z. You always have been my favorite flavor."

*Z*, that's what she'd called him that night by the creek. She'd whispered it breathlessly so many times he'd heard it in his midnight fantasies for weeks—*months? Years?*

"Willow." The heated whisper rushed out before he could stop it, and the lustful look in her eyes brought him closer. He closed his eyes as his mouth came down over hers—and she pulled away. His downward motion continued, and he lost his balance, catching himself with his palm in a glob of custard. "What the hell?"

She lifted a thinly manicured brow. "Just a kick-ass *actress* playing a role."

# CHAPTER THREE

AFTER WILLOW AND Zane cleaned her car, they took a walk down by the marina to discuss the elaborate backstory Zane had concocted for them. He'd just finished telling her that they'd supposedly been hooking up on the sly for months.

"Hooking up?" Boy, did he need lessons in coupledom. "Zane, couples that are serious about each other don't *hook up*. They get together, or sneak away, or . . . I don't know, but they definitely don't hook up."

"Good point. So, we've *gotten together* at least twice a month."

"I have a bad feeling about this. I tell Bridgette everything. Why would I keep this from her?" Her youngest sister had lost her husband to a tragic car accident shortly after Louie was born, and she owned a flower shop that adjoined Willow's bakery. Bridgette almost always knew where Willow was and why she was out of town. "And what about Talia? She's always coming to the bakery to grade papers. She knows why I leave town and when I do, too." Talia was her eldest, and most reserved, sibling. She worked as a professor at a nearby college, and although they weren't as close as Willow and Bridgette, they were close enough to make his story not quite so believable.

A breeze swept off the water and blew a lock of hair in front of her eyes. Zane tucked it behind her ear, like a real boyfriend—*fiancé*—might, and said, "Because what we have is private. Remember the weekend you told your family you were going to DC for the baking convention?"

"You mean the weekend I actually drove to DC and *attended* the convention?" Where on earth was he going with this, and how did he remember she'd gone to a convention in DC? That was months ago.

His eyes warmed. "Wills, you don't have to pretend with me. I remember that weekend like it was yesterday. We spent all afternoon holding hands and sneaking kisses along the streets of DC. We visited so many museums you said you felt like you should apply to be a contestant on *Jeopardy!*" He laughed as if he were lost in the memory. "We ate lunch on the lawn by the Washington Monument and made wishes with nickels in the Reflecting Pool because we were out of pennies. I told you our wishes would come true five times over, and, baby . . ." He lowered his voice. "Don't you remember how long we lay on the grass kissing? You said you wished we could lie there all day."

"I . . ." She was too caught in the fantasy to respond.

"I *know* you remember when you insisted we climb onto Lincoln's lap and take a selfie." His gaze, and his tone, were so earnest she *wanted* to remember it. "I have the picture hanging on the wall in my bedroom. Of course you know that, because we've spent so many steamy nights there. It sounds silly, but I still get sad every time I think of how you cried at the National World War II Memorial."

He pulled her closer, and she could almost remember the event that had never taken place.

"It's one of the reasons I fell so hard for you. You have such a big heart, babe." He cupped her face with his big, warm hand, moving his thumb lovingly over her cheek. "We forgot to eat, and we ended up having dinner at around nine that night at that little café. Remember? We ate by candlelight and shared an entrée because you said you were too happy to eat. But later that night, in the penthouse of the Marriott, we ordered dessert and . . ." He brushed his lips over hers, and she was too lost in him to react. "Well, what we did with the whipped cream was nothing short of sinful."

She blinked several times, reveling in the romantic rendezvous he described. She smiled, picturing all the things he'd just shared.

*Wait. What?*

*No.* He was doing it again, playing her for a fool.

*Ugh.* She pushed from his arms. "What was that? A role you've played or something?"

His eyes coasted over the grass, like he was coming out of a fog. He raked his hand through his hair and blew out a breath. "Uh. No, actually. Not a role."

"Oh." Now she felt a little lost, too. "I didn't think you knew what romance was."

He cleared his throat. "Right, I . . . um . . ."

They walked in silence for a few minutes, each lost in their own thoughts. Her mind kept circling back to each of the things he'd described. Had he experienced them with someone else? Was that why he was acting so strange? Jealousy clawed up her spine. Suddenly he grabbed her hand and pulled her into his embrace, snapping her mind firmly back to reality.

"What the hell?"

He pressed his mouth beside her ear, making her belly tumble despite her annoyance over the abrupt yank.

"Smile, sweet cheeks. We've got company."

Willow's eyes darted around the grounds, landing on a man with a camera pointed directly at them. "What the hell did you do?"

"Media, baby. That's why we're here."

She struggled to get out of his grip, wondering how he could have gone from one persona to another in the blink of an eye. And then she remembered. He was an actor. This was how he lived his life, jumping from one role to the next. She didn't even know who the real Zane

Walker was anymore, and she'd already committed to helping him. She clearly needed to step up her game if she was going to remain sane.

"Willow, relax. All they want is a few pictures of the happy couple. We need the public to buy our engagement, remember?"

*Where were they five minutes ago when we were both lost in your stupid fantasy?*

She was sure she had smoke coming out of her ears. "Is that who you were texting earlier? Tipping off the press? You set this whole weekend up *assuming* I'd agree to it!"

He leaned back, flashing a fake but loving smile, and gazed into her eyes as he spoke, smooth as butter. Leave it to Zane to play it up for the cameras. "It's not a bad thing that I know my fiancée better than she knows herself. Go with it, Wills. Think of the exposure for your bakery."

Two could play at this game. She wound her arms around his neck and pressed her body against him, knowing his weak points. Or rather, weak *point*. Flashing her own fake smile, she said, "How's this?"

"Mm. That's more like it." His hand slid to her ass, and she dug her nails into the back of his neck. Gritting his teeth, he said, "All in the name of believability, babe."

She ran her fingers through his hair, giving the press exactly what they wanted and telling Zane *exactly* what she thought. "Putting me in the spotlight without notice is low, Zane, and I don't do *low*. Enjoy these few minutes, because after this you're not getting anywhere near me. It's one thing to be used, but pulling this shit?"

"I seem to remember you using me in a much more intimate way." He touched his cheek to hers again and whispered, "I should have warned you, but I knew you could pull this off. I believe in you, Willow."

*I believe in you, Willow.* That's what he'd said to her when she'd confided in him about being terrified to leave Sweetwater and go away to school. He'd wrapped her naked body in his arms, and there beneath the stars, having just given her the most incredible night of her life, he'd confided in her that he'd been scared, too, when he'd gone to LA. Now, as her body remembered the feel of him cocooning her from her fears, he splayed his hands over her back, bringing their bodies flush and causing her nipples to spike. The rest of her body also remembered what it was like to be wrapped up safely within his arms, nestled against his naked body, gazing into his confident, caring eyes, and she felt herself moving against his hard length instead of focusing on her anger. *This was a bad plan. A very bad plan.*

"It's only a couple of weeks," he reminded her, kneading the back of her neck again.

*God, that feels good.* How did he remember how much she loved that?

Forcing herself to think past his scrumptious layers of seduction and focus on the annoyance that had simmered low in her belly moments earlier wasn't easy. But the lust surging forward threatened to drown her if she didn't get away from him. *Now.* "You've got three seconds to let go of me and get me out of that reporter's sight, or that breakup scene you're anticipating is going to happen a few weeks early."

ZANE WRESTLED WITH what the hell had just happened between him and Willow as he scanned the area for an escape before she blew this deal. He'd gotten lost in his own fantasy—only he had never fantasized about romantic walks and stolen kisses. His fantasies were dark and dirty, involving hot, sweaty nights with Willow's legs wrapped around his neck, or waist.

"Three. Two," Willow counted down.

His eyes landed on a fishing boat preparing to leave the dock. "Come on."

They took off running across the lawn and sprinted down the dock, leaving the photographer scrambling to gather the bags at his feet and run after them.

"Hold on." She toed off her heels and picked them up, holding them against her as they hurried up the ramp to the boat.

Zane whipped out a wad of cash and handed it to the crewman. "There's more where that came from if you can get us out of here *now*."

The burly fisherman grinned from behind his beard and dark sunglasses. "Damn, man. That's more than it costs to charter the boat for a day."

The photographer was on the dock, camera pointed at them as he hurried toward the ramp.

"I'll double it if you pull this ramp before that guy gets here." He nodded toward the photographer.

"Roll 'er out," the fisherman called to another guy at the front of the boat.

Zane put an arm around Willow's shoulder, shielding her from the photographer. He needed those pictures, but she was right. He should have given her a heads-up, and now all he wanted to do was get her out of the guy's sight. He ushered her into the cabin of the boat, where a brunette woman and two young boys with thick mops of dark hair were playing a game of Go Fish.

The woman smiled up at them. "I didn't know we were chartering today. I'm Cheryl, and these are my boys." She touched the younger boy's hand. "This is Tommy. He's five." She motioned to the older one. "And that's Kenny. He's eight. Say hi, boys."

"Hi," they said in unison.

The older boy studied Zane. "I know you. You're the guy from that movie Mom wouldn't let us see."

The woman squinted at Zane.

"*Guns Rebellion*?" Zane said. "You've got a good memory. That came out last year." He held a hand out to the woman. "Zane Walker. It's nice to meet you."

Willow cleared her throat.

"Oh, sorry." *Christ, I'm an idiot.* "This is Willow."

A blond-haired guy who looked like he pumped weights for a living, sporting a rich tan and eyes the color of the sea, came down from the deck, eyeing Willow appreciatively. He lifted his square chin in her direction. "How's it going?"

"Better now," she said flirtatiously.

Zane was a big dude at six one, but even so, the blond guy had a solid two or three inches on him. Zane didn't like the jealousy gnawing at his gut. He thrust his hand in the guy's direction. "Actor Zane Walker." *If you've got it, flaunt it.* "This is my fiancée, Willow."

*Whoa.* That felt weird coming out of his mouth. Pretending Willow was *his* suddenly took on a whole new meaning.

Willow glared at him.

The guy's eyes moved between the two of them. "Fred. Nice to meet y'all. Running from the press?"

"Yes. Sorry to crash your Friday afternoon," Willow said, even more flirtatiously than before.

Zane reached for her hand. "My girl hates the press. Don't you, sweet cheeks?" That earned him another piercing glare.

She turned happier eyes to Fred, taking a long, lascivious look at his muscular frame. "I don't love the spotlight, but Zane craves it. I guess as the number-one action hero he has to." She smiled at the woman and children. "He's also great with kids, and he *loves* to talk shop."

*What are you up to?*

"Now that we're away from the dock," Willow said with a hint of payback in her eyes, "I'm going to sit in the sun. Why don't you stay down here and tell these adorable boys all about what it's really like to be an action hero?"

"Yeah!" Kenny cheered. "Sit next to me. Do you know The Rock?"

Zane didn't mind children, but he sure as hell minded the way Willow was fluttering her lashes at Freddy *Beefcake* Fisherman.

"I'm not that familiar with boat safety," she said to Fred. "Would you mind giving me the rundown?"

Zane stifled the urge to call her out on the lie. She'd not only grown up on boats, but she'd worked at the marina for a few summers when they were younger.

"Happy to," Fred said.

Kenny tugged on Zane's hand, pulling him down to the bench beside him, forcing Zane to watch Fred follow Willow up the stairs.

By the time Zane extricated himself from talking about all things Hollywood with the curious little boys, more than an hour had passed. He found Willow up on deck, leaning back on her elbows, her face angled toward the darkening sky. One leg was stretched out along the padded bench, her other knee was bent, and her dress was bunched up around her thighs. *Playboy* centerfolds had nothing on Willow Dalton. Even in clothes she was hotter than any woman he'd ever known. She radiated confidence and beauty. He breathed a little easier knowing Fred was fishing a few feet away. At least she wasn't hanging all over the guy. Then again, he'd never known Willow to be a clingy, throw-herself-at-a-guy type of girl. She was too confident and smart for that, which was why seeing her flirt with Fred had thrown him off-kilter.

That's what he told himself, but it was a big-ass lie. It had nothing to do with what she was usually like and little to do with wanting to protect her from a lecherous guy. The truth was, he'd been jealous because she'd chosen to flirt with Fred instead of him. He didn't even know why it bothered him so much. He could have any woman he wanted, and he did. *Often.* But the whole time he was in the cabin, he'd been thinking about Willow, hoping she wasn't up here leading Fred on as she had down below.

He glanced at Fred, who was talking with Cheryl's husband, Jay, the bearded guy who had allowed them to board the boat. Jay had come down to the cabin to introduce himself shortly after Willow had gone back up.

Zane sat down next to Willow and stretched an arm across the back of the bench. "The sun's going down," he pointed out.

"Mm-hm. I don't care." She opened her eyes and blinked up at him, then closed them again. "Did you have fun with the kids?"

"They're cute, and very curious, which was cool. Way to ditch me, by the way."

"You have eyes," she said in a low voice, looking at Fred. "They don't make men like that in Sweetwater."

*Ouch.* "What am I? Chopped liver?"

"Like you need to hear how hot you are? *Please.*" She pushed up and sat beside him, wrapping her arms around her knees. "It's not just his looks. He's *nice.* Did you know they're brothers? Jay got sick last year. He couldn't work for four months, and Fred took over his charter business so Jay's family wouldn't lose the income, and he stayed on afterward. I think that's sexy, how much he loves his family."

If she classified Fred as nice, what did she think he was? *Oh, right, an asshat.*

*Well, that blows.*

It was no secret that he'd never been close to his unambitious parents, who had never done anything to better their low socioeconomic position, and they hadn't supported his desire to make something more for himself. Willow's parents had stepped in and given him the confidence he'd needed. They had not only told Zane to follow his dreams *and* his heart, but they'd made it seem possible.

"Listen," he said quietly. "If this is going to work, you can't pull that kind of crap. We're supposed to be a couple."

"You realize what I'm giving up to do this, right? If I weren't *fake engaged,* I could have a date tonight with a nice guy." She eyed Fred again.

He paused to regain control as the green-eyed monster reared its ugly head again. "I get that. I appreciate what you're doing for me, and I'll make it up to you in a hundred different ways. But I think I need to give you acting lessons if we're going to get through this."

Her eyes went flat. "Seriously?"

"Is it *that* hard to act like you're into me? I know I screwed up with the photographer, but you've got to understand, the focus group is demanding I clean up my act. That photographer is with TMZ. When I tip him off, he shows up. I gave him an exclusive on the story, but part of the deal was that he wouldn't publish anything until I gave him the okay next week, after we've had a chance to break the news to your family." Lack of privacy was just one of the many reasons he wanted to get out from in front of the camera.

She rested her cheek on her knees, watching him intently.

"And whose fault is it that you have to do this in the first place?" she asked sweetly, without judgment, as if she were asking what brand of cologne he wore.

He rested his elbows on his thighs, brought his eyes level with Willow's, and whispered, "I get it. I don't deny I'm the one who chose to live the way I have. I'm surrounded by beautiful women throwing themselves at me and expecting nothing in return but a few hours of hot sex. It's not like I'm cheating on anyone. Of course I'm going to indulge."

She lifted her head with a serious—*and hurt?*—expression. "You asked if it's hard for me to act like I'm into you, and the honest answer is yes and no."

He sat back and pushed his hand through his hair. He was used to women fawning over him, but Willow didn't fawn over anyone, least of all him. She'd always called him on his shit, and she was the only woman on earth who had the power to slay him.

"Because of my history with women?" He braced himself for the kick in the teeth he was asking for.

She smiled and shook her head. "I don't know. Because of all of it. Because I look at you and I remember things. Because I know the guy you were, and I can't help but look for him in everything you do. And at the same time, you're *Zane Walker*, the best-looking man and most talented action hero on the planet."

"Wills. Did you just stroke my ego?" He reached out and put his hand on her forehead. "Are you sick?"

She laughed, brushing his hand away, but he laced their fingers together and held on tight. Confusion filled her beautiful eyes, mirroring his own emotions.

"Just when I expect you to give me a cocky answer, you go and do something cute like that."

"Cute *and* the best-looking man on the planet?" Snarky answers were easier than trying to figure out why he was still holding her hand—and didn't want to let go. "Hell, baby, let's focus on those two things. That should make it easier for you to pretend to like me. And we're still doing those acting lessons, because that rolling-your-eyes crap is a dead giveaway that you're not totally, one hundred percent into me."

She rolled her eyes again. "I'd have to be actress of the year to make that happen."

"Then I'll kick up my game and make it so you can't help but fall for me." As the words left his lips, he knew he meant them. No matter what it took.

Cheryl and the boys came up from the cabin. Tommy and Kenny ran over to Fred and Jay.

Tommy hung on Fred's legs. "Can I fish, Uncle Fred?"

"Sure, buddy." Fred crouched beside the boy and helped him gain control of the fishing line.

Cheryl sat on the adjoining bench and zipped up her hoodie. She tucked her legs beneath her. "It's a nice evening, isn't it?"

"Gorgeous," Willow said.

"That's a beautiful ring," Cheryl said to Willow. "How long have you two been engaged?"

"We actually just got engaged earlier today." Zane draped an arm around Willow, pulling her against his side. Damn, she felt good, and he noticed she wasn't pulling away, which he liked even better.

"Really?" Cheryl said with a wide smile. "Congratulations. It seems like a lifetime ago for us. How did you propose?"

"He's told this story twice already today. I swear I'll never tire of hearing it," Willow said. "Every time he tells it, it feels like the very first time."

"Does it, Wills?" He shouldn't do it, but he'd been carrying the truth around for so many years, he was dying to get it out. Even if it was done only under the guise of telling a totally unrelated story. He took both of her hands in his, spurred on by the anticipatory look in her eyes. If she thought he was going to make a snarky remark, she couldn't have been more wrong. "Nothing has ever felt like that first night we came together. I knew then we'd end up here one day."

Her eyes widened just a hair before her cheeks flushed. He let that soak in for a beat longer before revealing what they were all waiting to hear.

"I had been wanting to ask her for a long time, but every proposal I thought up seemed like too much or too little. And then we came here for the weekend. We both snuck away under the pretense of being somewhere else." He lifted Willow's hand and pressed a kiss to the back of it, watching her intently. The pulse at the base of her neck was beating faster than before, and her lips parted, as if she were hanging on to his every word. Damn, he loved that look, and he couldn't believe she was giving it to *him*. He silently vowed to earn it over and over again.

He glanced at Cheryl. "We have to stay under the radar of the paparazzi, because my Willow really hates being in the spotlight." He dropped his gaze to Willow's hand, which had gone warm in his. "I'll never forget standing on that gazebo with the morning haze hovering over the water, and Willow . . ." He brushed his thumb over her knuckles. "She looked angelic with the sun rising at her back, like all the colors of the sunrise were made just for her. Just for that moment." He met Willow's gaze and said, "Just for *our* moment."

Her breathing hitched, and he knew she was remembering their night together, too, when he'd last said *our moment*. His throat was so thick with emotion he couldn't force his words out.

"He got down on one knee," Willow said just above a whisper, holding his gaze, saving his ass and owning up to the lie. *The fantasy?* "I'll never forget that moment. He looked at me like I was the only thing that existed. He didn't have to say a word. Even if he hadn't been down on one knee, I would have known what was coming." She reached a shaky hand up and touched his scruff, a small smile lifting her lips. "He said, 'There's only me and you, Wills. This is our moment.'"

*You remember.* He swallowed hard, trying to gain control of the resurgence of emotions he'd struggled to ignore for all these years, because Willow had made the rules, and the last thing he'd wanted to do was hurt her by breaking more of them than he already had.

# CHAPTER FOUR

WILLOW WAVED GOODBYE to Cheryl and the others as she and Zane headed down the dock in a bubble of awkwardness. Cheryl had made dinner on the boat, but Willow had been too nervous to eat more than a bite. Zane had been looking at her weirdly ever since she'd forgotten how to shut the hell up and had taken over his story.

*Oh my God, his story.* She'd been so caught up in his fake proposal that when he'd said, "Our moment," he'd opened some sort of floodgate to the past. It hadn't helped that when Zane had offered Jay the rest of the money he'd promised for letting them hijack their boat, Jay had pushed his hand away and said, "Keep it. It was nice getting to know you both. My wife always says those gossip magazines are full of lies. Now we know she's right. We hope you have a long, happy marriage." The color had drained from Zane's face, like he'd been caught having *real* feelings for Willow, and she'd felt the impact like a freight train slamming into the barriers she'd erected out of self-preservation.

She focused on the lights of the resort twinkling against the night sky instead of the frantic beating of her heart and the *whathefuckamIdoing* playing in her head. Every time she stole a glance at Zane, he shifted his eyes away, and a second later she felt the heat of his gaze burning into her.

This was crazy. They'd been friends forever. Even when they'd slept together, things hadn't been this awkward. One of them needed to break the ice. She looked up at the same time he looked over, and their eyes locked. *Lord*, he was looking at her *that* way again, with his chin tipped low and hunger in his eyes, but there was something else behind the heat. Something she'd seen only once in her life, as he'd lain above her down by the creek. Something she was probably mistaken about, given the totally effed-up state of her mind.

She said, "Hey, why don't we—" at the same time he said, "Let's go—"

He raked a hand through his hair, his laughter breaking the tension. She loved the sound of his laugh when he wasn't trying to be *the* Zane Walker. He had a wonderfully deep, carefree laugh that reminded her of fun-filled summer afternoons at the lake and family barbecues after he and Ben had played a winning football or baseball game.

"Whiskey?" he suggested.

"Make it a double."

They headed across the lawn toward a long deck that led to an outdoor bar overlooking the water, weaving through a sea of people who were dancing and laughing, shouting out one toast after another. At the center of a mass of twentysomethings was a dark-haired couple wearing sparkling crowns. A band played at the far end of the deck. They'd obviously stumbled upon some sort of bachelor/bachelorette party. *The perfect distraction.*

Zane plowed through the crowd, making a beeline toward the bar.

Willow followed him between two guys. "Sorry," she said. The crowd seemed to swell, and they pressed in on her. *Are you shitting me?* She felt a hand circle her waist and turned, catching the threatening glare Zane gave the guys before he tugged her out from between them.

"What are you doing?" His eyes darted around them.

"Me? You plowed ahead and left me to trail behind." She wrenched free. "Not exactly the way a fiancé should act, I might point out."

An apology rose in his eyes. "Sorry, baby."

With his arm securely around her, he pushed through the crowd and flagged down the bartender.

A beautiful blonde with breasts that looked like they were ready to tumble out of her low-cut blouse leaned across the bar. "What'll it be?" she shouted over the noise.

"Two whiskeys, neat."

"Make them doubles," Willow added.

Zane chuckled.

"What? I don't want to fight the crowd again in five minutes."

A few minutes later the bartender slid their glasses across the bar, and Zane paid. He draped an arm possessively around Willow, holding her tight as they moved through the crowd to a spot near the railing. Women began whispering behind their hands, with hope and flirtation lighting up their eyes as they ogled Zane. They stood up taller, arched their backs to show off their assets, and fluttered their lashes in his direction.

Willow rolled her eyes and turned to face the water. She had wondered how long it would take for people to recognize him. Zane was hard to miss with all that hotness wafting off him. Even when he wasn't trying to be hot, he sizzled. And despite his smartassery, he was charming in his own way. Or maybe that was years of repression refusing to be held back any longer. She'd always loved his smartassery. Almost as much as his badassery. And his ass in general.

With a viselike grip on her, he put his mouth beside her ear and said, "Is this better?"

His hot breath sent shudders of lust rippling through her. She gulped a mouthful of whiskey, reveling in the burn as it slid down her throat like lava. She'd rather have frosting, but since she wasn't in the kitchen, liquid courage would have to do. When Zane tightened his grip, mashing her body to his, she downed another gulp.

"Slow down there, sweet cheeks. You're liable to get drunk."

"Sweet cheeks?" She rolled her eyes.

"I thought we were done with those eye rolls. Meet me halfway, Wills."

She was painfully aware of the women watching him, even if he was acting like he hadn't a clue. She wasn't used to the jealousy whipping through her, or the twisting in her gut from being on the receiving end of stink-eyes from a pack of women just a few feet away. Willow didn't play games, and she didn't do drama. It was one of the reasons she loved her hometown so much. She had a nice life where she could wear her jeans or shorts and not worry about measuring up to anyone. She glanced down at her belted lavender dress, feeling even more out of place among an ocean of little black dresses. Sure, she had double Ds she could flaunt with the best of them, but she hated them. She'd hated them ever since she was thirteen, when they hadn't sprouted like cute little nubs and then blossomed into perfectly perky boobs that fit her body. They'd bloomed overnight, making her feel like a young, awkward Dolly Parton. To make matters worse, she also had rounded hips and a smallish waist that made her boobs look even *bigger*. She'd grown up dealing with boys talking to *the girls* instead of her, and while she'd thought that might change as the guys matured, she spent her life dodging men who did the same.

Zane moved in front of her, bringing her eyes up to his. He had never made her feel like other guys did. Even when she had been his for the taking, he'd focused on her—her eyes, her emotions, her hands. God, she remembered the way he'd kissed each of her fingers before intertwining them with his as she lay beneath him. It was like he hadn't seen her boobs at all. He'd seen only *her*. Now he was looking at her again. Heat sizzled and popped between them.

She shifted her gaze out over the inky water. She was romanticizing their friendship again, just like she'd promised herself she wouldn't do all those years ago. She'd failed miserably then, too.

"Hey, Wills. Look at me."

She reluctantly met his gaze. He was smiling in a playful way that reminded her of his younger self. She liked that younger, playful guy a whole lot. He tapped his glass to hers and pressed a kiss to her cheek, leaving her skin warm and her body tingling with anticipation. Or maybe that was from the whiskey. It was hard to differentiate when Zane's incredible body was pressed against her.

"To us." He lifted his glass to his lips.

His Adam's apple moved like he did, smooth as sin and alluringly tempting. She had the urge to seal her mouth over that sexy moving target. *Lord have mercy.* What was wrong with her? She downed the rest of her drink, wincing at the burn, feeling it pool in her belly like liquid fire and giving herself over to the blissful deadening of her nerves.

He raised his brows and finished his drink, watching her intently as he took her empty glass and set it with his on the railing.

His hands snaked around her waist, holding her impossibly closer. "Talk to me, Wills."

"Isn't this weird for you? Holding me like this and pretending to be engaged, when you're surrounded by gawking, available women? I mean, your photographer doesn't seem to be stalking us, so . . ."

His eyes narrowed and drifted around them, lingering on the women who had been giving her the stink-eye. He touched his cheek to hers again, instantly making her insides go soft. "I promised I'd make a concerted effort to ensure this works, and I never break my prom—"

When he drew back and gazed into her eyes with a serious and thoughtful expression, her pulse went a little crazy. She reminded herself this was his most important role yet.

"I try never to break my promises anymore," he corrected himself. "And no, Wills. This isn't weird for me. It would be weird to try to act like this with anyone other than you."

"Zane, I'm being serious. Don't feed me lines, okay?" She glanced down at the gaudy—and stunning—ring he'd rented. When she was a kid, she'd gone through a phase where she loved princess everything, from dresses to gems. Didn't all young girls? But as an adult, as a baker—as Willow Dalton—she wanted nothing like this when and if she ever got engaged. The diamond would only get in the way, and it was too flashy. It wasn't *her* at all. *Patch picked it out.* Another good reminder of why she shouldn't romanticize their relationship.

"It wasn't a line." He began swaying to the music with her in his arms. "Dance with me. I need the distraction."

"From those girls?" She ached at the idea that he wished he could be with someone else. This would be easier if being with him didn't make her remember what it was like to be touched like she was more than a piece of ass. To be touched like she was precious *and* sexy and looked at like she was the only woman he ever wanted.

The muscles around his mouth twitched. "No, Willow. *Jesus.* I know I've been with a lot of women, but whose insanely sexy body is crushed against mine right now?"

The anger in his tone was underscored by hurt, and it took her by surprise. She might not approve of his current lifestyle, or the reasons behind this grand scheme they were taking part in, but she'd agreed to do this for him, and he was making an effort. She needed to get past the ghosts of their past that were sucking up half the oxygen, to kick that elephant from the room so she could make the effort he deserved—the effort that, without the ghosts, and without that damn elephant, wasn't an effort at all.

"Do you really think anonymous women mean a damn thing to me? They're a way to pass the time. You're my *friend*. You know me better than anyone else in the world ever could. Everything's different with you, Wills. It always has been, and I'm really trying not to screw this up."

The way he said *friend*, like it was the most important thing he'd said all night, pushed all that other stuff out of the way. The person he'd been was still in there, drawing her closer. She wound her arms around his neck, wanting to dig deeper, to bring out more of the guy she'd loved so deeply.

"That's better. It's just us, babe. No one else matters."

His hands slid to the base of her spine, and she felt herself melting against him, believing him, feeling safe with him. *Wanting* him. She rested her cheek against his chest and closed her eyes. It had been a long time since she could be herself with a man, and if Zane was nothing else, he had always been that guy. He accepted her for all her quirks. It felt incredible to be in his arms again. Her mind tiptoed down a dangerous path.

*Maybe just one night . . . ?*

ZANE CAME OUT of the men's room and heard Willow's feathery laughter tickling his ears. He scanned the crowd in the bar, which had thinned out over the last few hours as they'd drank and danced. He wasn't sure if he'd imagined the wanting looks Willow had been casting his way all night or if he'd conjured them up with wishful thinking, but the longer he had her in his arms, the harder it was to remember they weren't a real couple.

They'd met Liz and Mark, the happy couple celebrating their upcoming wedding, which was taking place tomorrow morning by the lake. After a few awkward moments of them and their friends gushing over Zane's celebrity status, Willow had held up her hand and announced that they were engaged, shocking the hell out of him. She'd finally embraced their ruse, and good-time Willow had come out to play. He was sure the alcohol helped, but damn, he loved the way she draped herself all over him, playing up their relationship for their audience.

She laughed again, and he followed the sound to a tall table at the other end of the bar, where she stood with a handful of people. She wore Liz's crown, and everyone else was watching her.

*What are you up to now, baby doll?*

Endearments came so easily when he was with her and when he thought of her. He never called women anything other than their names, but he'd called Willow just about every affectionate name under the sun for as long as he'd known her. He grinned, recalling her annoyance at his use of *sweet cheeks*. She'd always hated that one, which made it even more fun to say.

As he approached the table, two good-looking guys stepped up beside her, one unabashedly leering at her cleavage. Zane curled his hands into fists.

Willow tossed something up in the air, and it landed on the table. A coin, he realized as everyone leaned in to see it and cheered. Her eyes widened, and a gorgeous smile spread across her face as she reached down and untied her belt.

*What the . . . ?* Zane quickened his pace and narrowed his eyes as she whipped the belt around over her head like a lasso and tossed it in the air with a loud *whoop!*

The leerer snatched it out of the air and leaned down, whispering something to Willow. Zane grabbed his shoulder, dragging him backward.

"Dude!" the guy hollered.

"Hands off my fiancée, buddy." He grabbed Willow's belt from his hand and pushed past him.

Willow, oblivious to him, tossed the coin in the air again.

He put his arm around her and said, "Time to go, Wills," as the coin landed on the table and cheers rang out again.

Eyes wide and glassy, Willow grabbed his shirt and tugged him closer. "Z! You've *got* to play this!"

The others began chanting, "Drink, drink, drink!"

Willow downed a shot, grabbed Zane's face with two hands, and smashed her mouth to his. It happened so fast he didn't have time to think past the heat blazing a path straight to his groin. She pulled back, blinking those unbearably long lashes up at him with a shocked look on her face.

He hauled her to her feet—her *bare* feet? "Time to go, Wills. Where are your shoes?"

"Aw, come on. We were just getting started," a guy called out.

Zane ignored him, focusing on Willow. "Shoes, baby. Where are they?"

She looked down and giggled, turning those mischievous green eyes on him again. Then she shrugged and wrapped herself around him like a second skin. "Lost them in Flip, Sip, or Strip."

*Flip, Sip, or Strip? Holy shit.* He made a mental note not to let Willow drink without him. *Ever.* "Come on, sweet stuff." He slid his arm around her waist and guided her toward the resort.

"But we were playing." She pointed over her shoulder.

"And now you're done."

"You didn't kiss me back." Her lips were pouty, and her brows furrowed.

Aw, hell. She was killing him. He *wanted* to kiss her, and not just to see her smile again. Grinding his teeth against the urge to do just that, he focused on getting her to the resort.

"Why didn't you kiss me?" She stumbled off the edge of the patio and into the grass.

"You're drunk." He swept her into his arms, nearly groaning at the feel of her warm, lush curves pressed against him. Heaven and hell collided, and he was the lucky recipient of their torturous impact.

"So?" She wound her arms around his neck. "I bet you make out with drunk girls all the time."

"Wills." His warning was clear. He focused on the music fading in the distance, the water lapping at the shore. The sound of the frigging adrenaline rushing through his ears. Anything except the woman in his arms who was too drunk to realize what she was saying. She pressed her hands to his cheeks and turned his face toward hers. Jesus, she was too sexy, all pouty and angry, a flush from too much alcohol pinking her cheeks. He tried to ignore the thrum of heat building inside him, but when she licked her lips, he felt it below his belt.

"Why. Won't. You. Kiss. Me?" she demanded.

He shifted his eyes away. "Put your head on my shoulder and chill, Wills." *Before I take you up on your offer.*

"Am I not hot enough for you?" She pulled his face toward hers again. "Not skinny enough? Not pretty enough?"

"Willow, stop." He carried her into the resort and directly to the elevator.

"Put me down." She pushed against his chest.

"Sweetheart, you're drunk. Just let me put you to bed." *Fuck.* Now he was thinking about her in bed. The elevator arrived, and they stepped inside. He pushed the button for their floor.

"I'm *not* drunk." She struggled until he finally set her on her feet. She swayed, and he gathered her in his arms. Sadness replaced the anger in her eyes. "Am I not slutty enough?"

He was *this close* to giving in. "Stop." His demand came out as a whispered plea. He thought he was strong, but she tore at him in ways no other woman ever could, breaking him down one word, one look, one *blink* at a time.

"That's it, isn't it? I'm not slutty enough. You probably like those girls who flaunt their boobs and get down on their knees without asking."

"Damn it, Willow," he snapped. "Stop this shit."

"Then tell me!"

He turned away, running through the possible outcomes of telling her the truth. None of which were good. She'd either call him a liar or he'd ruin their friendship. The elevator stopped at their floor, and she pulled out of his grasp, storming down the hall. She looked sexy as hell stomping her little tanned feet, her incredible ass swaying angrily. He was so screwed.

She reached their room and stood with her arms crossed and an angry scowl on her face.

He swiped the keycard and pushed the door open.

She shoved past him, tugging at the ring on her finger. "Why did you do this, anyway? Why *me*? Go get someone you can at least kiss, because obviously I'm not the type of woman you like anyway, so no one is going to believe it." Her face was red with frustration. The ring was stuck on her finger. She pushed his chest. "I can't take it off!"

He grabbed her wrist. "Because you aren't supposed to."

She was breathing so hard, smelled so good, but that desperate, sad look in her eyes did him in.

"Tell me why, Zane." She seemed to sober up. Her words were clear, her body steady. "Why wouldn't you kiss me out there? I'm trying to play your game. I guess I found the line between being your adoring arm candy that you can press your lips and body to whenever *you* see fit and your don't-touch-me friend. Clearly we're not that good at crossing lines these days unless it's done by *your* rules."

He stepped forward, still holding her wrist, and her back met the wall with a *thud*. "Stop. Talking."

"No. I want to know why you won't kiss me."

"You don't want to kiss me, Willow." He heard the greed in his voice. "You're just drunk."

"Maybe I just needed the liquid courage to act on my feelings. Maybe I'm just like all those other women who want you."

"Don't even joke about that," he snapped. "You're nothing like them."

She arched against him, her hand surfing over his ass, her eyes turning sultry and dark. "That's why you don't want me?"

"Damn it, Willow." He grabbed hold of her other wrist, pressing both against the wall beside her head. "Because if I kiss you, I won't want to stop, and we can't go there."

Challenge rose in her eyes.

"Wills," he warned. "You'll regret it in the morning."

She bowed away from the wall, brushing her thighs against his. "One kiss."

He pressed his body to hers, and her back met the wall again. She had to feel what she was doing to him. Had to know how much he wanted her. He should walk away, take a cold shower, and figure out how to get through the next two weeks, but he was drawn to her like metal to magnet. He wanted to peel her out of that dress and consume every inch of her.

"Why?" He had to know why she was pushing him so hard.

She ran her tongue over her lower lip, leaving it slick and enticing. "For old times' sake."

He touched his cheek to hers, and she shuddered against him. As he breathed in her feminine scent, he realized why he'd held her like this so many times over the past few hours. It had been how he'd calmed her down all those years ago. She'd been so nervous, trembling even as she'd tried to act tough, just like she was now. But he'd known the truth. She was terrified. Was she scared now?

"Your body remembers us," he whispered, and he couldn't refrain from sweeping his tongue around the shell of her ear, as he'd done that night. "My body remembers us." He rocked his hips against hers and gazed into her eyes.

"Z," she said on a long, heated breath, reminding him of the breathless girl of almost eighteen who had captured his heart.

"I can't sleep with you, Willow. I care about you too much to jeopardize our friendship again."

Her eyes narrowed. "You're an arrogant man. I want your mouth, not your cock."

Jesus, his Willow was back in charge. Her confidence was an aphrodisiac—always had been. He held on to his control by a fraying thread. "Seeing your pretty mouth say that dirty word, baby . . .

You have no idea how many times I have fantasized about that filthy mouth of yours. A kiss will never be enough. For either of us."

He tightened his hold on her wrists to keep from filling his hands with other enticing parts of her. She slid her knee up his inner thigh, tempting him to the edge of reason. He crushed his chest to hers and touched his lips to her forearm, aching to be buried deep inside her. She watched, breathing harder with each press of his lips as he kissed a trail down her arm. He moved his hand from her wrist to her fingers, holding her palm open, and circled it with his tongue, earning a heady moan from her.

"Zane," she begged.

He brushed his lips over hers again, torturing them both as she craned forward, trying to catch his mouth. But he wasn't sure he'd be able to stop once he got ahold of her luscious lips. He kissed her neck, loving the way she craned back, offering him more. He dragged his tongue down the center and along her breastbone, then kissed his way back up again. Her eyes were closed, her lips parted. He laced their hands together again, still holding them against the wall, struggling to maintain control of the desires stacking up inside him.

"Promise me you won't take off that ring."

"I won't," she panted out.

"Promise me you won't hate me for being weak. You've always owned me."

"I . . ." Her eyes came open, confusion and desire gazing back at him.

He'd stunned them both with his confession, but he didn't have time to explain. He needed her more than he'd ever needed anything in his life. "One kiss, baby."

"Yes—"

He cupped her jaw, the fear of what they were risking causing his fingers and thumb to press too hard into her flesh as he angled her mouth beneath his. "Promise you'll push me away if I get carried away."

He didn't wait for an answer, couldn't wait another second. Their mouths crashed together in a desperate, fervent kiss. She tasted sweet and hot, meeting his efforts with insatiable hunger. His emotions reeled. He'd fantasized about kissing Willow again for so long, he couldn't hold back, and he took the kiss deeper, kissing her rougher. She was right there with him, opening wider as he plundered and took, and took, and *took*.

ZANE DIDN'T JUST kiss Willow; he *possessed* her with his arms, his hands, his wicked tongue. He delved into the far recesses of her mouth, unleashing a surge of heat that first flooded, then consumed her from the inside out. She had almost forgotten what a *real* kiss felt like. The way his kisses could draw the energy from every limb, until she felt it creeping beneath her skin, moving toward his talented mouth. His kiss reached into her core, stoking a long-ago forgotten fire, breathing spirals of ecstasy into every iota of her being. She grasped at his arms in an effort to remain erect in her dizzying world. Just when she was sure her heart would explode, his fingers fisted in her hair, and he tugged her head back—*hard*.

His eyes were volcanic, and seeing him so desperate for her, so lost in *them*, sent her pulse skyrocketing.

"Stop me, Wills," he pleaded.

His roughness electrified her. No way was she stopping either of them. She pulled his mouth to hers again, *claiming* him. Then his hands were on her ass, lifting her higher. Her legs circled his waist, her dress bunched around her middle, and she didn't care. No, that was wrong. For the first time in forever, she *did* care. She cared a hell of a lot. She wanted her dress to melt off. Panties, too. She didn't want anything separating them.

His touch was controlling, his kisses raw and sensuous. She became aware of his hardness pressing against her center, his rampant breathing as he intensified their kisses, the scratch of his whiskers against her cheeks, and the air moving over her skin as he carried her across the room. They tumbled down to the mattress in a tangle of limbs, never breaking their connection. His weight pressing down on her was exquisite, and the intoxicating scents of whiskey and *man* made her head spin. She wanted to lick him, to drink him, to *consume* him, from his mouth to his ankles and every deliciously hard inch in between.

Desire pounded through her veins as they rocked against each other, sparking so hot she was surprised the sheets didn't catch flames. He reached over his shoulder and pulled his shirt off, like he'd done all those years ago, when he didn't want anything separating them. He was giving her a green light, and she wanted to zoom right past it. Her eyes fell to the dusting of dark hair on his chest. She'd seen his body in magazines and in every movie he'd made. And when he'd come back to Sweetwater for visits, she'd seen him playing basketball with Ben shirtless. But she hadn't looked closely, and she certainly hadn't been able to touch. It was one thing to see him from afar, but up close and shirtless, when she knew what his body had looked like as a boy on the cusp of manhood? Nothing could have prepared her for the man gazing down at her like she was a pretty little rabbit and he was a hungry wolf. He lowered his mouth to hers again, and she readied herself for his cruel ravishment. She wanted it. God, how she wanted it. But he kissed her so softly, so tenderly, he took her breath away.

His hand moved over her hip, up her ribs, and then his warm, strong hand left her body, avoiding her breast and stroking her cheek. A rush of emotions swamped her. *You remembered.*

"One kiss," he whispered. "It was never enough."

Her entire body arched off the bed, begging for his touch as he pressed his lips to hers in a series of provocative kisses. She wanted to touch his chest. *Needed* to feel that coarse hair on her fingers so she could recall the memory for her late-night fantasies. But she knew, without a shadow of a doubt, if she touched, she'd want to taste. And if she tasted, she'd want to follow that treasure trail lower. And that was out of the question.

One kiss, she'd told herself.

One kiss to get him out of her system.

One mind-blowing, panty-melting kiss, to ease the mounting tension between them.

He sealed his teeth over her neck and *sucked*.

*Oh, sweet baby Jesus, your mouth.*

Her nipples burned with the need to be *in* his mouth. All that grinding he was doing was creating delicious friction. Oh, wait, she was grinding, too. *Stop. Stop grinding.* Her hands moved to his ass. And what a fine ass he had. It was firm and round, and every time she squeezed it, he thrust harder. *Yes, yes, yes!*

His mouth was on a mission to drive her out of her mind. *Out of my clothes.* She squeezed her eyes shut, trying to wade through her tangled emotions. Wanton desires battled with reality. This could never go anywhere. They were playing roles. Or at least they had been. But this passion was as real as the man nipping at her lower lip.

His dark, lustful gaze brought reality rushing in. The years had only kept her feelings at bay. He was her pièce de résistance. She wasn't anywhere near over him. He was her cherry on top, the summit of a five-tier wedding cake. He was her strength and her weakness.

He must have seen her conflicting emotions, because he drew back and said, "I know," so tenderly, she wanted to yell, *No. You don't know. Ignore my waffling emotions and take me. Just take me.* But she didn't, and he kissed her again, slow and sweet and painfully delicious. He rolled onto his back and draped his arm over his eyes. "Alcohol wore off?"

"The minute you picked me up after we left the bar," she said honestly, trying to catch her breath.

He rolled onto his side, taking her hand in his, and smiled down at her. "You weren't out-of-your-mind drunk when you kissed me in the bar?"

She shook her head. "I had only one shot after our drinks. I was tipsy. Maybe very tipsy. But not drunk."

He flopped onto his back again, exhaling loudly. "So you were fucking with me?"

She pushed up on her elbow and ran her fingers through his chest hair. It was just as magnificent as she'd dreamed it would be. "Not really. I needed the liquid courage to get past not wanting to kiss you."

"*Not* wanting to kiss me? Christ, Wills. Way to stroke my ego."

She laughed and pressed her lips to the center of his chest. "I'm sure your ego will remain intact despite anything I say or do."

He hooked an arm around her neck and tugged her down, half beside him, half on top of him. "You're wrong, you know."

"About what?"

"Nothing," he mumbled, and rolled on top of her, pinning her beneath him. "I need a cold shower." He brushed his lips over hers again. "Want to make it a hot one and join me?"

She laughed, her mind still foggy from making out. "We had our fun. Now get that fine ass of yours off me and go introduce yourself to your right hand."

He gave her one last loud kiss and moved to the edge of the bed. His broad shoulders rounded forward, and he lowered his face to his hands, breathing deeply. She lay in the middle of the bed, watching him and wondering how they'd gotten there. She was supposed to be catering an event, not helping him fix his bad-boy reputation, and definitely not making out with him and opening all the doors to the past.

He pushed to his feet and stretched. The muscles on his back flexed, making her mouth water. He moved slowly, pulling his wallet, keycard, and phone from his pocket and tossing them on the nightstand. He glanced over his shoulder, and their eyes locked, stirring the emotions she was trying to pretend didn't own her.

"Last chance, sweet girl."

She closed her eyes to avoid falling into his. "I'm good, thanks."

She heard him walk into the bathroom and listened for the door to click shut, but it never did. The sounds of the shower brought her eyes open, imagining Zane stripping out of his jeans and boots. Knowing the only thing separating them was a few inches of drywall made her anxious. And *hot*. She pushed to the edge of the bed, digging deep for the courage to follow him, and rose to her feet too fast. All her blood rushed south. She reached for the wall to steady herself.

*Am I really going in there?*

She stood frozen, listening. For what, she wasn't sure. She imagined his naked body as he fisted his cock to relieve the pressure they'd built. Her knees weakened, and she dropped back down to the bed.

She wasn't ready for this. For *him*. For what would inevitably be a painful end to their two-week sham. She'd had her fun. Now she just needed to find a way to satisfy the throbbing ache between her legs *without* Zane.

AFTER A LONG, hot bath, Willow was clearheaded and strong in her resolve not to let their impromptu make-out session allow her to digress. She tiptoed out of the bathroom, hoping Zane had really gone to sleep as he'd claimed he was going to when he'd come out of the bathroom wearing nothing but a pair of black boxer briefs, looking like sex on legs. Mark Wahlberg had nothing on him. Zane could have modeled for a *Boogie Nights* commercial with that viper in his drawers.

The bedroom was dark, but there was no missing the form of a large, nearly naked man sprawled across the bed. *Ugh.* He was supposed to sleep on the couch. She eyed the narrow couch, then the bed. What woman in her right mind would turn away Zane Walker? *The one who knows firsthand what sleeping with Zane means.* A night of unforgettable pleasure, even her first time. A night of caring whispers and tender touches, and later, with the first two times under her belt, *combustible, explosive, passionate sex. To be followed up by certain heartbreak when our fake engagement comes to an end and I'm still hung up on you.*

Was it sad that the best sex of her life had been when she was just shy of eighteen and knew *nothing* about it? She'd tried to get lost in passion with the men she'd been with since, but no one had ever come close, which was a great reminder of why she couldn't do it again. Because *no one* has the best sex of their life at that age. She'd obviously romanticized them and fictionalized their sexual encounter to heights no one could ever live up to.

She gently moved his arm and leg to the other side of the bed and crawled in, huddling close to the edge. The sheets smelled like him. She buried her nose in them, closed her eyes, and at some point the sexy fantasies drifting through her mind lulled her to sleep.

# CHAPTER FIVE

WILLOW AWOKE TO warm breath against her cheek, a heavily muscled arm around her middle, and a hard cock nestled against her ass. This was *not* happening. But it sure felt good.

*No, no, no!*

She carefully lifted Zane's wrist between her finger and thumb, thinking she'd extricate herself without any need for conversation. He curled his fingers around her ribs and pressed his body tighter against her. She closed her eyes, willing herself to move. *But, but, but . . .* One of her teenage fantasies realized in a few glorious seconds. *Mm-hm, and what comes next? A shattered heart, you idiot.*

*That* was enough to set her into motion. "Zane," she whispered.

He didn't respond.

"Zane," she said louder.

He moved his leg over hers, trapping her with his powerful thigh. *Lovely.* "Zane, get up."

He snuggled in a little closer. Every hard inch of him squished between her ass cheeks.

"Jesus, Z," she mumbled.

In the space of a breath, he was on top of her, straddling her hips and gazing down at her with that devilish grin that probably burned off half the panties in LA.

"No," she said.

"No what?" He waggled his brows.

She eyed his enormous cock. "No *everything*."

He looked down at his erection and laughed. "You're going to give him a complex."

"*Z!*" She pushed him off and jumped from the bed, settling a hand on her hip. She tried to glare at him, but he lay there looking sexy and playful and so very *Zane*, she couldn't do more than laugh.

He patted the bed. "Come on, Wills. Let's play."

"We played last night. You were supposed to sleep on the *couch*."

"Oops. I forgot." His eyes cruised down her body, and she felt herself go damp. "Damn, baby. You look even finer in the morning than you do in my fantasies."

"What*ever*." She threw the pillow at him. "I'm taking a shower, and when I come out, that viper of yours better be sleeping."

He pushed up on one elbow. "Only one way that's going to happen." He eyed the empty side of the bed.

"Dream on, big boy." She grabbed her clothes from her suitcase and headed for the bathroom—locking the door behind her. That was to keep her in, rather than keep him out. A quick glimpse in the mirror caused her stomach to plummet. Her T-shirt wasn't so big after all. Zane had gotten a clear view right *through* her white lace panties to the part of her that was begging her to get right back in that bed and *do* the big, hot, arrogant actor.

A long while and two self-pleasured orgasms later, she left the bathroom and found Zane pacing the balcony in those tight black briefs. Her body stirred again. Two weeks of this was going to kill her.

She needed space to clear her head . . . *again*. She went to the balcony and whispered, "I'm going down to get breakfast."

He pointed to the phone and mouthed, *Sorry*.

The look in his eyes told her he really was.

She grabbed a muffin and coffee from the café and took them out to the lawn, gazing out at the beautiful mountains bordering the water. The resort made Lake George feel fancy and upscale. Sitting on the grass in her skinny jeans and T-shirt, she kicked off her sandals, and a cool breeze swept over her feet. If it weren't for the wedding preparations taking place on the opposite side of the lawn, she could almost pretend the elaborate resort didn't exist. Every once in a while, Willow thought about what it would be like to be the bride instead of the baker. Between baking wedding cakes and catering the receptions, it was hard *not* to think about weddings. But she wasn't like some women who *needed* a man. No, Willow was too independent to need anyone.

Her thoughts turned to Zane. *I needed to kiss you last night.* But where did that leave them now? Wishing she had answers, she forced herself to think about her motivations. She sighed, picking at her muffin and thinking about when she'd gone off to college after they'd slept together. He *had* done her a favor. She hadn't wanted to go away to college as an inexperienced virgin, and he'd given her experience. The problem was, no man could ever live up to what she'd built that night up to be in her mind—or in her heart.

She'd been naive to think she could sleep with him and not feel anything. She and Zane had continued texting for the first few weeks, but it wasn't like they'd texted love notes or had developed a real relationship. At least she'd stuck to *that* end of the bargain and kept her true feelings to herself. But she'd hoped that at some point their relationship might naturally develop into something more, and she'd gone out with her new friends and had boudoir pictures taken, intending to send them to Zane and win him over. But then he'd stopped texting, and with his radio silence, she'd chickened out. She'd never gone back to pick up the photos. And it was a good thing, because it might have taken her several months to finally move past her first all-consuming love, but knowing the kind of man Zane had turned into painted a pretty clear picture of what he'd wanted. If she'd sent those pictures and he'd turned her down, she would have been mortified on top of being heartbroken. And if she'd sent them and by some miracle they'd tried to have a relationship, he probably would have cheated, and that was the kind of pain she might not ever have recovered from.

She pushed those painful memories aside. Sometime later, after finishing her coffee and muffin and thinking about the Spider-Man cake she was going to bake for Louie's birthday, she was in a better mental place and determined not to go back to being that vulnerable girl again. From here on out, this was a business deal that wouldn't, *couldn't*, blur the line between friends and lovers.

Feeling more in control, she picked up her sandals and went in search of Zane, thinking about last night again. The man had more willpower than she did, and she was glad he'd finally given in. She had really believed he hadn't wanted to kiss her, and she had been surprised at how much that had hurt.

The gazebo came into view, and she recognized Zane's unmistakable profile: the sharp ridge of his nose and strong jaw, hair that looked as wild and free as his smiles did. He sat beside Liz, who was in her wedding gown. Willow's pulse kicked up as he leaned closer to Liz and took her chin in his hand, moving her face toward his. Willow froze, her fingers curling into fists. Was he hitting on the *bride*? Did Zane have *no* scruples? She stormed across the lawn, preparing to give him hell. And what was that stupid bride thinking? So what if he was Zane Walker! She was supposed to be in love with Mark. Didn't love mean anything anymore? Had the entire world lost their minds and turned into sweet-and-sour tarts? *Be sweet. Or be sour. But don't pretend to be one when you're really the other.*

Liz turned red, puffy eyes in Willow's direction as she approached, and Willow's stomach plummeted. He'd made her cry?

"Hey, sweetheart," Zane said softly. "Liz is having a case of cold feet. I was just telling her that means she's truly in love with Mark."

She wanted to ask what he knew about *true love*, but the lump in her throat only allowed an empathetic mew to escape. She stepped into the gazebo, and Zane reached for her like it was the most natural thing in the world and pulled her down on his lap. He brushed her hair over her shoulder, and his honest eyes made the lump in Willow's throat expand.

"I know a thing or two about cold feet," he said. "I was so afraid Willow would say no when I proposed, I wasted weeks trying to get up the nerve to ask her. You're just afraid of being hurt, Liz. But I'm sure Mark feels about you the way I feel about Willow. Like his world wouldn't be complete without you."

He turned his warm brown eyes on Willow, and she felt herself sliding down a slippery slope, wanting to believe him.

"She's my whole life," he said with a tender smile. "I can't imagine going a single day without seeing her beautiful face. I dream about seeing her belly round with our babies and about taking long walks when we're old and gray, so hard of hearing we have to shout just to hear each other."

"Gosh, you guys are so in love." Liz wiped her tears with a wad of tissues.

If Willow didn't know Zane was just playing a role, she'd have said the same thing. Part of her believed every word out of his mouth. But she pushed that vulnerable, naive girl down deep. Then she stomped on her head a few times, burying her even deeper. She followed Liz's gaze across the lawn and found Mark approaching, looking handsome in his tuxedo, a concerned expression etched into his face.

"Come on, baby," Zane said to Willow. "I think Liz and Mark should be alone." He squeezed Liz's hand and said, "Marriage takes an act of trust. In some ways it's a blind bargain, because by nature people and life are fluid. They're destined to change, which is what makes them so wonderful." His arm circled Willow's waist, and she wondered if he'd had relationship lessons for breakfast. "But if you both make an effort, you grow together, not apart. You've got this, Liz. Be happy."

He led Willow away from the gazebo. She waited for him to brag about how good an actor he was, or fish for kudos for a deed well done, but he remained silent. That silence endeared him toward her even more. These glimpses into the guy he had been were piling up inside her like sprinkles on her Zane cupcake, making her hungry for more.

His phone rang, and he pulled it from his pocket and glanced at it. "I've got to take this. Give me a sec?"

Willow watched him walk away, silently reprimanding herself for jumping to the worst conclusions about him. She vowed to stop and to try to gain control of her jealousy, which had spurred that awful thought in the first place. She watched him pacing, his hand cruising through his hair so many times she knew he was dealing with an issue. He downplayed his job whenever she brought it up over text. *Show up and look good. Nothing to it.* But she knew him better than that. She knew he'd probably studied and rehearsed relentlessly in order to have this time off. She also knew it would be far easier for him to have asked an actress from LA to play the part of his fake fiancée. *It would be weird to try to act like this with anyone other than you.*

She hadn't paid enough attention to his answer when he'd said it. Or maybe she was reading too much into it now, wondering if he really believed it, because for her it was one hundred percent true. She could never act like she had a serious relationship with anyone else. She'd found that out when she'd brought home another guy the Christmas after she and Zane had slept together. Faking it had made her sick to her stomach. She was thinking about that painful holiday when he returned to her side with a disgruntled expression.

"Come on, we've got to pack."

"What's wrong?" She hurried to keep up and followed him into the resort.

He looked even more distraught when they entered the elevator. "We need to go see your parents."

"My par—" She grabbed his hand. "What happened?" She patted her pockets, but she'd left her phone in the room. "Did Ben call? Did something happen? Are they okay?"

He grabbed her by the shoulders as panic swallowed her. "Wills, look at me."

She met his gaze, and in it she found solace.

"Your parents are fine, babe, but the papers picked up our story. It's all over the Internet."

"What? How?" Her mind reeled.

The elevator doors opened, and they rushed toward their room.

"Some idiot took pictures of us last night. People do this shit all the time. They sell pics for big money and the press makes up stories. You *know* that. My PR rep said they had pictures of us dancing and of me carrying you toward the resort. The headlines said something about our 'secret engagement.'"

It was going to be bad enough to try to lie to her family, but for them to find out from an article made it a hundred times worse. She followed him into the room and scrambled for her phone. One glance at the messages from her family told her they'd already seen the news.

"This is bad, Zane. Really bad. What am I going to tell them?" She rushed into the bathroom and began gathering her things. "I don't know why I thought I could lie to them. This will kill them. They'll never trust me again."

ZANE THREW HIS belongings into his suitcase, wishing he could track down the asshole who had taken the pictures and pound the shit out of them. No part of his plan called for Willow or her family to get hurt. In fact, he'd thought he'd taken measures to avoid that. It was hard to believe there had been a time when he'd craved this type of radical attention. He'd been an idiot to believe he'd needed it to validate that he'd *made it*. After a decade of acting, he was over invasions of his privacy. He'd had a hard enough time with the idea of one photographer at his beck and call, but he'd be damned if he was going to let Willow and her family get caught in the Hollywood bullshit crossfire.

"We'll fix this, Willow. It's not like you've lied to them."

She stopped stuffing clothes into her bag. "Isn't there a 'yet' missing?" She shoved the rest of her clothes in the bag and zipped it up. "Wasn't that the whole idea? We'd go back to Sweetwater and lie to everyone? Give them your made-up story about us and hope they bought it? I don't know why I agreed to do that. We have to tell them the truth."

He slung her bag over his shoulder, wondering how he could navigate this without screwing it up. "Wills, we can't tell them."

"We *can* and we *will*." She crossed her arms. "You're asking me to lie to my *family*."

"I am," he admitted, guilt suffocating him. "That makes me a shithead, but I promise you I'll take all the blame afterward. If one person slips up and says this is fake, the whole thing is blown."

"It's ridiculous anyway," she seethed. "Who will ever believe you would settle down with one woman? You don't even know what that means."

He clenched his jaw against the truth, but it broke free anyway. "You're so fucking wrong, you're on the wrong planet. You don't know everything about me, Willow, so don't stand there and judge me like everyone else in the fucking world does."

She scoffed. "Oh, please. You've never even had a long-term girlfriend."

He stepped closer, heat thundering in the space between them despite their dispute. "Maybe that's by choice, and not because of whatever reasons are floating around in that beautiful head of yours." He raked his hand through his hair, mired down by guilt. "Look. I need you, but I don't want to hurt you or your family. If you need to tell them, I'll announce to the press that they've got it all wrong. The ring is not an engagement ring, and we're old friends. I'll make sure your reputation stays intact."

Her gaze softened. "But what about the focus group and all that stuff about fans not buying you as a romance hero?"

"I'll figure something out."

"Goddamn it." She plopped down on the bed.

Zane crouched beside her. "I'm sorry, Wills. I love your family. They've been better to me than my own family ever was. I didn't think this through. I can't expect you to lie to them, and you can't tell them and expect them to keep it a secret. I'll call the photographer and put an end to the ruse right now. I'm sorry I got you involved." He slid his phone from his pocket and scrolled through his contacts for the photographer's number.

"Don't call him," she relented.

He lifted his eyes, and she rolled hers.

"I made you a promise. You kept yours when I needed you before college. It's only fair that I keep mine now."

He was filled with gratitude and admiration, but he didn't want her to feel pressured by their past. "Willow, this is different from what happened between us back then. If you do this, please don't do it out of some warped sense of obligation. I will adore you whether you agree or not. I don't want to hurt you or your family. It was an impetuous plan, regardless of how much I thought I'd planned it out. I missed this giant piece, and I don't want to hurt you."

She nodded, her gaze softening. He lifted his phone, and she put her hand over his, lowering it to his side again.

"It's only two weeks," she said, shocking the hell out of him. "They'll be mad when we finally tell them the truth, but if anyone will understand, it's my family. They go to crazy lengths for their friends, and they *love* you."

He cocked a brow. "I'm not sure Piper's on board with the whole loving Zane thing." Piper was a year and a half older than Willow and a year younger than him and Ben. She'd always treated Zane as if she didn't quite trust him, though he couldn't figure out why.

That earned him a sort-of smile. "Piper will probably be annoyed with both of us for a while, but she'll get over it."

He sat beside her. "Are you sure?"

She held out her left hand, the diamond sparkling in the bright lights. "What kind of fiancée dumps her man when things get tough? We've got this."

He wrapped her in his arms, and they both fell backward to the mattress. He kissed her smack on the lips. "I owe you big-time for this." He pressed his hips to her thigh. "I can make up for it right now if you let me."

She pushed him off, still smiling. "I'm *so* going to regret this."

He pulled her up to her feet and tugged her against him. "I promise you won't. I'll be the perfect fake fiancé. You're going to fall so hard for me, you aren't going to want this fake engagement to end."

# CHAPTER SIX

WILLOW TEXTED HER family before they left the resort to let them know they'd clear everything up when they arrived. They hadn't responded, which she took as a comforting sign, but Zane was so quiet on the way home he made Willow even more nervous. He was never quiet. She'd been surprised to learn he didn't have a car with him at the resort, but she shouldn't have been. He'd planned to spend the next two weeks in Sweetwater, which meant he had probably planned to drive back with her. It was all part of his *big plan*. She'd never known him to be a planner, but he seemed to have thought out just about everything to substantiate this shenanigan, with the exception of the guilt that went along with it. She realized that was probably why he was quiet, and it endeared him to her even more.

As the miles passed and they turned off the highway toward Sweetwater, the usual sense of calm her hometown brought evaded her. Zane's leg began bouncing repeatedly, another of his nervous habits. She'd forgotten about that one.

"You look even more nervous than me. You okay?" Willow asked.

"Yeah. Just thinking about Ben." He raised one shoulder in a half shrug.

She curled her fingers tightly around the steering wheel. Of course he was thinking about Ben. It was anyone's guess how her older brother would react to their news. Despite Zane's claim that Willow knew him better than anyone, she believed *Ben* knew him better. They were too close for him not to have shared his sexual conquests with her brother, and Ben was more than a little protective of his sisters. Willow was glad she didn't know all of Zane's secrets. Just thinking about him and other women made her feel a little sick. She'd been pretty good about not thinking about it over the years, but this fake engagement made her feel possessive of him in ways she probably shouldn't. Where did a person in a fake relationship draw their boundary lines?

"Maybe because you spend your life acting," she suggested, not unkindly. "And we're the one family you've never had to act around?"

He rested his head back, and a genuine smile, which was a world away from his mischievous or seductive smiles, slid across his face. He looked so *real*, Willow almost reached for his hand.

"Yeah. I think you nailed it, babe."

She slowed the car as they entered the narrow cobblestone streets of Sweetwater, which was located at the base of the Silver Mountains. Sugar Lake came into view, and as she turned onto the main drag, driving by the old-fashioned storefronts she adored, she thought of the seasonal festivals and community events she loved so much. But as she drove parallel to the lake, she had the urge to flee. Being on her turf made their situation even more real, and her stomach clenched tight.

"Can I ask you something?" she asked to distract herself.

"Anything."

"Don't say that. There are things I don't want to know."

He laughed. "Fair enough. You can ask me anything you want to know the answer to." He reached across the car and kneaded the tension that had settled in her shoulders.

He knew her so well, and his touch felt incredible. She could get used to this. *For a couple of weeks, anyway.* "You know how you call me *babe* and *sweetheart* . . . ?"

"Let's not forget *sweet cheeks*." He smirked.

"I'd rather forget that one."

"Admit it, you *love* that one the most."

His hand circled the back of her neck, massaging the knots at the base, and she heard herself moan. She clenched her mouth shut against the telling sound.

"Ah," he said. "Looks like I hit your sweet spot."

She glared at him.

"Admit it, Wills. I know how to hit *all* your sweet spots."

She rolled her eyes.

"Hey. No more eye rolls, remember?"

"I remember," she said in a singsong voice. "Can we get back to my question?" She turned down the road that led to her parents' house and felt like the elephant in the room had settled on her chest. "Why do you call women by those names?"

"What names?"

He stopped rubbing her neck but kept his hand there. His skin was so hot it felt like he was branding her with his handprint.

"Um. *Babe, sweetheart,* those kinds of names."

He began massaging her neck again, and despite her resolve to remain detached, his touch brought a world of comfort.

"Then maybe I asked the wrong question," he said, his hand stilling again. "What women are you talking about?"

She pulled onto her parents' long driveway and parked behind her siblings' cars. At least she had a clear path for an escape if things went poorly. "Are you really going to make me say it?"

"Wills, you need to clue me in. Who do you think I call those names? I try not to call women much of anything other than their names."

Searching his eyes for the truth, she'd swear it was staring back at her. "That doesn't make any sense. You call me everything *but* my name most of the time."

He shoved his door open and stepped from the car. "Stop picking me apart and let's get this over with." He came around and offered her his hand. "Come on, baby cakes. Let's go show your family how in lust we are."

Lust? That was easy, but fooling her parents into thinking they'd been secretly dating all this time? Not so much. "This is not going to be a walk in the park."

"Nothing worth its salt ever is." He motioned toward her parents' two-story white Victorian. "Ah, the Grand Lady. She still looks as beautiful as ever."

Her father had given their five-bedroom house that name because it sat high on a hill at the end of a cul-de-sac, as if it were watching over the other houses on the street. From Willow's childhood bedroom on the second floor, she could see all the way down to Sugar Lake. The house wasn't enormous, but it was big by Sweetwater standards and sat on three acres of land.

"My parents are talking about selling again. Maybe you can help talk them out of it while you're here. They're back to complaining about how big it is, and the upkeep."

"It is too big for them, babe."

She sighed. "I know, but I have so many good memories. It would make me sad to see it leave our family."

"I'll do my best," he promised, and slid his arm around her waist, holding her tight.

She didn't even try to fight it. She was getting used to being attached to him at the hip, and right then she needed every bit of support she could get.

ZANE PRAYED TO whatever gods might be listening and hoped to hell he could pull this off. He was more nervous than he'd ever been, with the exception of the night he and Willow had snuck out to take care of her V-card. He raked his hand through his hair and stared at the house he'd spent enough time in to know exactly which stairs creaked (the third from the second-story landing) and how many steps it took to walk from the front of the house to the rear (fifteen). He and Ben had figured out which windows were easy to climb out of by the time they were ten, and by sixteen they'd figured out how long it took Ben's parents to fall asleep after they'd gone to bed, so they could sneak out those windows. But perhaps his most treasured memory wasn't of the interior of the house; it was of standing in the dark corner of the back-yard waiting to meet Willow at midnight, sure he was going to have a panic attack or experience premature ejaculation from the mere thought of having sex with her. He'd never known fear or elation as he had while standing there watching Willow sneak out the back door to meet him. Even now it was his most treasured, and most terrifying, memory.

"How are we going to pull this off?" Willow asked.

She suddenly looked fearful and vulnerable. He took her in his arms and gazed into her eyes. "Baby, all you have to do is kiss me *once* like you did last night and nobody will ever doubt us."

She rolled her eyes.

"But if you follow it up with an eye roll, they'll never believe you."

"I'm sorry." She lowered her voice and whispered, "I'm so freaking nervous. I never lie to my family."

He cocked his head, giving her a look he knew translated as *I can think of at least one time that you did.*

"Anymore," she said sharply.

He smiled and pressed a kiss to her forehead. "We've got this, baby. They know we're friends. They know we text."

"Yeah." She laughed incredulously. "Bridge knows you proposition me all the time, too."

"Then it's an even easier transition. You took me up on a proposi-tion, which is true. That's all you have to say."

She drew in a deep breath, nodding. "Okay. I can do that."

"And I'll be right there with you. In fact, I'll do all the talking if you want."

"You might have to," she said as they walked toward the wide front steps.

He patted her butt. "No prob, sweet cheeks."

She glared at him.

He chuckled as Willow's mother, Roxie Dalton, came around the side of the house. Her wild blond curls were as unruly as ever. She threw her arms up in the air with a wide smile. The sleeves of her blue batik top hung like wings from her arms. Her colorful skirt wafted around her legs as she hurried across the grass.

"I thought I heard Chloe! Zane Walker, you sly little devil you." She pulled him into her arms and kissed his cheek. "How long have you been pulling the wool over our eyes?"

"My whole life?" Hey, that wasn't a lie.

Roxie laughed, and behind her Willow rolled her eyes.

"I always wondered if you two would figure out how good you'd be together," her mother said.

Zane's stomach knotted up. He'd always thought they would be good together, too, but knowing the woman who had been like a second mother to him bought their lie hook, line, and sinker, without so much as an explanation, brought guilt crashing in again.

Roxie's eyes teared up as she embraced Willow. "Baby girl. Oh, my sweet baby girl."

"Hi, Mom. I'm sorry you found out like this." Willow glared at Zane over her mother's shoulder.

Reality slammed into him, bonding with the guilt. *You're risking everything for me.* The same way she'd risked it all those years ago when she'd *chosen* him. Only this time *he'd* chosen *her.* Hell, he'd always chosen her.

"I want all the special details, but first—" Roxie reached for each of their hands, her eyes catching on the ring. "Well, isn't that sparkly and gorgeous?" She tipped a curious gaze to Willow.

"Yeah," she said. "It's . . . *big*. And beautiful."

He knew the ring was all wrong for Willow, but there was nothing he could do about that now.

Roxie drew in a deep breath. "You need to know that not everyone in the family is as on board as I am. Benny, Piper, Dad. They're . . . well, they're concerned. Talia has a lot of questions. And, baby girl, I think Bridgette is a little hurt. So, kid gloves, okay? She isn't here. She said she didn't want Louie around whatever went down this afternoon."

Sadness shadowed Willow's gaze, and Zane felt his heart crack open.

"I'm sorry, Mrs. D. The whole secretive thing was my idea. Willow wanted to be honest, but with my reputation and her hatred of being the center of attention, I thought it best to protect her for as long as we could." He took Willow's hand, and when he gazed into her eyes, his emotions poured out. "I know how hard it has been for Willow to keep our secret from her family, and I'll spend the rest of my life trying to make up for it."

As if on cue, Willow sighed dreamily.

"Oh my word," Roxie said a little breathlessly. "No one could deny the love between you two."

# CHAPTER SEVEN

IF LOOKS COULD kill, Zane would be laid out in the Daltons' back-yard. Piper glared at him from where she was repairing a picnic table bench beneath a giant tree. She had a hammer in her hand, and from the look in her eyes, she wanted to use it on Zane. Piper was a petite blonde at five two or three, and she probably weighed all of a hundred and ten pounds soaking wet, but Zane felt the threat of her stare as if she were a formidable opponent. And as Willow's sister, she was.

"There they are. Congratulations, sweetheart." Dan Dalton, Willow's father, swept her into his arms. He had been a college profes-sor before retiring and focusing on his second passion as a custom-home builder. He and Piper ran Dalton Contracting, and while he looked more like a professor than a builder—tall and slim, with close-cropped salt-and-pepper hair—he and Piper were both excellent at their craft.

Dan passed Willow to her eldest sister, Talia, who shared their father's dark eyes and his love of all things academic. She worked as an English lit professor at a small private college just outside Sweetwater, and she was the most serious and careful of Willow's siblings. She was a pretty woman, with thick, dark brows, high cheekbones, a slim, perky nose, and long, wavy hair almost as dark as her father's and Ben's, all of which softened the straightforward, geeky smarts that sometimes tumbled out of her mouth.

"Congratulations," Talia said after hugging Willow and embracing Zane. "Needless to say, we were all a little shocked."

Willow glanced nervously at Zane. He draped his arm over her shoulder and kissed her cheek, letting her know he had this. "I think we were, too," he admitted. "But when it's right, it's right."

Ben came out the back door of the house carrying a cooler and set it down on the patio table. He was a venture capitalist and a shrewd businessman, but in his cargo shorts and tank top he looked more like a frat boy. That was one of the things Zane loved most about the Daltons. They didn't put on airs. He and Ben had been best friends since the third grade, when they'd pried a bully off another kid in the schoolyard. Zane and Ben spoke over the phone often, and their friendship had never suffered for the distance.

"Zane." Standing shoulder to shoulder with Zane, Ben pulled him into a manly embrace and lowered his voice. "We should talk."

Zane had tried to prepare himself for Ben's reaction, but hearing the concern in Ben's voice messed with his head. "Sure."

"I'm putting an addition on my house. Stop by and check it out," Ben suggested.

"Absolutely. You still running?"

Ben patted his abs. "You know it. You?"

"Of course. I'd like to hit the pavement together, but I'm not sure I'll have time."

"If you can fit it in, hit me up. I'll try to go slow enough not to leave you in my dust."

Zane laughed. *Same old Ben.*

While Ben greeted Willow, Piper sidled up to Zane.

"Hey, Piper." Their embraces were always a little chilly, and today was no different.

"Hi." A curious smile lifted her lips. He'd take that over the scowl she'd flashed when she'd first seen him. "Engaged, huh?"

He pushed a hand through his hair and shifted his eyes to Willow. His heart rate kicked up, bringing genuine warmth to his words. "I couldn't let her go unclaimed for another day."

*"Unclaimed?"* Piper laughed. "She's not a dog at the pound."

"Jesus, Piper. Cut me some slack. It's a little nerve-racking to know we let you guys down by keeping our relationship to ourselves. What I meant was that I wanted the world to know we were together. I was done playing games, sick of hiding my feelings." The words exploded out of him much more forcefully than he'd expected, but he'd held them in for so long, he couldn't pretend anymore. The confession shocked the hell out of him, but it was the truth, and he didn't *want* to pretend anymore.

Piper eyed him skeptically. "Hm."

*Hm is right.* He stole another glance at Willow, and his protective urges surged forward. He was determined to make sure no one questioned his love for her. It was time to step up his game for his most important role yet.

"We're here to rescue you," Talia said as she and Dan came to Zane's side.

"Piper giving you hell, son?" Her father placed a hand on Zane's shoulder.

Piper laughed and went back to repairing the bench.

Zane met Dan's kind gaze, a smile instantly forming on his lips. Dan had been like a second father to him over the years. When he'd first gone out to Los Angeles to try to make it as an actor, Dan had connected Zane with his old college roommate, a big-time producer who had given Zane a place to stay and introduced him to several people in the industry. Zane owed Dan more than the lies they were feeding him. *Pile another log on the guilt pile.*

"Nah. She's just watching out for Willow," Zane said. "How's it going, Mr. D?"

"Pretty darn well these days. Looks like we'll be planning a wedding."

"Sure will." Zane breathed a little easier. "I hear you're thinking about selling the Grand Lady."

"We're kicking the idea around," Dan answered. "More seriously this time. We're not getting any younger."

"He's been talking about it for ages, but he can't let it leave the family any sooner than we could," Talia said. "So, Zane. What's the real story?" She set a serious gaze on him. "We had no idea you guys were even dating, and suddenly Willow gets a catering job at a resort and comes back engaged."

"Talia," her mother cautioned.

"I'm just curious." Talia glanced at Willow, who was talking with Ben.

Zane reached for Willow's hand. "The truth is, Willow and I have been seeing each other for a few months. But we've kept it under the radar because . . ." Willow's palm began to sweat. He hated that they had to live this lie, but they'd gone this far with her family. They couldn't back out now. "Well, because we didn't want the added stress of the media making our relationship into a circus act."

Piper set her hammer on the picnic table and crossed her arms. "How did you avoid the media for all this time?"

"It's not that hard when it's your goal." Zane launched into a diatribe about evading the press and blending in. He rambled for so long he wasn't even sure he was making sense. Beside him, Willow fidgeted with her ring.

"But, Willow," Talia said, "didn't you go out with Billy Crusher two months ago?"

Jealousy burned through Zane. Billy had been a year behind him in school. He was a good guy then, and if Willow had gone out with him, he was probably still a good guy, but that didn't make thinking about her in his arms any easier.

"I . . . um . . ." Willow stuttered.

"That was all part of the plan," Zane interrupted. "Keeping things as normal as possible so we wouldn't raise suspicions. We've had to be covert for so long, it feels good to finally have things out in the open."

"Listen, son," Dan said. "We love you like our own flesh and blood." He glanced at Willow. "But that girl there? She *is* our flesh and blood. I'm not going to pretend I don't hear the gossip. Not that I believe it, but it's a wild world out there, despite how homespun we are here in Sweetwater. Just give me your word that my little girl isn't going to get her heart broken, and I'll believe you. I need to hear it from you."

"I give you my word that I will never purposefully hurt Willow." Zane was surprised at how easily and honestly his answer came.

"Oh my God." Willow threw her hands up in the air. "I can't take this anymore."

The pit of Zane's stomach sank. "Willow."

"No." She held up her left hand and flashed her ring. "See this ring? We're engaged. *Yes*, we've been sneaking around to see each other, but would any one of you have believed we could ever really make it together otherwise?" She pointed at Talia, her words flying fast and hot. "You question everything to death. I wish I had hotel receipts to show you, but I don't. And, Piper? For whatever reason, you've never trusted Zane, so why would you now?"

She turned angry eyes on Zane, and he was sure the jig was up. His mind reeled, grasping for the right apology for Willow and her family, because even if she never forgave him, he wouldn't be able to live with himself if her family held this against her.

Before he could get a word out, Willow said, "But this man." She closed the distance between them, a loving smile softening her anger. "This warm, caring, funny, *arrogant* man has been trying to win me over for months. And—"

She was breathing so hard Zane expected another explosion, but she grabbed his face and crushed her mouth to his. Stunned, it took a moment for his addled brain to kick into gear, and when he did there was no holding back. There never was when it came to kissing Willow. He deepened the kiss, dipping her back like it was a grand kiss in a movie. But this was no movie, and this kiss—*holy hell, this kiss*—was nothing short of amazing, and it went on far too long for a kiss witnessed by family, but Zane was in no hurry for it to end.

When their mouths finally parted, he was so overcome with emotions, "God, I love you," came out before he could stop it.

"Glad to hear it," her father said. "Now let's get you a beer."

WILLOW AND ZANE had dinner with her family. By the time they finally left, Willow felt like she'd been through the wringer. Thankfully, her family had stopped peppering them with questions after she'd attacked Zane with the kiss that topped all others. But ever since, things had changed between her and Zane, and that was more nerve-racking than her family's questions. She couldn't look at him without her body heating up, and that was dangerous territory.

"I'm *so* glad that's over," she said honestly.

Zane placed his hand on her thigh, and her mind went straight to the gutter. How would she make it through the next two weeks when one kiss could set her body ablaze?

"You nailed it, Wills. That kiss was kryptonite to your family's interrogation."

"Whatever it takes, right?" She drove down the street toward the bakery, telling herself she'd kissed him for the sake of selling their ruse, not because she'd been waiting for an excuse with every breath she'd taken since last night. "I need to talk to Bridgette. I hate that she's hurt."

"I know, babe. Why don't we put our stuff in your apartment and go get a drink? After she puts Louie to bed, we can talk to her."

She eyed him. "We?"

"I'm not letting you take the blame."

*It's like you really care.*

He peered through the windshield intently. "Don't stop the car."

"Why?" She spotted two guys standing outside the bakery. "Oh God. Are those your reporters?"

"They're not *my* reporters, and no. The guy from TMZ already lost his exclusive. He's moved on to bigger and better stories. Those must be locals looking to make a buck."

"Great. So now I can't even go back to my own bakery? How am I supposed to get to my apartment?" She lived above the bakery.

"I've got an idea. Head down to Dutch's Pub, but drive around first in case they're watching the cars."

"You think they won't find us if we're sitting in a bar? They'll get bored of waiting and end up there anyway." She passed the bakery and kept driving until she was several blocks away before looping around the block and heading down toward the marina.

"We're not staying there. I just want to talk to Harley." Harley Dutch was a bear claw, big enough to share and sweet to the very core. He had gone to school with Zane and Ben. He'd had a thriving financial management business in New York City until a few years ago, when his father had gotten ill and he'd returned to Sweetwater to help with the family pub. She knew Harley still helped Zane and Ben manage their investments.

"I'm supposed to make Louie's Spider-Man cake tonight for his party tomorrow."

"Do you want to deal with those reporters? I'm used to it—"

"No! I've had enough stress for one day."

"Then I'll help you make the cake tomorrow. We'll get up early and make it before the party."

"The party isn't until the afternoon. I guess that'll work."

He took out his phone. "Let me text Harley." After he was done, he said, "Okay, we need to swing by Harley's house," and went back to texting. "Can we make a quick stop at Everything and More?"

Everything and More was a small-scale department store owned by Dennis Preacher, a crotchety old man who had growled at customers ever since he'd lost his wife to cancer eight years ago. Willow couldn't help but love Dennis and often made him special pastries just to see if she could earn a smile. It worked about a third of the time. He was definitely an acquired taste, like molasses cookies.

When she pulled up in front of the store, Zane jumped out and told her he'd be right back. Nearly twenty minutes later, she was debating going in to find him when he finally returned carrying two enormous shopping bags, which he tossed into the backseat. A pillow stuck out the top of one of them.

He slid into the front seat. "Sorry it took so long. Penny Preacher was working tonight. She texted me when she heard we were filming in Sweetwater and asked me to stop by. I figured I'd give her a thrill."

Penny was Dennis's granddaughter. She was a year younger than Willow and had won Strawberry Queen three years in a row at Sweetwater's annual Strawberry Festival. She was a definite fruit and custard pastry puff, beautiful inside and out.

"Give her a thrill? Is that short for . . . Never mind. Don't answer that." She sped out of the parking lot, trying to remember how to breathe.

An hour later, after meeting up with Harley, who lived down the road from the pub, they were in a rowboat loaded up with camping gear and whatever else he had bought at Everything and More. The water swished off the oars as Zane rowed them out toward the island, and Willow was still stewing over Zane giving Penny a *thrill*.

"This is your big plan? We're going to row out to the island and *camp*?" She lifted a bottle of her favorite wine from one of the boxes Harley had given them. At least she'd have *that*. They used to take rowboats out to the island with her siblings when they were kids, and Zane almost always came with them. Talia would read on the shore, Piper built forts, and Willow and Bridgette would pretend they were on a tropical island, ordering Ben and Zane around as if they were cabana boys. Most of the time Ben would ignore them, but Zane usually played along. It made sense now. Even back then he was honing the craft that would make him famous.

"Do you have a better plan?" His voice strained as he rowed faster. "If we stay at the B and B, they'll just hound the place and drive the owners crazy. This way you'll have a place to chill without anyone bothering you. Besides," he admitted a little sheepishly, "I seem to remember a certain girl telling me she dreamed about being whisked away to a remote island."

"How do you even remember that? It was—" *The night we slept together.* Butterflies took flight in her stomach. She silently chastised herself again. *Do not over-romanticize this!* It was hard not to when he remembered something she'd said a decade ago. "A *long* time ago. This wasn't exactly what I had in mind."

"I could have borrowed Harley's motorboat, but that would have alerted the reporters on a quiet night like this." He stopped rowing and gazed out at the lights of the town fading in the distance. "Besides, you don't need a yacht to be treated like a princess."

Her breathing hitched. "What did you say?"

"You don't need a yacht to be treated like a princess."

He began rowing again, moving through the water at a fast clip, while she tried to get ahold of her whirling emotions. Last summer he'd texted and invited her to join him on a yacht for the weekend, and he'd promised to treat her like a princess. Her response had been, *No, thanks. I don't need a yacht to be treated like a princess.*

She crossed her arms, gathering the courage to call him on it, but every time she opened her mouth to speak, something inside her fluttered with appreciation. He remembered two things that anyone else might have found insignificant. What did that mean? She watched him more carefully, taking in the way his jaw flexed with his efforts, his strong hands gripping the oars like he'd been rowing every day of his life. She doubted he'd even been out on a rowboat since they were kids. She lifted her gaze and found him watching her, arousing the lust he'd been stirring like an out-of-control blender.

"What are you doing, Zane?" she finally managed.

"Rowing us out to the island." When he spoke again, his voice was laced with seduction. "What are *you* doing, Wills?"

*Falling for you again.*

The island came into view, and without breaking their connection, he dragged one oar in the water, guiding the boat toward the land.

"You know what I mean," she challenged.

His lips quirked up. "You mean, what am I doing, as in saving you from the media hounds? You're my fiancée. It seems like the right thing to do. Don't you think, sweetheart?"

"*Fake* fiancée," she said softly, gazing down at the ring. Maybe he didn't remember that text after all. She wished she could get his comment about Penny out of her mind, or at least stop feeling like she was falling for him again. Because the two conflicted so harshly she was left feeling like half-risen dough.

"What's the matter, Wills? Nervous about spending the night on a remote island with your man?"

She swallowed hard against the truth. She wasn't worried about Zane making a move on her. It was her own lack of control around him that concerned her.

"No," she said too sharply. "And you're only my *fake* man."

"I assure you, I'm one hundred percent *real* man, even if I'm your *fake* fiancé. But don't worry, baby cakes, I brought *all* the provisions we'll need."

She imagined he meant condoms, and she was as turned on as she was annoyed by the idea.

He docked the boat on the shore and reached for Willow's hand to help her out. She was flustered and still feeling a little prickly about Penny.

"I've got it." She jumped out of the boat, and her foot sank into the mud. "Ugh."

"Why don't you go up on the beach and I'll get the gear."

"I can help." She reached for a bag, which was heavier than it looked. "What's in this?"

"All the stuff we need."

She peeked into the bag. "Towels?"

"You didn't think I'd leave my skinny-dipping girl hanging, did you?" He waggled his brows and grabbed two boxes.

Willow had always loved skinny-dipping. Her family knew she'd sneak down to the lake at night and take a quick dip. She'd been caught skinny-dipping up in the mountains by her friend Logan Wild a few years earlier, too, but she didn't remember mentioning that to Zane. "I can't believe you remembered I like to skinny-dip."

"Are you kidding? I used to set my alarm so I wouldn't miss your dips in the lake."

"For some reason I believe that."

He laughed and they headed into the woods. Leaves and twigs crunched beneath their feet. Willow stayed close to Zane in the dark forest, wondering if he really had watched her skinny-dip. She had always been careful to walk down by the boathouse, where no one was ever around after dark. A thrill ran through her at the prospect of his naughty peeking.

"Pick a spot, beautiful."

"I can barely see."

He set down one of the boxes and turned on the flashlight app on his phone.

"You lead. I'll follow." He leaned closer and lowered his voice before saying, "Just like old times."

Her pulse quickened as they wove through the thickly wooded area, but her mind kept jumping back to *giving Penny a thrill*. It wasn't like he'd been in the store long enough to do anything, but the way he'd said it still bugged her.

"How are we going to set up a tent here? And what about a bathroom? This feels a little extreme for avoiding photographers. We don't even know if they *were* photographers."

"They were. A few local photogs, as I suspected. I texted my security guys. They've probably already taken care of it, and you won't have to be bothered for the rest of the time I'm in town."

"You sound like a drug dealer or a Mafia man." Lowering her voice an octave, she said, *"My security guys."*

"If you're going to bitch about photographers, you can't give me shit about what needs to be done to get rid of them."

She couldn't argue with that. "But you need the media. Aren't they part of the focus group's plan? You can't screw that up."

"I'll figure something out. But I'm not going to screw up your life in the process. We'll be seen enough around town without you being hounded by the press."

"What if the focus—"

"Wills, I've got this. Let me deal with it, okay? No one is going to make you feel like a prisoner in your own town. At least not because of me." They came to a clearing, and he set down the supplies. "This is perfect. I'll get the rest."

"I'll go, too."

"Only if you hold my hand."

She hesitated, still thinking of Penny. "Why?"

"Because part of acting is immersing yourself in your character." He stepped closer, a glimmer of seduction in his eyes. *"Immerse* with me, Wills."

"Maybe you should have brought Penny." She stepped away, but he grabbed her hand and hauled her back.

"Green is not your color, baby."

She rolled her eyes, struggling against him as his arms circled her, holding her captive.

"Now we're back to eye rolling?" Tightening his grip with one hand, he ran his finger along the edge of her jaw. "You're the one who keeps pointing out that this is a *fake* engagement."

"It is."

"But you keep forgetting, no one here is supposed to know that. Not your family, not Harley, and definitely not Penny Preacher."

He pushed his hand beneath her hair, cupping the back of her head, and angled her face toward his as he had right before they'd kissed last night. He held her gaze for so long, her stress turned to anticipation.

"More importantly," he said in a husky voice. "Fake or not, I'd never embarrass you by hitting on another woman when I'm supposed to be with you. I might not be a saint, but I'm not a cheat. Besides, why would I ever drive a Honda when I have a Bentley in the garage?" He cocked a brow. "Coming?"

*Not yet.*

*Holy smokes. Seriously?* She was definitely losing her mind. "No. Go ahead." She pointed toward the boxes. "I'm going to find the wine."

# CHAPTER EIGHT

WHEN ZANE CAME back from getting the supplies, he found Willow sitting on the hill with her back to their campsite. She'd always needed time alone to cool down, and if she was feeling their sizzling connection even half as strongly as he was, she'd need a lot of space. He glanced up the hill, catching her silhouette against the moonlight. Her legs were stretched out in front of her, and her head was tipped up toward the sky. She looked peaceful and beautiful and so frigging sexy he could stare at her all night long, which was precisely why he returned his attention to setting up their campsite.

Inside the tent, he finished laying out the sleeping bags and spread the Egyptian cotton sheets he'd bought over them, set the pillow at the top, and checked the string of LED lights he'd hung around the entrance one last time before setting out the goodies he'd brought. He took care of a few more things, tossed his phone in the middle of the bed, and went to join her.

"Hey," she said as he dropped down beside her.

"You okay?"

"Mm-hm. Sorry about before."

He put an arm around her. "As I said, green's not your color. If I hinted at wanting to do anything more than letting Penny feel happy that I remembered she'd texted me, then I'm sorry. I was just killing two birds with one stone."

She rested her head on his shoulder. "I'm just a little messed up right now."

"I think I've already stolen that title. Your rep is clean." Pressing a kiss to her temple felt natural, and really, *really* good. How many years had he wished for time alone with Willow? "I'm sorry for putting you through this, but I'm glad we're getting this time together."

She gave him a long, assessing gaze. "Are you?"

*More than I ever realized I would be.* "Hell yes."

"But why? You're stuck out in the woods when you could be anywhere else."

"But you wouldn't be there."

For years they'd kept each other at arm's length, and now heat and the past and something much bigger seemed to twine together, tethering them with an unbreakable bond. His body moved of its own accord, leaning forward, wanting her, *needing* her in his arms. Her eyes said, *Take me*, but he knew he'd never stop at one kiss. There was no way. Not this time. Before he could get carried away, he pushed to his feet, grabbed the bottle of wine she'd been drinking, and pulled her up beside him.

"Come on. I've got a surprise for you."

"A better surprise than a fake engagement and photographers stalking my work and home?"

He turned her by the shoulders in the direction of the tent. The lights twinkled against the dark forest.

"Oh, Z—"

His heart thumped harder. That breathless whisper did him in. He took her hand and led her down to the tent. "Go on in, princess."

She went down on her knees on the edge of the bed. He watched her beautiful eyes drift over their comfortable bed and the cupcake he'd set off to the side.

"I'm sure it's nowhere near as good as yours, but I figured you might want something to go with this." He set down the wine bottle and knelt beside her, handing her his phone. "Turn it on."

She pushed the button, and the screen came to life, revealing the opening credits of the movie *The Notebook*. She covered her mouth, her eyes warm and dreamy.

"There's a whole playlist if you're not in the mood for that one." He reached over and navigated to Willow's Playlist, watching as she read the titles—*You've Got Mail, Titanic, 50 First Dates, Sleepless in Seattle, Love Actually, Pretty Woman* . . .

Scrolling through the twenty-plus titles, she said, "All my favorites."

"Yeah."

"How . . . ?"

"Ten years of being blown off is a long time. Each time you blew me off, you revealed a little more about yourself. Your favorite movies, that you like the Strawberry Festival better than any of the others, your penchant for custard instead of cream filling, your hatred of blue skirts and guys with no chest hair . . ."

*"Oh my gosh"* slipped out like a secret.

"I know I'm putting you through hell, Wills, lying to your family, taking you off the market for the next two weeks, but I'm really glad you're with me."

"This was my choice." She looked at the playlist again. "I thought you were just messing with me all those times you texted."

"So did I," he admitted.

She grabbed his hand, as if she needed it for stability. *Hold me, baby. Hold on tight.*

"Z," she whispered, emotions warring in her eyes. "I'm having trouble defining the line between real and fake."

He cradled her warm, soft face in his hands, the scent of wine and sweet, luscious *Willow* drawing him closer. Desire throbbed through his veins, his hands shook with the anticipation of finally touching her again, and he didn't even try to restrain himself any longer. "Then let's not define it."

She leaned forward, but the second before their lips touched, he tangled his hand in her hair, holding their kiss at bay.

"This time *I* make the rules," he said too harshly, but he was half a second away from tearing off her clothes and taking *all* of her, and there was no way in hell he would deny himself the chance to *feel*.

She swallowed hard, clutching his arms so tight her nails carved half-moons into his skin, and sweet Jesus, it felt *good*.

"This time we *feel*," he demanded. "We feel as much and as hard as we want. And we don't worry about anyone else. *Anything* else. Got it?"

She was breathing so hard, "Yes," came out as a plea.

He dragged his eyes down the length of her body, earning a shuddering inhalation, and in that moment his internal fire changed to an inferno; his desire turned greedy and dark. "Tonight you're mine, Willow."

He waited a beat to see if she changed her mind, but she was right there with him, so he pushed a little harder. "From this moment on, baby"—he brushed his lips over her cheek, and her breathing hitched—"I'm yours."

ZANE'S MOUTH CAME down over Willow's slowly, in complete control. God, she loved that about him. He never lost his cool. She gave herself over to their kiss, to his possession, no longer surprised that she wanted him so desperately. Their mouths moved in perfect sync. Intense and deep and so very *real* she could barely breathe. He lowered her to the bed, the weight of his hard body as intoxicating as a bottle of whiskey. This was how it had happened last time. They'd come together as if it were the only place they were ever meant to be. She drank in the taste of his mouth, disappeared into his scent, surrendered to the seduction of his hands moving over her skin like he owned her. He did own her. He always had.

His mouth moved down her neck, skipping over her breasts, and claimed the tender skin around her navel. She ground her hips, tugging his shirt up until he finally tore it off, revealing all his glorious planes of flesh, hers for the taking. He worked off her shoes and then removed his own. He watched her intently, electricity sparking between them as she wriggled out of her jeans and panties. Drunk-on-Zane Willow had serious game, obliterating the side of herself that usually held her back.

She eyed his jeans. "Off."

Salivating to taste him, aching to touch him, she watched as he visually devoured her. His piercing stare made her tremble and wet in anticipation of finally—*God, finally*—getting another chance at experiencing what she'd spent years searching for, the feelings he'd given her when she was too young to appreciate how good it had been, too stupid to realize that not every man possessed the capability to make her heart *and* body sing. She, too, had become an actress, lying about *amazing orgasms* and how men made her feel, when each and every time they'd paled in comparison to Zane. She tore her shirt over her head, and he breathed harder. Holy cow, she loved that. She reached behind her to unhook her bra.

"Willow," he practically growled. "You don't have to."

He was the only man who had ever really known her, who understood what it meant for her to bare her breasts. The others had never deserved that trust, and she'd never given it to them. "I want to."

She unhooked the clasp, and her breasts fell hot and heavy against her skin. He inhaled a long, uneven breath that made her feel like she'd given him a magnificent gift.

"Sweetheart."

The word was so full of emotions she felt it like a caress. He stripped off his briefs, and she got her first look at another part of him that had ruined her for anyone else. She didn't think as she sank down to her knees and took him in her mouth, earning a low, heady groan, spurred on by the raging fire in his eyes as he pumped his hips. She had dreamed about what this might be like, loving him with her mouth, but nothing could have prepared her for the overwhelming need for *more*. She wanted to feel him inside her, to be wrapped in his arms until she couldn't tell where she ended and he began. She wanted to disappear into *them*.

He must have sensed her desires. He came down to his knees in front of her, his gaze boring straight to her soul. "I've waited so long to touch you."

She couldn't breathe, couldn't think, could only guide his hand to her breast, gasping with sweet agony at the feel of his rough palms loving the parts of her she'd spent her life hating. He kissed her neck, her shoulder, inciting sparks beneath her skin. She leaned forward, wanting him to take more of her, but he was in no hurry, caressing her breasts, dragging his tongue along the swell of each one torturously slowly. Taking one nipple between his finger and thumb, he lowered his mouth to the other, teasing over the peak and blowing warm air on the wetness he'd left behind.

She arched against him, and he moved to her other breast. "Zane—"

She was ready to beg and plead for him to give her more as he continued the agonizing tease, dragging his tongue around her nipple, over the peak, until she was barely breathing. Her hips began moving in time to his talented tongue, currently lavishing her other breast with the same tantalizing attention. As he lifted her breast to his lips, he kissed the tingling peak, leaving her panting and barely breathing at once.

"You're so beautiful, baby," he whispered, pinning her in place with a hungry stare as one hand moved down her belly to the juncture of her thighs. He pressed one long finger firmly between her swollen lips, and stilled. She grabbed his arm, rocked against that thick digit, urging him to give her what she so desperately needed. A gratified grin lifted his lips.

"You're my heaven, Willow," he whispered, and kissed her slow and deep until her legs shook.

Just when she thought she couldn't take it anymore, he drew back just enough to slide his tongue along her lower lip, teasing her as she leaned forward, aching for more rough kisses. He kissed the corner of her lips, then slicked his tongue over the bow of her upper lip, and she imagined his mouth between her legs. A moan escaped, and he dipped his tongue inside her mouth, kissing her so softly she whimpered. Even on her knees, she feared she might crumble to pieces, and gripped him tighter.

His thumb moved in slow circles over her sweetest spot, and she closed her eyes, hypnotized by his touch. Tremors built in her thighs, rising in her chest and vibrating beneath her skin, building pressure of staggering proportions. His mouth left hers, and as she opened her eyes, his lips closed over her breast at the same moment his fingers entered her, lighting thunderous explosions inside her. He sucked her breast harder, and she clutched his head, unwilling to let his mouth release her despite the needlelike darts shooting from her nipple to her undulating center. Just when she thought she'd lose her mind, he tore his mouth from her breast and sealed his teeth over her neck. She cried out with the exquisite pain and all-consuming pleasure as her orgasm crashed over her, as turbulent as a riptide. Her knees gave out, and she collapsed against him.

"I've got you, baby," he whispered.

He lowered her trembling body to the bed, gazing down at her with a look so unfamiliar it nearly stopped her heart. She felt him shaking, and when he asked, "Still with me?" it was all she could do to nod.

He kissed her tenderly at first, then urgently and exploringly. Passion pounded through her veins, blood rushed through her ears, and when he moved down her body and brought his mouth to her sex, she thought she might pass out from the sheer pleasure radiating through her. He brought her right up to the peak, holding her there so long she was sure she'd stopped breathing, and then she shattered into a million pieces, time and time again, until her body went limp. When he reached for his wallet and tore open the little square package with his teeth, she feared she had no energy left. But as he sheathed his hard length, her body awakened again, pulsing and quivering with anticipation.

She felt the broad head of his cock at her entrance, his powerful thighs nestled between hers. He came down over her, and she rose to meet him, crushing her mouth to his and kissing him like she needed him to breathe. And at that moment, she *did*. Maybe she always had.

"Look at me, baby," he said into the kiss.

Entranced by his words and the emotions in his eyes, she tried to hold his gaze, but as he entered her, the pleasure was too intense. He unraveled her, inch by glorious inch, and as emotions she'd been carrying for years flooded her, her eyes fluttered closed.

He touched his cheek to hers, whispering as he buried himself deeper inside her, "Jesus, I've missed you."

His arms pushed beneath her, cradling her body against his, until even air couldn't fit between them. Their mouths came together as they began to move, and he kissed her so deeply, so *lovingly*, years of pent-up emotions came rushing forward. Her legs wound around his waist. He penetrated deeper, took her rougher. She clawed at his back, pleas streaming from her lips. She felt free for the first time in forever, and when he buried his face in her neck and said, "Come with me, baby," there was no holding back.

"Willow, Willow, *Willow*," he ground out as they found their mutual release, and she knew her name would never sound the same again.

# CHAPTER NINE

ZANE LAY ON his back beside Willow as they came down from the explosive pleasures of their lovemaking. He rid himself of the condom, then pulled her close again.

"Jesus, Wills. That was even better than I remembered, and I remembered it as pretty damn amazing."

She pushed up on her elbow. Her golden hair spilled over her breasts, tickling his chest. "I should hope it's better. We were kids. What did we know back then?" She brushed her fingers over his chest hair. "Well, you knew what you were doing, but I was totally lost."

He grimaced against what he'd led her to believe. "You weren't lost. You knew exactly what you wanted and you'd planned it to the nth degree, from your fluttering lashes while you convinced me to believe your ridiculous notion that we wouldn't feel a damn thing."

Her brows knitted as she reached across his chest for the cupcake. Feeling her breasts crushed against him as she scooped frosting onto her finger and sucked it off brought another rush of heat, and he felt himself getting hard again.

"It wasn't ridiculous. It worked." She scooped up another heap of frosting.

"If you put that finger in your mouth, I can't be held responsible for the outcome."

Her eyes narrowed, and she swirled her tongue over the frosting.

"Willow," he warned, gripping her arms.

She closed her lips around her finger with a challenging look in her eyes. "Mm."

In one swift move she was beneath him, laughing as he reached for his wallet again.

"How many of those do you carry?" She rose and kissed his chest.

"Stocked up before I met you at the resort. Just in case."

She gasped and laughed at once. "You pig. You knew we'd end up having sex!"

He eyed her as he tore open the package. "Hoped."

"Whatever." She was still smiling.

He held the little square packet out. "You don't want this?"

She trapped her lower lip between her teeth, but her unstoppable smile gave away the truth. Still, he needed to hear it from her. He was already in too deep. His emotions hadn't just gotten away from him; they'd obliterated everything except what he felt for Willow.

"Tell me, Wills, because if the game stops here, I need to know. I meant what I said about us." He lowered his body over hers, kissing the edges of her lips. "I want to *feel*." He nipped at her jaw, feeling her arch up beneath him. "I want to *touch*." He slanted his mouth over hers, kissing her so intensely it should be criminal. "I want *you*, baby."

"Me, too." She smiled up at him. "I just wish I was the one who had tricked you into this fake relationship."

He couldn't hide his surprise.

"What?" she snapped. "I hate that you orchestrated this. It gives you control."

He rolled off her and onto his back, waving toward his body. "Control me, baby. Every which way you'd like."

Her eyes flamed, and just as quickly, a lethal calmness washed over them. She eyed the condom, eyed his cock, and licked her beautiful lips again. He loved seeing her set the vixen inside her free, but *fuck*, she was determined to make him lose his shit. He saw it in her eyes as she straddled him, trapping his erection flat against his abdomen. She laced their hands together on either side of his head and began sliding along his hard length. Her hair tumbled around them, curtaining their faces.

"You have no idea how many times I've wanted to torture you," she said with sultry huskiness.

"Sweetheart, you've been torturing me for years." He craned up to capture her mouth, but she drew away with a wicked—*and gratified?*—smile.

"I have better things in mind for that mouth of yours." She arched above him, lowering one heavy breast toward his mouth.

*Good fucking Lord, you can torture me anytime you please.*

Between her breast in his mouth and her slick heat moving hard and quick over his erection, he was going to lose it. She controlled the speed, shifted her breast to give him access to the other, still holding his hands prisoner.

"Baby," he said as she reached for a condom. "Another minute of that and I'm going to come."

She sheathed his cock, guided him inside her, and pinned his hands beside his head again. They both moaned as her body swallowed him to the root. She arched back, riding him as adeptly as a rodeo champion, her incredible breasts bouncing just out of reach. Every time he thrust his hips, she stopped moving, her sharp green eyes driving into him. She wanted complete control, and it was killing him to hand over the reins, to allow her to slow her efforts as she climaxed again and again, bringing him to the brink of madness. Just when he didn't think he could take another second of her tightness pulsing around him, she quickened her pace, releasing his hands and catapulting them both into an earth-shattering release.

Willow collapsed on top of him, trying to catch her breath. "Wow."

He ran his hands over her slim waist, along the flare of her hips, and gave her ass a smack.

"Hey!" She lifted her eyes to his.

"That's for torturing me." He pressed a kiss to her shoulder. "Jesus, baby. You blew my mind."

She made a sleepy sound, snuggling against him.

"Wills, I need to get rid of the condom."

She whimpered, and he wrapped his arms around her, not wanting to move a muscle, either, but unless they wanted a mess, he needed to deal with this. He shifted out from beneath her, earning another whimpery, moany complaint as he took care of the condom.

He kissed her shoulder again, coming down beside her.

Her eyes popped open. "Skinny-dip?"

He laughed. "I thought you were sleepy."

"I was, but then I remembered we have the lake to ourselves." She grabbed a towel from the bag and wrapped it around herself.

He knew a lot of wild women, but there was a huge difference between *wild* and *Willow*. She was her own brand of wild. *The very best brand.*

She peered into one of the bags. "You didn't by any chance pick up soap, did you?"

He reached into the bag and tossed her a bar of soap wrapped in pretty tissue paper. "They didn't have lilac."

She put it up to her nose, inhaling deeply as she unwrapped it. "Mom's lavender and chamomile. One of my favorites."

He grabbed a towel and stepped out of the tent, reaching for her hand. "Come on, sweet cheeks."

Her eyes dropped to his cock. "Um, don't you want to put on that towel?"

"Not really." He grabbed her sandals and set them in front of her. "Better wear these so you don't hurt your feet." He shoved his feet in his boots, and she laughed. "What?"

"You're buck naked and wearing black leather boots. You look like you belong on an X-rated Tumblr page."

He scoffed. "Not a chance. I'm not stupid enough to let anyone take compromising pics of me."

The amusement left her eyes, and just as quickly she was smiling again. "I'm going to get a picture of you like that. The perfect blackmail."

"No, you're not."

"Wanna bet? I have *no idea* how you managed to get me naked and let you do all those dirty things to me," she said with a taunt in her voice. "You probably drugged the wine or something. A girl needs assurance, and a picture is the perfect way."

"You have no idea, huh?" He tugged off her towel, and she ran toward the water, shrieking and laughing.

He chased her down the beach, dropping their things in the sand. She kicked off her sandals at the last second and ran into the water, squealing. He tugged off his boots in record time and followed her in. His arm swept around her waist, and he carried her toward the deeper water while she laughed, struggling to be set free.

"You want to blackmail me?"

"Yes!" She laughed harder, turning in his arms and clinging to him like a koala to a tree. Her smile was as radiant as a summer sun. She tightened her legs around his waist, trembling and clinging to the soap. "How did we end up here?"

"Standing in waist-high water in the middle of the night?"

She shook her head. "Naked. Together. In this crazy fake relationship."

"Oh, *that*."

She rolled her eyes. "I'm serious. I have been anti-Zane for a *long* time."

"That's a little cruel, don't you think?" He walked into deeper water to try to warm them.

"True, though. Self-preservation." She pushed away, floating on her back. The tips of her breasts broke the surface, and her hair fanned out around her like a halo. She was *stunning*.

He swam to her and took the soap from her hand. "Let me." He began washing her. "Self-preservation? Is that why every time I came back for a visit you made sure we were never left alone?"

She grabbed the soap and swam away.

"Wills," he called after her. Moonlight glistened off the water, threading over her skin. "Do you regret it?"

"Tonight?" She rubbed the bar of soap from shoulder to wrist.

He wanted to ditch the soap and run his hands all over her until he'd memorized every dip and curve of her body. "All of it," he said. "Any of it."

She disappeared beneath the surface. He felt the current change seconds before she broke the surface in front of him and wound her arms around his neck. She was going to be the death of him. Every time she touched him, his entire being wanted more.

"Is it possible to regret it and cherish it at the same time?"

Hell, that couldn't be good, but he understood what she meant. "Yeah. I think it is."

"Then that's how I feel. I don't regret the first time, because until tonight it was the most wonderful experience of my life."

"Wills . . ." Her name came straight from his heart.

"I just regret how I handled it afterward—back then, I mean. And I don't regret tonight. It was bound to happen, and I think I knew that when you first propositioned me about this plan of yours. Maybe we both did." A sexy smile lifted her lips, bolstering the emotions he no longer wanted to hide.

"God knows I must be crazy," she teased. "But I actually *like* you. I'm more myself with you than I've ever been with any other guy, which is why I've tried to keep you at arm's length. You're too easy to get swept up in. And despite knowing that I might regret this when these two weeks come to an end, I'm not going to pretend that I don't want this. I want to *feel* and *crave* and *take*, and I want those things with you."

Her honesty was almost too much to take. It wasn't fair to either of them to have let them go so far. But if he'd been weak then, he was ten times weaker now, after having tasted and felt and experienced Willow. There was no turning back. He didn't want to turn back. Not now, not *ever*.

His chest constricted with the magnitude of the realization, and his response came without hesitation. "Then let's not let it end."

A soft, confused laugh slipped from her lips. "What are you saying?"

"It all makes sense now, Willow. Why I remember everything you have ever said or texted to me when I'm too wrapped up in my own life to care what any other woman says or does. Why we've never let go of each other after all these years." His pulse raced as the pieces of his reckless, stubborn life became crystal clear.

She pushed away, treading water to keep afloat. Her smile crumpled right before his eyes, and she turned angry and sad at once. "You're losing your mind. This is a ruse, a game."

"But it *can* be so much more. Don't you see?" He swam out to her. "We're not scared kids anymore. We're not trying to find our way. We *know* who we are."

Sadness tugged her beautiful mouth down at the corners, slaying him anew.

"Right, Zane, and I know you're a player. You don't do monogamy, and I don't do . . . whatever it is that you want."

She swam toward shore, but he grabbed her hand, pulling her to him. He planted his feet firmly in the lake bed, needing the stability to combat her tears, which were shredding him into a million little pieces.

"I fucked up, baby. I never should have followed your asinine rules. I should have told you how I felt then."

"Who are you kidding? You went back to LA and forgot all about me. You didn't feel then, and you don't now."

"You're wrong, Willow. Dead wrong."

She pushed at his chest, and he held her wrists so tight he feared he'd leave marks, but she needed to hear the truth, and damn it to hell, he needed to say it.

"When I went back to LA, we kept in touch with texts, and I adhered to your stupid rules. I didn't talk about what we'd done, not with you, not with anyone. At every audition, it was *your* face, *your* texts that pulled me through. Did you forget that we kept in touch until I got my first gig and my life got away from me?"

"Yeah." Her voice cracked. "I remember it more like you dropping off the face of the earth."

"Three months of grueling work, Wills. That's what it took to nail the part. Working twenty-four-seven with my acting coach, going to meetings, rehearsing with my costars so I wouldn't fuck up *their* careers. I wasn't out at bars fucking everything on legs."

Her eyes narrowed. "No? Well, that celibate phase sure didn't last long."

"Goddamn it, Willow. Take some fucking responsibility." Ten years of anger and hurt came roaring out. "Do you know what it was like texting you after that night? I tried to follow your rules, but I couldn't *not* feel. I fell so goddamn hard for you, I came home that Christmas ready to tell you the truth despite your need to control everything in your path. You were my first, too." There it was, all his truths splayed out before her, leaving him vulnerable as he owned up to his lies—all of them. From the teenage comments he'd made to look cool about supposed conquests to the gut-wrenching ache he'd been left with by following her goddamn rules. More anger came tumbling out, and there was no stopping this runaway train. "Did you ever slow down enough to think that maybe, just maybe, *I* had feelings that you *couldn't* control?"

Her jaw dropped open as if she were going to speak, but no words came.

"Of course not, because you were too busy protecting yourself. Well, baby, you made it clear where I stood. When I came home for the holidays, you had already moved on with some college prick. *You* moved on, Wills, not me. Not by then."

"But . . . you never . . ."

"If I *never*, it was because I was trying to honor your rules. But I loved you, Willow. I fucking loved—*love*—everything about you, and seeing you with that other guy?" He winced against the memory. "When I left Sweetwater that winter? That's when I gave in to peer pressure and became the guy you read about now. Yeah, that's right. Think about it, Willow. Was I that guy before then? *Fuck, no.* What did you expect? You *broke* me, and if it makes me an asshole that I filled that void with whatever willing woman I could, that's okay."

She went slack in his arms, and he spoke in the calmest voice he could manage so she had no choice but to hear him. "Because what I didn't realize then but I see too goddamn clearly now is that I have looked for pieces of you in every woman I've ever been with. And not one of them has even come close. That's the truth, and you may not be willing to admit that this thing between us—this lifelong deception we've existed in—is real, but I sure as hell can. And I'll prove to you that I'm the *only* man you'll ever love. Because what we had, what we *have*, has lasted ten years in a world where nothing is real. We're real, Willow. We're as real as it fucking gets."

He released her, wishing he had kept his mouth shut. Wishing he could have just allowed himself to take whatever amount of time she was willing to give. But he was done lying to himself, and now, by the look in her eyes, he knew he had new guilt to carry. On what could have been the most beautiful night of their lives, he'd fucked up again.

His truth became her burden.

WILLOW'S LEGS SHOOK violently, and her mind spun out of control, too overwhelmed to hold on to any one thought. Some part of her had always hoped to hear everything Zane had just said, but how could she believe a word of it? *I was your first?* She'd heard rumors of girls sleeping with him when he was in high school. He'd hinted at it himself. He'd loved her? He loved her now? This was all too much. Nothing made sense anymore.

"What is this?" she finally managed. "I'm supposed to believe you're unburdening yourself from a life of self-inflicted torture and . . . *what?* Pledge my never-ending love to you?" She trudged toward the shore, her world spinning on its axis.

"I didn't plan this, Willow," he pleaded. "But it's the truth."

He held a towel up for her, but she wrenched away, shoving her shaky feet into her sandals, and grabbed the other towel.

"This is just another role for you, remember?" she snapped as she covered up. "There's no role you can't *nail.* Well, now you've nailed your leading lady, too. Just like always. And I did it willingly, Zane. So don't play me for a fool. We have to convince everyone else, not each other."

Fresh tears tumbled down her cheeks.

"Willow—"

He reached for her, but she turned away, unable to process his confession and deal with her own, which was clawing to be released.

"Willow, you were my first. That was the truth. And you're the *only* woman I have ever wanted when I was lonely, not any of those women I settled for. But you made it clear every damn time I reached out that I was barking up the wrong tree. I don't blame you. I'm the one who fucked up. I'm the one who promised to abide by your rules and was too weak to do it. I'm the one who led you to believe I was experienced and could play your game. I was the one who turned off my emotions when I lost you."

Her breathing went shallow, and she forced the truth from her lungs. "I had to protect myself."

"From . . . ?"

She paced, more confused than ever. "From you. From *me*. From being hurt again."

"Now I'm confused. I followed your rules. How could I have hurt you?"

She crossed her arms, needing a barrier between them. Or maybe between her and the truth. "*I* broke them. I went to college and I thought . . ." An unsteady laugh fell from her lips. "I thought we had a connection, and when you disappeared—"

"Got lost in my first acting gig," he corrected her.

"Right. But it doesn't matter. I was heartbroken, and it took me forever to find my footing again." She'd forced herself to make it through her classes, from one day to the next, one month to the next, and finally one year to the next, until she'd built a life. A happy life, even if a piece had always been missing. She'd spent years searching for a man who didn't exist. Only now he was right there in front of her.

He existed, and he wanted her.

*But for how long?*

He closed the gap between them. "We were both hurt," he said tenderly. "We were young and stupid."

"We *were*, and maybe I wasn't the only one who got hurt, but . . ." She turned away, trying to stop her gut from roiling. "But you tricked me" slipped out before she could think.

"Damn it, Willow. I never tricked you. I abided by your rules."

"Not then." She faced him again, and reality came bursting out. "*Now*. The resort, the catering job. How can I trust you when you couldn't even be honest with me about that? Is this what our relationship would be? One lie after another?"

He pushed his fingers through his hair, turning away and uttering a string of curses. She felt her heart crumbling, and when he turned with a defeated look in his eyes, the hurt pummeled her from the inside out.

"But it wasn't *all* a lie, Wills. I needed to clean up my rep, and I knew you wouldn't have agreed if I had been honest with you. That's who we *were*, baby. But it doesn't have to be who we are."

A thunderous ache swelled in her chest. She turned away, willing herself not to fall apart. But she *was* falling apart, and there wasn't enough will in the world to stop it from happening. She needed time and space to try to weed through her tangled emotions—but she needed to be there with Zane in equal measure.

Zane stepped into her line of vision, prolonging her torment.

"I'm sorry, baby. I didn't mean to ruin tonight. This hit me as out of the blue as it did you, but it's been there all along. I have a lot to make up for, and mark my words, Willow, I will make up for this. For all the years we lost. For not knowing how you felt all those years ago. For *everything*."

She wanted to wrap her arms around him and say she believed him, that they would figure this out together. But she was terrified by the intensity of her emotions and just as terrified of losing him again. Her legs gave out, and she dropped to her knees.

He crouched before her, causing another rush of emotions to implode inside her. Tears welled in her eyes.

"Willow, I think we should go back. I'm sure the photographers are gone by now, and I know you, baby. You need to wrap your head around this."

She wanted to stay right there in the haven of his embrace, but she couldn't, and he knew that. Knew it in a way no one else ever could, and that confused her even more.

"Z," she managed before emotions clogged her throat and she collapsed into his arms.

"It's okay, baby," he whispered. "I've got you."

She closed her eyes, soaking in his comfort.

He held her until her breathing calmed, and the hurt and fear wound into one numbing sensation, buffering her from it all.

"Come on, baby. Let's get you home so you can rest."

She didn't even try to respond.

Zane insisted she not help disassemble their camp, but she had to move. She needed the distraction. Or at least she thought she did. When the tent fell into an unusable heap, it felt like a metaphor. Zane expertly folded up the nylon into a nice neat package, taking care of the loose ends, making it appealing again. She didn't know how to do that. How did a person take years of fear and pain and love, years of living within the barriers they'd built out of self-preservation, and let the person who caused the need for the moat and the walls and the arsenal in for good?

She sank to her knees and stuffed a pillow into the bag. If she didn't take time to clear her head, she'd forever live in a middle ground, wary of his motivations, disbelieving his true feelings. Every incredible thought of being with Zane was chased by memories of her devastating heartbreak.

"Wills." Zane knelt beside her, bringing the heat only he could create, and it seated itself deep in her chest. "I—"

"Don't. Please." She finished shoving the supplies into the bag and pushed unsteadily to her feet. He deserved to know the truth. She had to try to tell him what was in her head, but she couldn't even see straight. "You're . . . I . . ."

Tears welled in her eyes again, and she blinked them away. She was not going to fall apart. *No, no, no.* How could she tell him he was the gasoline to her fire, the wind to her sail, knowing their immense love came at a huge cost? He could annihilate her without even trying. And she was all too aware that she had pulled the trigger all those years ago. From what he'd said, he didn't even know how she'd clung to their weekly texts and hoped for more. *She'd* built those barriers, and *she'd* locked herself in with the guns aiming at the wrong person. "I'm sorry. It's not fair. I wish I could deal with this now, but . . ."

"I'm not asking you to, baby," he said softly. "I just want you to know that I'm here."

*For now.* Hating herself for the seeds of doubt she let pepper his confession, she forced her legs to carry her toward the boat.

They rowed back to town in uncomfortable silence, giving her time to reflect on everything he'd said. It wasn't out of the realm of possibility that she'd been his first. She didn't know why, out of everything he'd said, *that* was the thing she was picking apart. But it nagged at her like a bee sting. He'd been so cool and confident. Had he been that good an actor all along?

She parked behind the bakery, and they took the back staircase up to her apartment. Once inside, she set her keys on the table by the door, feeling like she'd been away for a month, and waved to her couch. "You can sleep there."

He set her bags on the floor, his eyes never leaving her. She was so confused, so hurt, as much by herself as by this moment. Was it wrong to want to protect herself, even if part of her wanted to take everything he'd said, wrap it in gold, and praise it like a god?

He hiked a thumb over his shoulder. "I'm going to hit Ben up for a place to stay."

"But what about the focus group?"

"I don't give a rat's ass about the focus group, Wills. I want to finally do the right thing for us. I want to do right by you, no matter what the cost."

"But . . ." Her thoughts stumbled. "We lied to my family, and no one will believe we're engaged if you're staying at Ben's."

He pushed a hand through his thick hair and lifted one shoulder in an I-don't-give-a-damn shrug. "Then they don't."

He stepped closer and took her hands in his. Her confused heart skidded to a halt. His eyes brimmed with passion again, full of so many unspoken promises she felt herself getting lost in them.

"What do you want from me?" she asked meekly. "I'm so confused."

"You said you can be yourself around me. That's all I want, sweet girl. Don't put up your walls and lock me out. You have every reason not to believe me, and I have only one reason to try to convince you otherwise."

He pressed her hand to his chest, and she felt the sure and steady beat of his heart beneath her palm.

"It's always been yours, Wills. It's always been *you*. I just buried those feeling so deep, it took years to unearth them."

# CHAPTER TEN

"LET ME GET this straight. You and Willow aren't really engaged, but you want to be, because suddenly you *love* her?" Ben paced his living room like a caged tiger. "What the hell is really going on, Zane? You show up last night looking like hell and ask for a place to crash. You make me wait until the morning so you can *process* whatever's happened. And now you give me this load of crap?"

Zane had come straight to Ben's after leaving Willow last night, but he hadn't been able to think straight, much less figure out how to break the news to Ben that he'd been lying to him and was in love with his sister. Now, leaning against the back of Ben's couch, where he'd been for the last twenty minutes as he explained to Ben what had happened, he still wasn't sure what to say. He splayed his hands. "I know how it sounds. But it's the truth, Ben. I needed to clean up my reputation. Willow agreed to help."

Ben grabbed Zane's shirt with fisted hands, seething through gritted teeth. "You asked my sister to lie for you?"

"You think I don't want to pound the shit out of myself for this?" He knocked Ben's hands away. "I'm an asshole, Ben. Tell me something I don't know."

"Willow's never asked a damn thing of you. Why her? Out of all the women in this world, why ask her to lie for you?"

"Because that's what we *do*. We ask each other to do outrageous, unreasonable things, knowing we will." There was no way Zane would give up their secret, so he gave Ben the only thing he had to offer.

The rest of the truth.

"Because I love her, man." He dropped down to a chair at Ben's bar.

Ben paced again. "You don't know the first thing about love. I *know* you, remember? I know about your revolving bedroom door. You might be able to fool my sister, but you can't fool me."

"I'm not fooling her. I've owned up to everything I've done. I'm not hiding my past from her, Ben. Willow knows exactly who I am. She always has." He pushed to his feet, too restless to sit still. "I want her in my future."

Ben scoffed.

"You don't know everything about me, Ben. Did you know I've kept in touch with Willow all these years? That I've asked her to meet me somewhere every fucking month for *years*? She never took me up on it, but that didn't stop me from asking her too many times to count."

"You don't even know her anymore, Zane. You're fooling yourself."

"Am I?" He raked a hand through his hair. "Or am I finally doing what I should have done years ago? I know it's crazy, but it's true."

"Why?"

"Why?"

Ben closed the gap between them. "Yeah. Why? Why do you love her?"

"Do you even *know* your sister? She's smart as hell, more determined than any person I have ever known, and she's funny, Ben. She makes me laugh, and she irritates the hell out of me with her snarky comments, but it's the best kind of irritation, you know?" He sank down to the bar stool again. "And she's sweet and real, and I don't know, man. You're asking me to explain something people have been trying to figure out forever. Love is crazy and unreasonable. And you're right. I don't know the first thing about it. But I'm going to figure it out."

Ben crossed his arms, setting a steely gaze on Zane again. "Did you purposefully not mention her looks?"

"What?"

"You didn't mention her looks even once."

Zane shrugged. "She's beautiful, but what does that have to do with anything? You asked why I love her, not if I thought she was pretty. Jesus, Ben. She's a baker, and we all know how much she loves sweets. She could gain a hundred pounds and I'd still love her. What's your point?"

Ben sank down beside Zane, shoulders slumped. "I think you just made it."

"Now you've lost me."

"God, you're thickheaded sometimes." Ben glared at him. "I don't know what's gotten into you, but in all the years I've known you, you've talked about how hot women were. Never once did you mention anything *real* about a single one. I thought you were incapable of seeing past a woman's looks. I honestly was worried that you'd end up like one of those old guys who marry a twentysomething, money-grubbing piece of arm candy." His glare softened. "I believe you, man. So what's your plan?"

"I'm going to win her over. No matter what it takes." Zane smiled, knowing he'd taken a solid first step. "I sent her ten dozen roses. That should help ease the tension."

Ben laughed.

"What? Women love roses. That's like Romance 101." He'd given her a single rose the night they'd first slept together, and she'd swooned.

"Not Willow. She can't stand the sight of them."

"Aw, hell." Zane bolted for the door.

He had walked the eight blocks from Willow's apartment to Ben's house last night, and now he sprinted down the cobblestone streets toward the bakery.

"Hey, Zane." Aurelia Stark, the woman who ran the bookstore, waved as he ran past. "Congratulations!"

He waved back and picked up his pace, skidding as he rounded the corner onto the main drag. A crowd of people milled around beneath the pink awning at the entrance to Sweetie Pie Bakery, spilling over to the sidewalk in front of Bridgette's flower shop, Secret Garden. Two of Zane's security guys flanked the entrance to the bakery.

He slowed to a walk, noticing several people carrying pink Sweetie Pie Bakery bags and long-stemmed red roses. A tall blond woman pushed through the doors carrying a pink box and a single rose. Anxiety prickled his limbs. Was Willow giving away the flowers he'd sent her?

"There he is!" the tall blonde yelled.

The crowd converged on Zane like a swarm of bees, waving pieces of paper and calling out his name. Zane drew upon his inner actor, forcing the man who wanted to reach his woman down deep so he could win over the crowd as quickly as possible. He squared his shoulders and flashed a practiced smile. He'd mastered faking it until he made it and moved on to made it, and needed to fake it until he could get the hell out.

"Give Mr. Walker some room, please." Jacob Seton, the head of his security detail, formed a beefy barrier between Zane and the crowd, while Mort Penner, the other bodyguard, manned the door to the bakery.

A redhead thrust a newspaper past Jacob's arm. "Can I get your autograph?"

Zane grabbed it and scrawled his name, hurriedly moving on to sign a handful of others. Every time the bakery door opened, he caught a glimpse of another customer carrying a rose, tightening the knots in his gut. He needed to see Willow.

A man walked out of the bakery carrying a rose, and Zane's blood pressure spiked. What the hell was going on? He was *done*. He gave Jacob and Mort the secret nod, and the two burly men formed an impenetrable wall around him.

"I appreciate you stopping by, but that's all I've got time for. My fiancée awaits." His gut and heart warred with the statement as he quietly and quickly gave his security team instructions to ensure this type of thing didn't happen again, and made his way into the bakery, which was almost as packed as the sidewalk.

The bell above the door chimed, and Willow popped up from behind the glass pastry display. "Hi, I'll be ri—" Her smile tightened, and his hope plummeted.

She returned her attention to ringing up a purchase for a stout gray-haired woman. "Okay, hon. We've got two Loverboys and one blueberry muffin. Hopefully this will bring a smile to your granddaughter's face. I'm so sorry to hear about her broken ankle."

Zane kept his head down, hoping not to cause a ruckus as he had out front. He stuck close to the wall that adjoined Secret Garden. The archway between the two shops had no doors. The lights were out in the flower shop, and a single chain hung from one end of the archway to the other with a pretty hand-painted sign that read, **WE'RE BUSY PLANTING SECRETS. PLEASE COME BACK TOMORROW.** Had these shops been in LA, there would be impenetrable locked doors separating them. Zane smiled to himself. He'd wanted to get out of Sweetwater so badly when he'd graduated high school; he'd never recognized how monumental *trust* was in the community.

Zane inhaled the delicious aroma of fresh-baked pastries and the heavy floral scents of the roses. Sunlight streamed in the storefront windows, casting a warm glow over several round tables and on the self-service coffee station lining the far-left wall. He stole a glance at Willow, who stood behind the register at the right end of the counter. She was smiling at her customer, listening intently to something the woman was saying, and it was clear that she was trying not to meet his gaze. He took a moment to look around. The bakery was decorated in true Willow style, upbeat with a vintage flair. Distressed mint and pink cabinetry below wide glass displays spanned almost the full width of the store, with a walkway on either side. He knew Willow baked the items she sold each morning, and the cakes, muffins, and pastries were nearly sold out already. Behind the register were built-in shelves boasting packages of bakery paraphernalia wrapped with pretty pink and green bows. The original hardwood floors and elegantly detailed white crown molding gave the bakery a charming feel. The roses he'd sent were proudly displayed at each end of the counter and on several of the tables. Maybe Ben had it all wrong and she didn't hate them after all.

Willow picked up a vase of roses and handed it to the elderly woman. "Give her these, too. If the sweets don't do it, these sure will."

"Oh, Willow. Bless your heart." The woman turned with a pleased smile and carried the vase out the door as another customer stepped up to the register.

*What the hell?*

AFTER A SLEEPLESS night spent wishing Zane had stayed one minute and telling herself he'd done the right thing by leaving the next, Willow had come to work at 5:00 a.m. tired, confused, and longing to see the man who had singlehandedly turned her entire world upside down. She was in no mood for the flock of women who had invaded her bakery with the sole purpose of getting a piece of her fake fiancé, the man who was currently stalking her with a predatory look in his eyes. Lord help her, the man was brutally compelling in his tight, faded jeans, which hugged the assets that had doled out so many orgasms last night she'd lost count.

"How are you today, ca—Leah? What can I get for you?" Great, she'd almost called her *cake pops*! Willow often thought of her customers by what they ordered rather than their names. She tried harder to concentrate on her friend and ignore her fluttering stomach.

"I'll take a box of cake pops for Lisa's teacher, please," Leah said. "She just found out she's pregnant."

"Oh, how wonderful." Willow turned to grab a box, and Zane stepped behind the counter, snatching it off the counter with a puckish grin. She forced a smile for the sake of her customers and lowered her voice. "What are you doing?"

"Helping my fiancée." He held the box as she filled it with cake pops.

"You've turned my life into a circus," she whispered. He leaned closer, and her traitorous nipples peaked to attention.

"I'm sorry, Wills. Since when do you hate roses? I was trying to apologize."

She'd loved the note he'd included with the flowers. *I'm about as imperfect as they come, but my love for you is real.* But the roses had reminded her of the one he'd given her all those years ago, and she'd had trouble fighting the troubling emotions that came with the memory.

"Since *you know when*," she finally answered.

Understanding dawned in his eyes, and it killed her to see the hurt that followed. She wasn't being fair. Not now that she knew the truth about what had really happened back then.

Willow rang up Leah's order. The diamond ring turned as she used the register, slicing into the side of her middle finger as it had been doing all morning.

"Zane Walker," Leah said breathlessly, a blush rising on her cheeks. "I've seen every one of your movies."

Willow fought the urge to roll her eyes.

Zane stifled a chuckle and slid an arm around Willow's waist. "I hope you enjoyed them. I'm gearing up for my most important role yet, as this beautiful woman's husband. I'm truly a lucky man."

*Husband?* Her insides fluttered. He sounded so sincere she wanted to throw caution to the wind, pretend everything was perfect, and live in that fantasy forever. But she'd tried living in a fantasy once before, and it had backfired. *Big-time.*

*For both of us.*

If they were going to really give this a shot, she needed to make sure they were communicating honestly. No more secrets, no more tricks. Were they capable of that? And what about when he went back to his life in LA? Long-distance relationships weren't easy, and everyone in LA knew him to be just that. *Easy.* As if Zane were inside her head, his angry confession rushed in. *You broke me.*

"How's it going, Mr. Gray? What can I get you?" Zane asked the next customer, drawing Willow's attention from her befuddled thoughts.

"Morning, hon." She smiled at Martin Gray, and knew chocolate chip muffins were on tap. Martin reminded Willow of Robert De Niro, with beady eyes and an ever-present twitchy smile, which made him look like he was always on the cusp of making a joke.

"Good morning, Willow. You look beautiful today."

Always the flirt. "Thank you."

Turning to Zane, he said, "I'll take two chocolate chip muffins, please. It's no wonder the ladies came out of the woodwork. I've lived here all my life and never seen half those women. I guess it's not that often the star quarterback comes back for a visit." A hearty laugh rumbled out of his lungs.

Willow chuckled. Zane winked at her, and her belly fluttered again. She was as bad as she'd been as a teenager with a crush.

"I assume you've heard our happy news," Zane said to Martin.

"Sure have. I wondered who was going to sweep our Willow off her feet. But don't you even think about whisking her away from here, son. I need my Sweetie Pie muffins."

Carrie Warren reached over the counter, distracting Willow from her eavesdropping. She had gone to school with Piper and was about as gossipy as they came. "Let me see the ring, Willow. Oh my goodness. That is *huge*! Just *gorgeous*."

Willow thought of Carrie by what she resembled, not what she ordered. She was a lemon tart: *sweet-looking*, but one bite was often overwhelming. She glanced at Zane, catching his eye. "Yes, well, everything Zane does, he does *big*."

"I want all the details," Carrie gushed. "How did he propose?"

Curiosity shone in Zane's eyes, and Willow recalled the story he'd concocted about the proposal. "It was beautiful," she said, and a smile crawled across Zane's lips. She loved his smile, and it killed her to know how much she'd hurt him last night with her confused reaction. She turned back to Carrie before the longing she felt poured out of her mouth. "But I'd like to keep the details of our proposal private. What can I get for you?"

She felt Zane's gaze burning into her as she filled Carrie's order, but there was no time to stop and try to clear the air. The bakery was slammed, and she and Zane worked in tandem for the next few hours. Zane poured on the charm to each and every customer, touching Willow every time they passed in the narrow space behind the counter and whispering sexy innuendos until she sported an irrepressible, *bordering on* ridiculous, smile.

Now he was helping the last customer, a young brunette Willow didn't recognize, while Willow wiped down the tables.

Zane called across the shop, "Hey, babe. I need a good whipping."

Her mind went straight to the gutter. *Whipping? Are you into that? Am I? No. No way.* Her eyes darted to the customer, who was giggling. Only then did Willow notice the box of éclairs in Zane's hand. *Oh, thank goodness.*

After topping the éclairs with whipped cream, which brought more sexy innuendos than should be legal, she rang up the customer and locked the door behind her after she left. She felt Zane's presence before his arms circled her waist from behind, and his soft, warm lips touched her neck.

"We make a good team, Wills. Let me be the frosting on your cupcake."

*Yes, yes, yes.* She closed her eyes, willing herself to be strong. They needed time to talk before she could fall under his spell again. But first she had to get started on Louie's cake. A flicker of panic rose in her chest. Bridgette was probably furious with her for not calling last night.

"I can't think about *frosting your cupcake* right now. I haven't even made Louie's cake yet. The place has been a zoo since early this morning."

He turned her in his arms, and his seductive gaze bored into her. "Hi. Remember me? The guy who told you he loves you?"

Only he could make her laugh when she was so stressed. "I remember."

"My security guys got rid of the reporters."

"Yes," she said as firmly as she could, trying to claw her way back to having some modicum of a backbone. "But the people in town wanted to congratulate me, and I have no idea where all those girls came from, but they obviously wanted to get an eyeful—and probably much more—of *you.* I changed my mind. I don't want national exposure. It sounded good. Actually, it sounded too good to be true, but it's a big pain in the butt. I should have had time to make Louie's cake, but I haven't had time to *breathe.*"

"Then I'll help you. And all of this stuff will die down by tomorrow. I've already taken care of it. It happens every time we film in a new place. Fans come from neighboring towns to get a look at celebrities. I hate it, too, Wills. I hate it more than you could ever imagine. But it'll be over quick, especially without the media hounds feeding them articles every day."

"What a *nightmare.* I don't know how you deal with that kind of attention. I've decided that I'm happy with my quiet, small-town life. If my days were all this busy, I'd have to hire people to help me. I like having a business where I can hang a sign on the door and lock up because I want to run an errand and not have to worry about people mobbing the place. I want to do more catering, but all I *really* want is to make Sweetie Pie into a bakery and bookstore." Why was she suddenly a motormouth? She must really be nervous. "Aurelia's here for the week, and I'm going to talk to her when I get a chance. So please nix the exposure except where we have to be seen together to clean up your reputation. Just please keep them away from the bakery."

Aurelia Stark had been raised by her grandparents, who had owned the only bookstore in Sweetwater for more than forty years. She'd gone to school with Willow and had moved away after college. A few years ago, Aurelia's grandparents had sold the bookstore when Aurelia's grandfather had suffered a stroke and moved into a rehab facility on Long Island. Mick Bad, the attorney who purchased the building the bookstore was in, lived in New York City and had been looking for a small place in town to use as a weekend getaway. He'd gotten along so well with Aurelia's grandmother, he'd kept the store intact on the first floor, in case Aurelia's grandmother ever wanted to come back and run it, and used the apartment upstairs as his getaway. Aurelia came into town for a few days each month and opened the store to keep her grandmother's dream alive. Willow hoped she could convince her to go into business together and combine the bookstore with the bakery.

"Already taken care of." Zane leaned forward. "The exposure you've already gained, plus the catering for the set, should still help with getting your name out there. Even without the photographers hounding us, they'll be around the set, and stories will still make the papers."

She arched a brow. "Did I mention that I received an e-mail this morning from someone named Payton from craft services for the set? She's sending over the breakfast menu tomorrow. She said they usually have bagels and pastries for breakfast, but apparently some of the crew members have special dietary needs."

"Like I said, I'll help."

"I'm sure you have to study your lines and do whatever actors do." She glanced out the window at the two security guards. She hated that they needed to be there, but she had signed up for this.

Zane slid a hand to the back of her neck, brushing his thumb over her skin.

"Come on, Wills. Let me help you bake Louie's cake. Give me an inch."

"You'll take a mile." Her heart hammered against her ribs.

"That's true," he admitted. "I'm good at taking more with you. But in all fairness, I can't help it. Maybe I shouldn't have let us go so far last night."

"You? *Ha!* Aren't you the cocky one? That was *my* decision, too." She couldn't stop her voice from rising, and the emotions that had bottled up over the last twenty-four hours rushed out. She swatted at a rose, sending several petals sailing to the floor. "And I don't hate these!"

He crossed his arms, and despite her tantrum, he was perfectly calm. "You gave them away."

"I was angry. Or . . . *confused.* I was *something.*"

Amusement rose from his smile all the way to his eyes. "I feel like I should apologize. But I'm not sure about which part. Asking you to lie for me, or realizing I'm in love with you."

Her insides melted a little more. "Zane—"

"Hear me out." He stepped closer, his masculine scent engulfing her as he touched her cheek. "It was wrong of me to ask you to lie, but if I hadn't, we wouldn't have spent this time together. And there's no way in hell I'll apologize for my feelings."

His touch was a heady invitation, drawing the truth like a serum. "I don't want an apology."

He lowered his chin in that devastatingly alluring way he had, and she fought the urge to go up on her toes and press her lips to his. She couldn't tear her eyes from his mouth, remembering the firm press of it against hers, the openmouthed kisses he lavished on her neck, her breasts. *Between my legs.* Her body shuddered with the tantalizing memory.

"Are you going to tell me what you *do* want?"

His voice pulled her from her reverie. Feeling a little unsteady, and aware of the minutes ticking by, she headed into the kitchen. Her *lair.* The only place she felt grounded and confident despite whatever chaos went on around her. She began setting out mixing bowls and ingredients for Louie's cake.

Zane followed her in. "Last night was agony, babe. I've gone over this a hundred times, trying to figure out where I went wrong."

"Where we *both* went wrong." She carried the flour to the counter and pulled a measuring cup out from beneath.

"Bullshit, Wills." He waved at the counter. "How can I help with this?"

She pointed to the refrigerator. "Think you can measure a cup of milk and break six eggs into this?" She pushed a bowl across the counter and began measuring the flour.

"I'm on it." He tugged the fridge open. "I'm always happy to handle your jugs."

"Only you could joke right now." She tried to sound serious, but it rode out on another laugh.

"I wasn't joking." He smirked, and God help her, she loved his naughtiness. "Clearly this was my fault. One minute you were in my arms, and then I opened my big mouth and you were gone."

She dumped the flour into the bowl and leaned over the counter, tapping the sides of the vanilla and almond extract bottles over his bowl. Her ring spun on her finger, scratching the inside of her middle finger again. She turned it right side up, and the damn thing spun again.

"It *wasn't* your fault," she snapped, annoyed with the ring, not him. She drew in a calming breath. "Don't you think there's a chance you're just *in the moment*? And when the beautiful actresses and the rest of your Hollywood life roll into town, you're going to realize I'm just a small-town girl who will never be what you're used to?"

He looked up from where he was cracking eggs into a bowl with a serious expression. "No."

"When you're done filming, your life will get away from you again, and regardless of what you might or might not feel for me—"

"Jesus, Willow." He came around the counter with a wolfish look in his eyes. "These are *my* feelings. I *know* what I feel, and I know what *you* feel, because I see it in your eyes. I feel it in your touch." His voice went low, unleashing a whirl of passion in the pit of her stomach. She hated—*and loved*—that he had that effect on her with nothing more than his voice. No wonder his touch turned her inside out.

"You look at me like I'm a bucket of frosting and you want to dive in." He stepped closer, stealing all the air from her lungs. "I gave up too easily back then. I should have said 'fuck the guy' you brought home and done this—"

His mouth collided with hers, as punishing and angry as it was sweet and provocative. Shivers of desire sliced through her as he delved deeper, crushing her to him. Her thoughts fragmented, and every ounce of her thrummed to life, pressing into him, craving more than one kiss could ever give. His hands circled her waist, lifting her effortlessly onto the counter. He pushed between her legs, intensifying his possession and their kiss. *Jesus, this kiss.* It was a kiss for her hungry soul to melt into—and melt she did. He was an eagle soaring through the sky, and she was weightless, entranced by his intensity, completely and utterly lost in him.

He tore his mouth away, and she touched her burning lips.

"Yeah," she whispered without thought. "You should have done that."

"Then stop pushing me away and let me show you the man I can be, the man I *will* be for you."

"You can try," she said, struggling to beat her dizzying brain into submission. "But I'm warning you. I won't fall for you just because you set my body on fire."

He waggled his brows and pulled her closer, until she felt his hardness against her center. "I set your body on fire?"

"Oven," she said to distract herself from the delicious man rubbing against her like a cat. She was so into him, poor Louie would never get his cake. "I need to heat up the oven."

"I'm all for getting heated up." He dipped his head, ravishing her neck with openmouthed kisses.

"Z—" *We're never going to finish baking Louie's cake.* She was pretty sure the words never made it from her brain to his ears.

He took her in another plundering kiss, chasing away more of her brain cells.

"Louie's cake," she panted out between kisses. "Need to bake it."

"You bake, baby." He lifted her from the counter and set her feet on the ground, then turned her toward the counter. He ground his hard length against her ass. "I'll just . . ." He unbuttoned her jeans, slowly unzipping them from behind. "You'd better get mixing, or prepping, or whatever it is that needs to be done to get that little guy's cake in the oven."

She scrambled for the ingredients, trying to remember where she'd left off as he pushed his hand down the front of her pants, teasing her and nibbling on the back of her neck. She pressed her palms to the counter, trying to catch her breath. It was a losing endeavor.

"Finish up, sweet girl, so your big guy's cake can get in *your* oven."

She'd never made a cake so fast in all her life.

# CHAPTER ELEVEN

WILLOW PUSHED OPEN the front door to Bridgette's cottage-style home later that afternoon and inhaled the scent of home-cooked meals, mommy hugs, and little-boy smiles. The hardwood floors were spotless, the carpets freshly vacuumed. Balloons were tied to each banister, and a colorful birthday banner hung across the foyer. Bridgette was everything Willow wasn't, from her lithe figure and always perfectly brushed blond hair of various shades to her careful and methodical tendencies. She would make sure Louie's birthday party—as she did his life—was perfectly orchestrated to ensure his happiness *and* his safety.

"Hello?" Willow called out. "Bridge? Where's the birthday boy?"

"Upstairs, Auntie Willow!" Louie hollered. "We're getting ready for my party!"

She carried Louie's Spider-Man cake over to the stairs. Her body was still humming with memories of all the sexy things she and Zane had done earlier while the cake was baking. "Tell Mommy I'll put the cake in the kitchen."

Louie bolted toward his bedroom, and Bridgette's voice sailed down the stairs. "Mommy's right here."

Her sister appeared at the top of the stairs, looking cute in a pair of white capris and a peach tank top. Her strained smile cut straight through Willow.

"Where's your new *fiancé*?"

"He should be here soon. He had to pick something up. Do you have time to talk?" She inhaled a lungful of guilt. "I'm really sorry I didn't call last night, but it was a hard night."

Louie collided with Bridgette's legs in full Spider-Man garb. "My Spider-Man cake!"

Bridgette took his hand, slowing his little legs down as he descended the stairs. A pang of sadness nipped at Willow. She remembered what Bridgette had been like before she'd lost the love of her life. She could have been the poster child for rebellious, wild risk takers. At nineteen she'd gone against their parents' wishes and quit college to run away and get married to a drummer. Six months later she was pregnant, and almost a year after that one tragic car accident forever changed her and Louie's lives. The old Bridgette would have let Louie sprint down the stairs or slide down the banister. Willow adored Bridgette, but she missed the part of her that she had buried alongside her husband.

Willow crouched for Louie to see the cake. She could only see his eyes through the Spider-Man mask, but they were as wide as hard-boiled eggs.

"Wow! Can I have a piece?"

"When Mommy says it's time."

"What do you say?" Bridgette reminded him with a gentle hand on his shoulder.

"Thank you, Auntie Willow!"

Willow pointed to her cheek. "How about some sugar, sweetie pop?"

He gave her a loud, smacking kiss and took off running toward the playroom. Louie was the epitome of a rainbow-layered birthday cake, full of sweet happiness inside and out.

"Now that's more like it." Willow rose to her feet. "Kitchen?"

Bridgette followed her in.

Willow glanced out the glass doors to the yard, which was decked out with all things Spider-Man, from the tablecloth to the piñata hanging from the big oak tree. Helium balloons were tied to the backs of all the chairs around a long table.

"Want a drink?" Bridgette asked.

"Only if it's a stiff one." She set the cake on the counter.

Bridgette arched a finely manicured brow. "Trouble in paradise?"

"It's not like that." Willow leaned on the counter, eyeing the cake. Zane had helped her frost it, and she couldn't remember the last time she'd laughed so much. *Can you imagine if we really had the ability to create webs like Spider-Man? I could tangle you up and never let you go.* His tease had led to more sexy talk about being tied up, which had led to messy, frosting-covered kisses—and that was *after* they'd already made love on every possible surface.

"From the look on your face, I'd guess you meant something else by a *hard* night."

Willow laughed and felt her cheeks heat up.

"Ah, now we're getting somewhere. But *Zane Walker?*" Bridgette whispered his name. "I'm still getting over the shock of him being your first."

"I told you *three* years ago." She'd spilled her secret after too much wine, when Zane had texted twice to razz her about the Jets losing, since he was a Giants fan, followed by, *Come see me. I'll show you how a real baller plays.*

"It was very traumatic for me," Bridgette teased. "I mean, he used to spend the night at our house *all* the time. Don't you remember lying in the hallway spying on him and Ben when we were like seven and eight? After you told me, I started to imagine all sorts of crazy things about you two and wondering if I missed hundreds of secret make-out sessions."

"I assure you, you did not." Much to her chagrin, of course. She'd fantasized about exactly that time and time again when she was a teenager.

"Not even when you were tutoring him in math?"

"Not even then."

Bridgette wrinkled her brow, eyeing Willow's ring. "So you go away to cater an event and come back engaged." She pulled Willow's hand closer, inspecting the ring. "That's gorgeous."

"It's gaudy and awful," she corrected her.

"Well, it's not *you*, but I think it's stunning. How could I not have noticed you've been seeing him? Why would you keep that from me?"

"Can you keep a secret?" Willow worried over breaking her promise to Zane, but while it was hard to lie to her family, it was *impossible* to lie to Bridgette.

"What do you think? No one else knows he popped your cherry," she teased.

"The engagement isn't real, but he wants it to be."

"Holy shit," Bridgette whispered. "You're lying to Mom and Dad? Why?" She opened a cabinet and dug around, withdrawing a bottle of wine.

Willow reached for wineglasses.

"Mugs," Bridgette said. "Covert operation with the little one around."

Two mugs of wine later, Willow had told her the whole sordid story. "And now I'm in this state of limbo. And you can't tell anyone this is fake."

"This is a lot to process." Bridgette twirled a lock of hair around her finger, a nervous habit she'd had for as long as Willow could remember. "You never knew you were his first?"

Willow shook her head. "I told you how he was that night. He was so in control. Mr. Calm, Cool, and Collected. I never would have guessed that he'd never done it before. And when we were together last night? One epic orgasm after another, like my body has been saving it all up for him. No one—absolutely *no one*—has ever made me feel like I do when we're together. And it's more than just the sex, you know? I can be myself with Zane. Good, bad, whatever. And the way he looks at me . . ." She shivered and held her arm up for Bridgette to see. "Goose bumps, Bridge. *Goose bumps* just from thinking about him."

"That's how it was for me and Jerry. And just for the record, I don't want to hear about epic orgasms. I'm happy for you, but my girl hasn't been touched since Jerry died, and she's a little jealous."

They both laughed. "I'm sorry. But . . . *oh my God.* I can't lie. It's magical. We're combustible. Just like it was all those years ago, only different. *Better.* Because now we're adults, and . . ." She paused, still unable to believe what she was about to say was the truth and not a silly fantasy. "This feels *real,* and he wants it to be. But I'm scared shitless of getting hurt again."

"You were young, and you made up all those stupid rules."

"I told you about the rules?" She must have had way too much wine that night, because she didn't recall sharing those details with her sister.

"Let's see. No feelings, no talking about it after the fact, no looking at each other differently, no blackmailing, and he was to let you walk home alone. For the record," Bridgette said, "I'm still impressed that you did that and no one found out. But I can't help wondering. Do you ever wish you hadn't set up those rules?"

Willow shook her head. "I can't think about it. I drove myself crazy thinking about it for way too many months afterward."

"And now it's come full circle," Bridgette said. "You two have kept in touch like you're best friends or lovers. And you have sexual history, which begs the question . . . if you're *not* still in love with each other, why would you have kept each other in the loop of your lives for all this time?"

Willow looked up at the ceiling and groaned. "That's why I'm so confused." She leaned forward, and her sister met her halfway, like they used to do as little girls sharing secrets. "I don't think I ever stopped loving him," she whispered. "But the whole reason we're doing this charade is because of *who* he is. How can I be in love with a guy who sleeps around?"

A haunted look came over Bridgette's face, and Willow wanted to evaporate into thin air. Jerry had been madly in love with Bridgette, but he'd been a snake in the grass before they'd started dating.

The front door swung open, and their parents walked in carrying two big presents. Louie bolted out of the playroom as if he had a grandparent-homing device. "Grandma! Grandpa! Auntie Willow made me a Spider-Man cake!"

Their father lifted him into his arms. "Spider-Man doesn't seem to have a mouth. He can't eat cake."

Louie tugged off his mask. "I have a mouth, Grandpa! It's just a mask."

Bridgette covered Willow's hand with hers and spoke quietly. "All I can tell you is that I knew Jerry was right for me from the very first time we met. It didn't matter that he was in a band and everyone knew what kind of guy he was. *Nothing* would have kept me from marrying him, because I knew we were right, regardless of what happened before we met. Musicians and actors aren't that far apart where their endgames are concerned. Jerry used to say, 'A player will play while he's searching for his soul mate, and then they're all in.' Remember how I compared myself to all of his female fans at first? It was hard. Like, really *excruciatingly* hard when he was on the road, but one look in his eyes and I was toast."

"What is it about their eyes? I'm the same way with Zane. He does this thing . . ." She lowered her chin and looked at Bridgette through her lashes.

Bridgette laughed. "I hope he does it better than that. You look a little insane."

"You always make me feel better. I'm sorry I didn't tell you the truth right away, but everything happened so fast." She moved closer so there was no chance of anyone else hearing and said, "You cannot tell anyone that the engagement is fake."

"I never would." Bridgette hugged her. "I think there's a lot more to this. He could have just asked an actress to play the part, but he went to all that trouble to get you to do it. That says something."

"Yeah, that I'm an easy mark." Even as she said it, she knew it wasn't true. She'd compared every man to Zane for so long, and now she had the only man she'd ever wanted. But she was terrified of handing over her heart, afraid to believe what would make her the happiest woman in the world could really be coming true.

"Since when are you a pessimist? You're the *chosen* one. That's how I see it."

Their mother breezed into the kitchen and kissed the top of each of their heads. "Are you girls going to chat all day? The rest of the kids are going to be here in ten minutes."

"Come on." Bridgette pushed to her feet.

"Where's that man of yours?" their father asked on his way out to the yard.

"He'll be here soon." Willow glanced at her phone. It had been hours since Zane had left to pick up the rental car. She wondered where he'd gotten held up.

More than an hour later, ten little boys and girls were taking turns swinging a bat at the Spider-Man piñata, and Willow was chowing down on her second piece of cake.

"It's pretty bad when your fiancé stands you up." Piper stood beside Willow, stealing pieces of Willow's cake off her plate. "But it's even worse when he stands you up at your nephew's birthday party."

"Thanks for pointing that out," Willow snarled. It wasn't like she hadn't already run through the gamut of possible reasons why Zane was late. She chose to ignore the worst of them—a pretty fan catching his attention—and went with what was clearly less likely but more palatable: he'd gotten locked in a gas station bathroom and had no way out.

"Well, he *is* Zane," Piper said.

"Yes. My *fiancé*," Willow reminded her, feeling oddly proprietary of him. "So please tread carefully, okay, sis? This is an emotional time for all of us."

"Mm-hm. I'm sure he just got caught up with fans or something."

*Let's hope not.* "I know you don't trust him."

Piper tucked her stick-straight shoulder-length blond hair behind her ear and crossed her lithe arms. "It's not that I don't trust him, per se. It's just always bothered me that he used to lead you on. I worried you'd hook up with him and get your heart broken. I'm so glad you weren't that stupid."

Willow watched Louie swing at the piñata, hoping Piper couldn't read the truth in her eyes. "What are you talking about? He never led me on."

"Oh, come on. Don't try to pretend you weren't completely in love with him when you were a kid. He was always *right there* when you were baking, and asking you for help with math? He was two grades ahead of you. That was sort of ridiculous, don't you think?"

She decided to ignore the first accusation, because how many lies could one woman be expected to maintain in one day? "He was a kid who loved cookies. And I kicked ass in math." Could he have been flirting with her back then and not really lame in precalc? She didn't have a clear enough head to figure that out at the moment, and the truth was, she had been a tall, gangly girl with big boobs and an uncanny ability to work with numbers, while Zane could have had his pick of the most popular, beautiful girls. "But let's say that was true and he really did flirt with me. Shouldn't you be happy for us now?"

"Maybe," Piper said cheerily. Then her expression turned serious. "If I hadn't seen pictures of him with no less than three women in the last two months."

"That was all part of our plan to cover things up." Willow hoped she sounded casual, but she was pretty sure she sounded like she was lying.

"Then you're a better woman than me, because I'd never put up with that shit." She snagged another bite of Willow's cake.

"I was doing the same thing!" Willow whispered harshly. "You *know* I went out with Billy Crusher six or eight weeks ago and Xavier Frank last month. We explained this yesterday."

"That's true. I had forgotten about that. I just don't want you to get hurt, because if he hurts you, then I'd have to kill him. And then I'd go to jail, and look at me. I'm tough as nails out here, but in the pen? The whole scene isn't pretty."

Willow laughed and set her plate on the table. "You're a big pain in the ass for such a tiny person, but thank you for watching out for me."

"You're my little sister. I'll always have your back. Are you sure everything's okay? He's really late, and Sweetwater isn't big enough for him to get lost."

"Spider-Man!" Louie sprinted toward the side yard with nine screaming friends on his heels.

Talia sidled up to Willow and Piper as they headed for the side yard. Butterflies took flight in Willow's stomach as a tall, broad Spider-Man came into focus and lifted Louie into his arms. She would know that athletic build anywhere.

Ben's laughter sailed across the yard from where he and their father were heading toward the mayhem.

"Mom! It's Spider-Man!" Louie yelled to Bridgette, who was looking at Willow with an approving smile.

"Oh my God," Piper said with awe. "I've never seen Louie so happy."

"The only one missing from this party is your man, Willow," Talia pointed out.

"Not anymore," Willow said more to herself than to her sisters.

Spider-Man looked over the kids' heads, locking eyes with Willow. He lifted his shoulders in that simple, honest shrug that was so very *Zane* it made her warm all over.

"I concede," Piper said. "He might have just won me over."

"Me too," Willow whispered. His voice sailed through her mind. *Then stop pushing me away and let me show you the man I can be. The man I will be for you.*

She was done pushing. So very done.

"WHAT YOU DID for Louie was amazing," Bridgette said to Zane as she hugged him goodbye after the party. "He'll remember this day forever."

"He's a great little guy." Zane reached for Willow's hand, glad to see things between her and Bridgette seemed to be okay. "If you have time while I'm in town, why don't we all get together? We can do something kid friendly."

The smile Willow flashed made him want to suggest it again and again.

"Or we can have Mom and Dad watch Louie and we can do something adultish," Bridgette suggested.

"I'll call you, Bridge." Willow hugged her, and Zane heard indiscernible whispers pass between them.

They both came away smiling, which he took as a good sign, and Willow reached for his hand again.

"Thank you for being so good to Louie," she said as they walked down the driveway toward their cars. "I've never seen him so happy."

"I'm sorry about being so late. I thought I could get a costume at Walmart in the next town over, but they only had kids' sizes. I had to call a buddy from the city, and he met me halfway."

"You had someone drive halfway from New York City? You must have really good friends."

"Why does that surprise you?" He nudged her shoulder with his. "You know I'm a good guy."

"Yeah. I do."

"So you'll stop all the nonsense and give me a chance?"

"Haven't I already shown you that?" When they reached her car, she hooked her finger into the waist of his jeans and pulled him closer. "On the counter in my bakery kitchen? On the prep table? In my office?"

His body had been humming all afternoon from their sexy tryst. "Maybe you should refresh my memory." He backed her up, trapping her against the car.

"Do I have a choice?" she teased.

"Always."

She shook her head with a sweet smile on her lips. "Not when it comes to you I don't. I never have."

His mouth came down gently over hers in a kiss so warm and wonderful he never wanted it to end.

"Let's go by Ben's and get your stuff," she said between kisses.

"It's in my car."

"Geez. You could at least pretend like it was my choice."

He laughed as she climbed into her car. "Babe, I know you better than you know yourself. How many times do I have to say that before you realize it's true?"

Her smile faded, and she ran her finger along the edge of the steering wheel, avoiding his eyes. "I told Bridgette."

"I know you did."

Her eyes flicked to his. "How . . . ?"

He cocked a brow.

"Right." She smiled again. "You know me."

"I told Ben."

"You said you might." She reached up and grabbed his shirt, tugging him down to eye level. "I'm scared, Z. You need to know that. Like, scared-to-death scared."

"I know that, too, sweetheart, and I'm going to do everything I can to make sure you know you can trust me." He gave her a chaste kiss. "We're playing by my rules, remember? Let go of all the bullshit, and one day you'll wake up and realize I've been the frosting on your cupcake all along."

She laughed. "You're such a weirdo."

"What does that say about you? You're engaged to a weirdo." He glanced up at Bridgette's house. "I used to think the houses here were nondescript, but they're really cute as hell."

"You were in such a rush to get out of Sweetwater and on to bigger, better things, you snubbed your nose at a lot of things."

"I never snubbed my nose at you." He leaned in for another kiss.

She sighed. "Hashtag *truth*."

"Now who's the weirdo?"

"Definitely *you*. Think we can watch one of those movies on your playlist tonight?"

He closed her car door and leaned in the window, taking another kiss. "We can try." He winked and walked toward his rental car.

"What does that mean?" she called after him.

He glanced over his shoulder. The passion between them transcended words. *We're so right together. What the hell took me so long to figure it out?*

# CHAPTER TWELVE

WILLOW HAD FORGOTTEN that in all the years they'd been friends, Zane had only been in her apartment once, and that was last night when he'd dropped her off. It had been dark, and he'd been solely focused on her. There was no way he'd noticed anything else. She rarely thought of him as a wealthy actor, but it was hard not to realize it as he was standing in her one-bedroom apartment, which she was sure paled in comparison to the mansion he must live in. Piper and their father had done an amazing job of making it feel open and airy when she'd renovated, by adding cathedral ceilings and keeping the kitchen open to the living room, separated only by a breakfast bar. The recessed lighting, cream-colored walls with white moldings, and neutral furniture gave the space a cohesive feel. Of course, Willow being the pastry lover she was, she'd added mint and peach accent pillows for a splash of color.

What would Zane think of her cozy nest?

His gaze coasted to the windows overlooking the lake and fell to the couch below, where the yearbook she'd been poring over last night like a lovesick teenager sat like a beacon to her heart's desire. Her pulse kicked up. Could she casually pick up the yearbook and slip it beneath a pillow without him realizing it?

"Love your place, Wills."

"Um, thanks. Why don't you put your stuff in the bedroom?" She motioned to the door to their right and moved in front of him, hoping to block his view of the couch.

His eyes flicked over her shoulder, and his lips curved up in a knowing grin.

"Wills." He stepped closer, his arms circling her waist. "Were you feeling nostalgic last night?" He nuzzled his scruffy face against her neck, sparking a rippling effect of shivers and heat.

She touched her forehead to his shoulder, sheepishly answering, "Maybe."

He pressed a kiss to her neck, took her face between both his hands, and put his warm, moist lips on hers, kissing her as he smiled.

"I love that," he whispered. "Don't be embarrassed about drooling over your man."

She laughed and crossed the room to pick up the yearbook. "I wasn't *drooling*. I was cursing." She reached for it, and he grabbed her by the waist from behind and sank down to the couch, bringing her onto his lap.

"Cursing? That doesn't sound like a girl who's in love." He reached for the yearbook, and she pulled it away.

"Remember, this was last night, when your confession came on the heels of the most incredible sex I've ever had. So there was all this lust and confusion tangled up with the other stuff."

"Go on." He nipped at her lips. "I'm liking the 'most incredible sex' part."

She laughed again, and couldn't remember ever having as many happy moments with any man as she'd had in the last two days with Zane. Despite the turmoil, he was, *bar none*, the man who made her heart sing.

"It sounds *exactly* like a girl who is madly in love but has tried to ignore her feelings for so long it's clawing at every inch of her soul to be set free." She snuggled against his chest and draped an arm over his shoulder, speaking softer. "And then she remembered the pain of the past, and it chained that love to the wall, leaving the lovesick girl in a constant battle of wanting the infuriating man and being afraid of the emotions he incited."

He brushed her hair away from her face and kissed her again, dipping into her mouth like a flower blooms, gentle yet certain of its ability to consume the sun's rays. The yearbook fell from her fingers as he took the kiss deeper. She loved the way his kisses forced her to abandon all thought and become one with him. He knew when to be rough, when to be tender, and not a single second of their kisses felt forced or practiced. These kisses were beautifully real, making them that much sweeter.

"Baby," he breathed, gathering her hair over one shoulder. "When you want to curse me, do it to my face. We're *feeling*, Wills, and I'm not going to let either of us screw this up by keeping secrets about anything."

How did he know exactly what she needed to hear?

"I want to know when I piss you off so I can fix it or argue about it, and I want to know when I turn you on." He pulled the neckline of her shirt down and kissed the center of her breastbone. Her body pulsed with desire. "I want to strip away all the bullshit and get to the bottom of who we are. The good, the bad, and the frustrating."

She couldn't breathe. She felt like she was standing outside her body, watching a movie she'd wished for forever.

"And you're looking at me like you're not sure if I'm acting or not." He picked up the yearbook and sighed. "I don't blame you. Sometimes I have a hard time distinguishing between the two."

He pulled her closer.

"I actually wasn't thinking that I don't believe you. I was thinking that you knew exactly what I needed to hear. But the fact that you can't distinguish between real and fiction is a little scary."

"No, it's not, baby. It would be if I wasn't aware of it." He flipped through the yearbook to the drama club picture. "Do you know why I became an actor?"

"You said you loved everything about it, and you couldn't wait to get to Hollywood, to live a bigger, better life." She gazed down at the picture of the boy she'd fallen so hard for. It seemed strange to admit to herself now, but his senior year had been the year she'd dreaded the most. She'd expected to see less of him as he matured toward manhood while she was still finding her footing in that space between awkward and confident. But that hadn't happened. Even though Zane had been the varsity football team captain, mentoring junior varsity players, with cheerleaders fawning all over him, he still took the time to talk to her after football games, if only for a minute. He'd flash a smile and say something like, *Glad you made it.* She hadn't thought about those times in years, but now she remembered how he'd look in her direction between plays, and for a beat the rest of the kids had faded away. Had she always romanticized their friendship?

"That's what I told everyone," Zane said, pulling her from her memories. "But do you want to know the rest of the story?" He flipped through the yearbook to the picture of the football team.

"Of course."

His eyes remained trained on the photograph. He and Ben stood in the back of the picture, both of them tall and dark, their faces masks of cool confidence that boys of almost eighteen possessed.

"Growing up, I always felt like I was putting on an act, you know? Trying to fit in and make up for the things I lacked."

"Everyone does. That's part of figuring out who you are."

He lifted his eyes to hers. "You didn't. You've always been real."

"Only because I sucked at faking it." She thought about that for a minute, and she realized that wasn't exactly true. "Actually, I didn't really suck at it, so I haven't always been real." She flipped through the yearbook until she reached her class picture and pointed to the picture of herself. She'd always worn her hair long, but she'd had bangs back then. "That girl had been crushing on you for years, and I did a pretty good job of keeping that to myself."

He laughed. "No, you didn't."

"What? Yes, I definitely did." She bumped him with her shoulder. "You had no idea."

"No?" An amused smile lifted his lips.

"Oh my God. Piper was right." She covered her face with her hands. "How embarrassing!"

"Why? I was totally into you."

She rolled her eyes. "Yeah, right."

"Wills, are you kidding me? Do you know what kind of torture it was when you tutored me? Have you ever tried to concentrate with a raging hard-on?"

She gasped, laughing. "You did not have a raging hard-on! Please don't tell me Piper was right about that, too. She said you were really good at math and just trying to hook up with me."

"I did, too. Every damn time. But your sister is wrong. I sucked at math, geography, history, *and* English, which was another reason I felt like I needed to pretend to be something I wasn't." He closed the yearbook and set it on the coffee table. "But she *was* right about my being into you. I was *definitely* crushing on you."

"Holy shit, Z. You've just turned my entire world upside down. All those years I got excited when you'd talk to me, or look at me, or . . ."

"Or throw every football with the hopes that you'd be impressed?"

She stared, speechless.

"Don't look so shocked. You were funny and ballsy and so smart, baby. God, I was in awe of you. And you were the prettiest girl in Sweetwater. Still are."

She shook her head to try to snap out of the surprise and overwhelming happiness that consumed her. "I was gawky and awkward."

"You were beautiful and adorable." The loving smile he flashed warmed her from the top of her head to the ends of her toes and all the best places in between. "But Piper was also wrong. I wasn't trying to hook up. In fact, it was just the opposite. I *had* to study with you, because your mother suggested it when she found out I was failing math. How could I tell your mother no? She treated me like her own son. But trust me, the last thing I wanted to do was hook up with you."

"Gee, thanks," she said, only half teasing.

"Come on, Wills. You were my best friend's little sister. If anyone was ever off-limits, it was you."

She sank back against the cushions, her mouth open. "You liked me."

"I liked you."

"You got *hard* for me," she said with great satisfaction.

"I jerked off to thoughts of you." He shifted his hips.

"Ew!" She smacked his arm, then bit her lower lip as she thought about it. "Really? That's kind of hot."

Laughter sailed from his lungs. "God I love you." He crushed his mouth to hers, laughing and kissing at once. "I'll jerk off for you anytime you want."

"I'm holding you to that."

He touched his forehead to hers and said, "Good. I never told you what you'd be doing while I was jerking off."

He pushed a hand between her legs, rubbing her through her jeans, and she felt herself go damp. Her eyes dropped to the outline of his rigid cock beneath his jeans. "I love when you talk dirty," she whispered, and he made a low, gravelly sound in his throat.

"Don't tell me that." His jaw tightened. "We're too good at crossing lines."

"I crossed a big line for you. Cross this one for me. Don't hold ba—"

Her words were smothered in his demanding mouth, which was exactly what she needed to bridge the gap between the fear she hoped to leave behind and the trust she needed to move forward. He continued rubbing her through her jeans, stroking her into a greedy frenzy of need and want as he ravaged her mouth. When he used his broad chest to push her down to the couch, she went willingly, spreading her legs to accommodate his powerful hips. He grabbed her hands, pressing them into the cushion as he ground his hips in a maddening rhythm, matching every penetrating stroke of his tongue.

"I need you naked," he said, tugging her shirt up. "I need to have my mouth on you."

Her body quivered. "Yes," she panted out, rising off the cushion.

He tore off her shirt and hesitated for only a second before reading the approval in her expression and removing her bra. Perched on his knees between her legs, he tugged his shirt off and tossed it aside. His eyes rolled over her face, full of love and burning with desire. His gaze traveled lower, lingering on her breasts. Goose bumps chased the heat of his stare, pebbling her nipples into burning peaks. She felt more vulnerable now than she had on the island. This wasn't a game, driven solely by passion. This was truth and honesty twining together, bound by a ribbon of hope and trust.

"Christ, baby. Every time I look at you you're more gorgeous than the last." He brushed his hand over her stomach, causing her insides to clench and burn. "I can't do this here. I want too much of you."

He moved off the couch and took her hand, bringing her up in front of him. Her breasts grazed his chest, sending white-hot sparks darting through her veins.

With a finger beneath her chin, he lifted her eyes to his. "You're the sweetest thing."

"I'm *your* sweetest thing."

She took his hand and led him to her bedroom, leading him away from their past and welcoming him into her future.

WILLOW'S WORDS BURNED into Zane's mind. He'd waited a life-time to hear her say that she was *his*. He followed her into the bedroom, taking in the yellow walls and white trim, distressed furniture in muted shades of blue and green, built-in bookshelves flanking the doors to the balcony, and a king-size bed with a fluffy white blanket. He took her in his arms, her soft green eyes gazing up at him with wonder and trust and so much love he wanted to fall into them.

"I've fantasized about what your bedroom looked like and imagined it hundreds of different ways. But each and every time, *one* thing remained consistent."

"Tell me." She touched his chest, sending lust straight to his core.

"I was always in it." He lowered his lips to hers, breathing her in. "I promise you don't have to be afraid." He took her hands and guided them to the button on his jeans, knowing that even though she was telling him to play dirty, she still needed to know she had some power. "*You* are who I want. You are who I have *always* wanted."

A sexy sound escaped her lips.

He grabbed his wallet from his back pocket and tossed it on the bed, covered her hands with his, and helped her undo the button on his jeans. He pushed them off and stepped out of his briefs. There were many dirty things he wanted to do, to say, to experience with her, but he knew she was still scared despite her plea for crossing another line. Allowing her to leave her jeans on made him more vulnerable than her, and he hoped—God, he hoped—that nugget of fear in her eyes would dissipate.

"Touch me, baby," he said, desperate for her. "I want your hands on me."

She pressed her hands to his chest, and her lips followed. She was shaking as she kissed his pecs and slicked her tongue over his nipple. His hard length twitched between them. Her hands moved down his back, and she clenched his ass as she sealed her mouth over his nipple and sucked. His hips bucked forward, white-hot pleasures tearing through him.

"That's it, baby." He wound her hair around his hand. "Suck harder. I love your mouth."

His muscles tightened as she sucked and licked, giving the same attention to the other side of his chest. Grinding his teeth with every slick of her tongue, he rocked against her belly. "Feel how hard you make me."

Her hands gripped his sides as she kissed a path down the center of his stomach. Then she went up on her toes, reaching for his mouth. He tugged her head back, taking her in a kiss as roughly as he wanted to make love to her. He sucked her tongue into his mouth, showing her what he wanted next, pushed a hand between her legs, and rubbed her through her jeans.

"Touch me, Z. I need you to touch me."

"Oh, I'm going to touch you." He kissed her softer, loving how she craned up for more. "I'm going to touch you, and taste you, and love you until the sun comes up."

He filled his hands with her breasts, and she inhaled sharply.

"I want to bury my cock between these gorgeous breasts that you've always hated, and not because I'm a boob man. I'm a *Willow* man. And I want to love every inch of you. I want you to feel how much I love you in the way I touch you and obliterate all your fears." As he lowered his mouth and teased one taut peak, he watched her reaction, gauging how much dirty talk she could take.

Her eyes darkened, narrowed. Her fingers dug into his sides, and her lips curved up in a sinful grin. "What are you waiting for?"

*Oh, hell yes.* "In a hurry?"

"Only for you."

The challenge in her eyes turned him on beyond comprehension. He sucked her breast into his mouth, working the button of her jeans with his free hand. He hooked his hands into either side of her waistband and yanked her pants down to her knees.

"Leave them on," he demanded, loving the inferno blazing in her eyes as he pushed his hand between her legs and plunged two fingers deep inside her, taking her in a rough, possessive kiss.

She moaned as he sought the magical spot that would bring her up on her toes. Her fingernails dug into his skin as she clung to him, murmuring into the kiss. He brought his thumb into play, teasing her clit as he intensified the kiss even more. Her thighs tightened around his hand, and he knew she was close. He tore his mouth away and clamped it over her breast, sucking her nipple hard enough to send her over the edge.

"Z—*oh God. Don't stop. Harder. Oh my God.*"

He loved her through her panting pleas, through the peak, until the very last pulse of her climax. She went limp against him. He lifted her into his arms and strode to the bed. Pulling the pretty blanket to the foot of the bed, he laid her down and rid her of her jeans. She blinked up at him, looking sated and so very trusting it filled him to the brim. His desire to be dirty took a backseat to his need to take her in his arms and love her with all of the tenderness she deserved.

"More dirty talk, please," she said as sweetly as if she'd said, *Please pass the sugar.*

"You sure, baby? We don't have to—"

"I've never done dirty talk, and I trust you, Z. I want to do *everything* with you. I want you to do what you said you wanted to do. To put your"—her eyes dropped to his throbbing cock—"between *the girls.* I want to let go of all my fears and put it all out on the table."

He grinned at the thought of her spread-eagle on a table.

"We are *not* having sex on my table." She curled her finger, motioning for him to come closer.

"Christ, I'll never be able to deny you a damn thing." He propped up pillows at the head of the bed. "Get comfy, precious girl."

She scrambled up to the head of the bed with a wide smile and leaned back against the pillows like he'd just offered her an ice-cream cone. Her long blond hair cascaded over her breasts. Her cheeks were flushed, her eyes locked on his, anticipation glittering back at him. She was his every fantasy come true, only better. Because she was *Willow*, and she was *finally* his.

He shook his head slowly. "Touch yourself for me, dirty girl."

She trapped her lower lip between her teeth, and a second later it sprang free. "You first."

"I wasn't sure you'd really want to play this game." Boy, was he wrong. He held out his hand. "Lick my palm, sweetheart."

Just watching her lick him was erotic. He fisted his cock, giving it a long, tight stroke. He lifted her hand and sucked two fingers into his mouth, leaving them glistening as he guided them between her legs. Her skin flushed, and she touched herself tentatively, watching him stroke himself.

"Come on, baby. Show me how you like it."

She slid a little lower on the pillows and began moving her fingers quicker, breathing harder, and he was right there with her. Lust pooled at the base of his spine. Knowing how much she trusted him, how much he loved her, made everything more intense.

"Now will you do it?"

Her plea pulled him from the fog of lust consuming him. "Make love to you?"

She shook her head, looking sweet and seductive at once as she reached for him, then glanced down at her breasts. This was the biggest act of faith she could ever show, and the magnitude of it brought his mouth to hers in a kiss he hoped would convey how deeply he loved her.

"Baby, I adore you for *you*. You know that, right?"

"If I didn't, I wouldn't ask you to do this. Be dirty with me, Z."

He straddled her hips, his eager erection bobbing between them, and he hesitated. It was almost too much, holding her heart in his hands.

"Talk dirty to me," she whispered, reaching between his legs.

Her touch cut him loose. "Suck me, baby. Let me feel that wicked and wonderful mouth of yours around my cock."

Her hair tumbled forward as she took him in her mouth, her eyes trained on his, taunting him as much as she pleasured him. His primal instincts surged forth, pushing away the softer man who had tried to take over. He gripped the base of his cock, staving off his release.

"Get me nice and wet, baby, so we can fulfill our fantasy." Watching her slick her tongue over the tip and along his shaft nearly made him lose it.

She settled back against the pillows again and pushed her breasts together.

"Wills, you have no idea what you're doing to me." *Heart, mind, and soul.* He leaned his palm against the headboard, nestling his cock between her breasts. "Jesus. I could come like this."

"That would be a waste." She reached around him and smacked his ass. "Get to it."

He pushed his cock through her gorgeous breasts, unable to quell the greedy noises that came with the blissful feel of her warm skin engulfing him. She licked the head each time it appeared, surpassing even his most erotic notions and taking him right up to the brink of release.

"Slow down," she said. "Let me get my mouth around you."

He groaned in agony, slowing his pace. As the wide crown pushed between her breasts, her warm mouth clamped down around it, and her tongue swirled over the tip, fraying his restraint. When her hand disappeared between his legs to *her* slick heat, his resolve shattered. He swept her giggling, squirming, deliciously soft body beneath him and reached for his wallet, quickly sheathing himself.

She wound her arms around his neck and rose off the mattress to align him with her entrance.

"I like being dirty with you," she said with a wide smile.

"I'm not going to ask how you got so good at that."

"Lots and lots of porn."

His eyes widened, and she burst into laughter. "God, you're gullible."

"I was just picturing watching porn *with* you."

She wiggled her hips. "We could make our own porn, but you talk a lot during sex, so maybe not. I might have to gag you."

"Oh, baby. Now we're talking."

He gathered her in his arms, and she grinned up at him. "You never told me the real reason you went into acting."

"Now who's talking too much?"

She leaned up and kissed him. "Just tell me. Then you can make love to me until neither one of us has any energy left to talk."

"That was the plan all along, sweetheart."

"Z," she complained.

He gazed down at her and knew she'd push until he told her. "I thought acting was all I was capable of and that a fast-paced, bigger-than-life existence would be more fulfilling than what Sweetwater had to offer. But I was young and stupid. I didn't even know what *fulfilling* meant." He kissed her softly, weighing his answer. "But we're not going to talk about that now. All you need to know right this second is that there's more I want out of life than to look pretty on a big screen."

"Like?"

"Like you, baby. I want you."

She looked at him for a long moment with a serious expression, like she was contemplating world peace. "I want you, too, Z," she whispered.

He brushed his lips over her cheek and whispered, "You love me, Wills. Now stop talking and let me love you like you deserve to be loved."

"With whipped cream and sugary goodness?" she teased.

She was killing him with Willowness. "That'll be the second course."

"Third," she corrected him.

"Wills."

"Sorry," she whispered with another sweet giggle. She schooled her expression and said, "Do me, Walker, and stop talking. *Geez.* Where's my ball gag?"

As their bodies came together, he got lost in the loving words slipping from her lips and the complete and utter lack of fear in her beautiful eyes.

# CHAPTER THIRTEEN

WILLOW AWOKE AT two in the morning to an empty bed. Her heart sank with old heartache, and just as quickly, she chided herself. She wasn't going to allow her seventeen-year-old stupidity to stand in the way of her adult happiness. Blinking away the haze of sleep, she spotted Zane sitting out on the balcony overlooking the lake. He was shirtless, leaning forward. She pulled the blanket around herself and padded across the floor. He turned as she pulled open the glass door. His hair was still damp from the shower they'd taken after their sexcapade. It looked like he'd pushed his hand through it, pulling it away from his face, making his chiseled features appear even more defined.

The corners of his mouth tipped up despite the serious look in his eyes. "Hey, babe. I hope I didn't wake you." He reached for her hand, holding papers in the other, and guided her down beside him on the wicker sofa.

"You didn't. Everything okay?"

He pulled her closer, wrapping an arm around her shoulder, and kicked his feet up on the railing. "Yeah. I couldn't sleep."

"Worried about your film? Is that the script?"

He shook his head. "Don't you have to be up at the crack of dawn?"

She snuggled in closer and smiled up at him. "Yes, but when I go to bed with a hot guy and wake up alone, it kind of rattles me."

He pressed his lips to hers. "Sorry."

"So . . ." She eyed the papers in his hand. "If it's not your script, what is it that has enough power to drag you from my bed when I'm naked?"

"You mean besides the fact that you talk in your sleep?"

"I do not!" *Holy cow. What did I say?*

He laughed. "Maybe. Maybe not."

"Zane Walker, if I do talk in my sleep, it's about recipes or something innocuous."

"How do you know I'm not going to sell your trade secrets?"

"How do you know I didn't videotape last night to use as blackmail when you turn into an asshat?"

"Touché, sweet girl." He leaned in for another kiss.

"So what *are* you doing?"

He sat back, his eyes skirting over the lake. "I had forgotten how beautiful it is here at night."

"Nice change of subject."

He pushed a hand through his hair and faced her head-on. The tension around his eyes and mouth made her stomach knot up.

"You're right, and I'm sorry. I promised to be honest. I've never shared this with anyone before, so cut me a little slack." He waved the papers. "You know how I said I wanted more out of life?"

"Yes." She sat up a little straighter, preparing for whatever shoe was going to drop.

"I'm sure you've heard the reason I took this role was to drive my career in a new direction. Romantic suspense, which could then lead to romantic comedy and all those silly love stories."

"It was all over the media. You have to be excited about kissing Remi Divine. I assume you have kissing scenes." Remi Divine was his beautiful twenty-four-year-old costar. America's sweetheart of the moment.

"Wills." He shook his head. "Yes, I have to kiss her, but acting kisses aren't like real kisses."

"Do your lips touch?" she teased.

"Uh-huh."

"It's a real kiss." She snuggled closer. "But I'm not jealous or anything."

He cocked a brow.

"Okay, maybe a little. But I'm a big girl." *I know how to hide it well.* She pushed that green-eyed monster away and locked the door behind it. "Anyway, isn't the change from action movies to romance what started the uproar with your focus group?"

He shrugged. "Yeah, that and other things. The truth is, this role is just another role for me. I thought it was the roles I was taking that were leaving me feeling empty, but after filming so much of this movie, I know that wasn't it. As I said earlier, acting was the only thing I was good at. *Not good in class?* No problem. I'm athletic. I'll become the star quarterback. Girls didn't care that my family was poor. They saw a cute guy and made me popular. *Have a poor family that doesn't want to help themselves or help you become something more?* No problem. I'll do it on my own. Acting, acting, acting."

He pushed his hand through his hair again and shifted, putting space between them. "Making friends was easy because of Ben. Your brother didn't give a shit about my unambitious family or my crappy clothes or any of that. He saw *me. You* saw me. Your family saw me, except maybe Piper. I think part of her saw right through me."

Willow took his hand. It was hot, *nervous* hot, and her heart hurt at the thought of him believing that for all these years.

"Zane, Piper didn't think you were acting. She thought you were leading me on. That we'd hook up and I'd get hurt."

He slid her an uncertain look. "Well, she was right."

"But we hurt ourselves. You didn't hurt me. I know that now." She moved closer, needing the connection for what she was about to ask. "Do you feel like you're acting with me now?"

His eyes warmed, and he pulled her closer. He lifted her chin and kissed her softly. "For a long time I wasn't sure who the real me was. Nobody in Hollywood talks to me about anything real. They talk about movies and women and parties and awards that I don't give a rat's ass about. It's easy to be the wild guy. *Good-time Zane*, the partier who lives life on a whim. But when I came home for your parents' anniversary party in the spring and we went fishing with your dad, things changed."

He looked down at the papers in his hands, and when he met her gaze again, his eyes shone with new light. "Not a single person in your family asked me about acting, or the latest gossip, or what movie I was doing next. You mentioned wanting a bookstore in your bakery one day, and Talia and I brainstormed about ways to get through to kids who have trouble with academics so they don't end up feeling lost. It's so different when I'm here. Ben and I played basketball, and Piper gave me hell about anything she could. And your mom tried to get me to use her Sweetwater Spice soap. Remember?"

He laughed, and it brought a lump to Willow's throat.

"You remembered . . ." *All that?*

"And more. Your dad asked me what my goals were for this year, and when I answered, I realized I had told him the truth. Not the Hollywood bullshit I spewed out in LA. You guys know me in a way no one out there ever could."

"That's called *family*," Willow said softly, knowing it was a touchy subject for him.

Emotions swam in his eyes. "Yeah. Being back here is *torturous* bliss. It's the place I desperately wanted to escape to prove myself, and in doing so, I got lost. But you never let me fully disappear. You were always there, a text away, turning me down but reminding me of the person I really was. I am not acting with you, Wills. Maybe sometimes when you'd blow me off and I needed to suck it up to remain sane I'd hide behind that fun-guy mask. But not now. No."

"Z—"

He touched his lips to hers in a tender kiss that felt as though he was sealing a vow.

LYING NEXT TO Willow, listening to the even cadence of her breathing as she'd slept in his arms, had changed everything for Zane. He knew she was worried about his reputation, but he also knew, from every second they spent together, that she was it for him. Willow was as real as real could be, and he didn't just want to show her how much he loved her; he wanted to be the best man he could *for* her. He'd gone out to the balcony to read over the project he'd been toying with recently.

"After talking with your dad, I went back to something I'd started—and put away—a long time ago." He laid the papers he'd been holding in her lap and placed her hand over them.

She glanced down with confusion in her eyes.

"Go ahead, take a look."

She picked up the papers and scanned the title page. "*Beneath It All?* A screenplay by—" Her eyes widened. "You wrote this?" She flipped to the first page without waiting for an answer.

Anxiety crawled up his spine. "I haven't shown it to anyone, and it's probably crap. It's gritty and not at all like what you're used to seeing in the theaters."

"Shh." She leaned her back against his side and pulled her feet up on the cushion. The blanket parted, revealing a flash of skin between her breasts.

"Wills, are you naked under there?"

"Mm-hm. *Shh.*" She flipped the page and continued reading.

He ground his teeth together. Well, that took care of his nerves. Now he was too busy thinking about her naked to worry about what she thought of the screenplay.

# CHAPTER FOURTEEN

WILLOW PULLED THE last tray of muffins from the oven and set them on the cooling rack with the others, filling the oven with two more cakes to bake. She set the hot pads on the stainless-steel table, then grabbed the powdered sugar and sprinkled it over two trays of doughnuts, inhaling the sugary sweetness she knew she'd never get enough of. She pushed the trays of doughnuts off to the side and pulled two trays of mini tarts from the other oven. The heavy door complained with a piercing screech.

"You need to get that fixed, baby girl."

Willow startled, nearly dropping the tarts. "Mom, you scared me half to death. It's fine, just noisy." The oven was on its last leg, but she wasn't quite ready to say goodbye to it yet, and she needed to save a little more money before she could replace it. She slid the trays onto the table as her mother placed a box on the butcher-block counter at the other end of the kitchen.

"I'd say you're too sentimental, but I can't. Look at who you're marrying." Her mother sighed. "I'm happy for you, honey. And holy moly! There are roses on every surface out there. He really did fill the bakery with roses. I thought the girls had exaggerated. It smells even more heavenly in here than usual. Plus . . . *bodyguards?*" Her mother's springy blond curls framed her face.

Willow rolled her eyes. She was glad the crowds were gone, but it still felt weird to have Zane's brawny security guys standing in front of the bakery. She'd given them each a muffin and coffee when she'd arrived. They were nice, if not a little stoic.

Her mother's wide-legged pants nearly swept the floor as she went to check out the muffins. "I made you some of that jasmine body butter you love so much."

Her mother had been making soaps, shampoos, and fragrances since Willow was a little girl. It had started as a hobby, but the ladies in the community had quickly caught wind of her lovely fragrances, and before Roxie knew what was happening, she had more requests than she could handle. Now she sold them in local stores and did a moderate amount of online sales as well. She claimed to put magic potions into some of her fragrances, only she never told them which ones. It was a running joke in the community. Whenever someone got engaged, someone always blamed it on Roxie's wares. Willow had enough of her mother's handiwork to stock an entire store. "I have plenty of the lavender lotion you made me a few weeks ago. You should give that to Bridgette." Mini tart shaper in hand, she began pushing the centers of the tarts down to make space for the cream cheese filling. "You're early today."

It was seven o'clock Monday morning, and although Willow was at the bakery every morning by five o'clock preparing for the 8:00 a.m. rush, her mother, who babysat Louie, rarely came by before seven thirty, when Bridgette arrived to open her flower shop.

"It just hit me. We have a wedding to plan! And I wanted to drop off the body butter. You know how soft the jasmine body butter makes your skin." Her mother waggled her brows.

*"Mom."* She thought about bathing in the lake with the soap Zane had bought. And last night, after they'd showered, he'd helped her put on the lavender lotion her mother had made. *I love how everything smells on you.* An old fear shivered through her, and she stomped it down deep. She wasn't guilty of over-romanticizing their relationship

anymore. She smiled to herself. She'd fallen asleep reading his screenplay in bed and had woken to the alarm wrapped in Zane's arms. She would have liked nothing more than to stay there, but she had too much to do. Including, she hoped, reading more of the screenplay and getting in touch with Aurelia to talk about the possibility of partnering with the bakery and the bookstore.

Her mother pointed to the muffins. "Are these my favorite?" Roxie Dalton was a sweets lover, and she'd passed her mouthful of sweet teeth down to Willow. The way Willow had it figured, she could thank her mother for her curvy figure, thick blond hair, and inability to ever hold her tongue. Her father, on the other hand, had supplied her with the stubborn genes she wore so proudly.

"Blueberry cinnamon, yes, and let's keep the eyebrow wiggles to a minimum." She finished preparing the centers of the tarts as her mother chose a muffin. She had a feeling if her mother had any idea how dirty she really wanted to get with Zane, she'd be gasping in horror. She gently twisted the tarts, removed them from the tins, and set them aside to cool.

"What? Can't I be happy for my baby girl? Zane has always been like family. He was your first real kiss, for goodness' sakes."

"A mistletoe kiss when I was seven does not count as a real kiss." Her mind spiraled back to the first kiss that *did* count, when he'd stood before her dripping with confidence and eagerness and holding her so lovingly it had felt like a dream. *Don't be nervous. I've got you.*

"Every kiss counts, sweetheart." Her mother took a big bite of the muffin.

Until the night at the lake, Willow had dismissed her and Zane's first real kiss from counting. But now that she knew the truth, that first kiss had shifted back into the place she'd once held it, making it a treasure once again.

"There are plenty of kisses that don't count. Think of all the frogs I kissed over the years." *When I was trying to find someone to fill the emptiness Zane left behind.*

"I disagree. If you hadn't gone out with those other men, you'd have no perspective about what's true love and what's nothing more than lust or physical attraction. I'm glad I dated a few men before your father. He might be a proper gentleman now, but your father had his own bout with recklessness."

"Daddy?" Willow couldn't imagine it.

"Oh yes. He was quite the catch, and he knew it. I wasn't even sure I wanted to compete, even though your father had set his sights on me *big-time*." Her mother took another bite of the muffin. "Mm. This is incredible."

"Thanks." Willow set up the blender, her thoughts turning introspective. "How did you know you could trust him?"

Her mother's eyes drifted up to the ceiling, and she sighed. When she met Willow's gaze again, there was a well of wisdom in her eyes that Willow wanted to learn from.

"I didn't know. I *hoped*, and every day he showed me I could trust him." Her mother reached over and squeezed her hand. "I know you, baby girl. You're thinking about the actresses that will flock here next week and wondering how you'll handle it."

"No—" She couldn't lie to her mother any more than she already had. "I mean, yes, but not because I don't think I measure up. Just because . . ."

"Because yesterday every woman and their sister came from over the hills and across the mountains to see him?"

Willow turned on the blender, remembering how frustrating that had been.

"I know, honey, but the man sent you dozens of roses and *ran* through town to see you."

"How do you know that?"

"Nothing spreads faster than gossip in Sweetwater, and you two *are* all over the Internet. He had his security guys put out the word that if anyone comes near your place to gawk, he'll get a restraining order."

She turned off the blender. "What?"

"I'm pretty sure you don't have anything to worry about. The man is in love, Willow. And I think he always has been."

A little thrill raced up Willow's spine. "Why do you say that?"

"Mother's intuition. Now can we talk about the wedding? Have you set a date?"

She turned on the blender, working out her thoughts. Restraining orders? He wasn't kidding when he'd said he'd taken care of it. The back door swung open, and Piper breezed into the kitchen with Bridgette and Louie at her heels.

"I told you she'd be here," Piper said as she snagged a doughnut. She came in most mornings for breakfast on her way to work. Her hair was tied up in a high ponytail, and her jeans were worn so thin along the thighs Willow was sure they'd split any day now. She slid her perky size-two butt onto a stool and took a big bite of a doughnut.

"When am I ever not here?"

"Um, when you have a hot fiancé lying in your bed." Piper smirked.

"So now you're pro-Zane?" She liked that a whole lot more than she'd realized.

"Let's just say that what he did for you-know-who was beyond amazing."

"Hi, Auntie Willow." Louie hugged her legs, getting flour all over the front of his shirt. "Mommy said I could only have half of a dough-nut today."

"Did she, now?" Willow arched a brow at her youngest sister.

"He already ate a bowl of cereal and a banana." Bridgette peeked into the box their mother had brought. "Jasmine body butter?" She and Piper exchanged a knowing look.

Willow rolled her eyes. "It's for *you*."

"Oh no, it's not," her mother said. She opened her arms and knelt down for Louie. "Come here, sugar pop. Let's get you that doughnut."

Louie leapt into her arms. "Yay."

"Seriously, Bridge. Take the body butter." Willow finished preparing the filling and began spooning it into the tarts.

"No way. I don't need one of Mom's magic love potions right now. I've got a little boy who takes up all my energy." Bridgette began brushing the flour off Louie's shirt. "I should have brought him a change of clothes."

"Little boys are supposed to get dirty, honey," their mother said as Bridgette wiped powdered sugar from Louie's chin. "Louie and I can finish baking if you want to spend this morning with your man."

"Mom, what did I *just* tell you? Implying sexy stuff to your daughter in any fashion goes along with eyebrow waggling." Her family's approval had her giddy inside, despite the tiny amount of trepidation she still held on to about when Zane eventually left for LA. "Where is Talia when I need her? She'd tell you it's inappropriate to suggest those things."

"Talia had an early meeting with a student this morning," their mother said. "Besides, *sexy stuff* is part of being in love. How do you think you three got here?"

"Ew," the girls said in unison.

"I have to get into the shop," Bridgette said. "But did Mom ask you about the engagement party?"

Willow concentrated on the tarts, placing pieces of strawberries and whole raspberries and blueberries on top of the filling. "Nope. She skipped right to the wedding planning."

"When *are* you getting married?" Piper slid off the stool and washed her hands in the sink.

"I love you guys to pieces, but we just got engaged." She caught a supportive look from Bridgette. "Can you give us a little breathing space, please? Let us enjoy the newness of our engagement before we throw a party. Zane starts filming next week. There's going to be enough craziness around here."

Piper leaned closer to Willow and whispered, "This is all Mom's doing." Then louder, "I have an estimate to give in ten minutes. I need to boogie. Thanks for breakfast." She grabbed a muffin and headed for the door.

"And I need to open my shop. You know your fiancé called me about the roses, but I didn't have the stock to fill your bakery with them." Bridgette raised her brows and said, "The guy's got serious game, sis."

Louie kissed Bridgette. "'Bye, Mommy."

"Bridge, take the body butter," Willow pleaded while Bridgette fussed over her little man.

"No way." Bridgette headed out of the kitchen. "If too many Zane seekers come by and drive you crazy, text me and I'll come save you."

"Thanks, Bridge. Don't blame me if your phone starts vibrating like a"—she looked at her mother—"phone."

Roxie laughed. "Honey, I really can finish the baking."

Willow closed her eyes for a second, breathing deeply and trying to channel her inner calm.

Her mother chuckled and reached a hand out to Louie. "Come on, sugarplum. Let's go work in the garden and leave Auntie Willow to her baking." On the way out the door, Roxie lowered her voice and said to Louie, "Maybe tomorrow she'll let us take over."

Willow grabbed a doughnut and shoved it in her mouth to keep from accepting her mother's offer and hightailing it upstairs to be with Zane.

ZANE TRIED TO give Willow space so she didn't feel smothered, but every minute was a test of his willpower. She'd kept him at arm's length for so many years, he wanted to soak up as much time with her as possible. A brief phone call with Jacob told him that his threat had helped, but after going for a run, studying his lines, and weeding through e-mails, he couldn't stay away another minute.

The bell over the bakery door rang, and Willow looked up from where she was bent over the counter. Her hair was pulled back in a long braid, making her damp green eyes look even more devastating. She dabbed at them with a wad of napkins, her lips curving up in a strained smile.

Zane's heart lurched as he closed the distance between them, vaguely aware of the customers sitting at the table saying hello to him as he passed. "What's wrong?"

She pushed from the counter and waved his screenplay at him. "This. Z . . . ?"

"It's that bad? I knew it was rough, but—"

"Shut up. *Rough?*" She thrust the papers against his chest, and a tear slid down her cheek. "This is heartbreaking, and beautiful, and suspenseful. It's not at all what I expected."

"Thanks?" He wiped her tears with the pad of his thumb and kissed her softly. In a blue T-shirt and cutoffs, she looked deliciously sexy. "I missed you, and you nearly gave me a heart attack. I thought something had happened."

"Something *did* happen." She inhaled deeply and shook her head.

"She's been crying the whole time I've been here." A gray-haired woman rose from one of the tables and smiled. "You don't remember me, do you?"

"I'm sorry. It's been a long time," Zane answered.

"I'll give you a hint. You brought me groceries and cut my lawn after my husband left." She pulled her purse over her shoulder, and recognition dawned on him.

"I'll be right back," he said to Willow, and came around the counter, unable to believe his eyes. "Mrs. Gerstone?" He *had* cut her lawn and brought her groceries from the time he was thirteen until he left town for good. She had been so heavy for all those years, she could barely walk. "I'm sorry I didn't recognize you."

"It's funny what losing a hundred and thirty pounds does to a person's appearance. And their health." She touched his cheek. Her palm was cool against his face. "You were my inspiration. Bless you, Zane."

"Me?"

"Oh *yes*. I buried my unhappiness about the hand I'd been dealt in food. You used yours for motivation. And look where you are now." She looked at Willow and then back at Zane, who was floored by her admission. "Engaged to our Willow, the kindest woman in all of Sweetwater."

Willow came around the counter. "She's only saying that because I make her special nonfat muffins and sugar-free tarts."

"Bless you both," Mrs. Gerstone said. "I'm glad you never forgot your roots, Zane. You always were a nice boy."

They talked for a minute longer, and after she left Willow said, "You know what you said about my family knowing the real you?"

"Yeah."

"I think the people here know the real you, too." She looked down at the screenplay as they walked back to the counter. "But after reading this, I wonder how much of you I really know. You blew me away. You're brash and cocky, but this . . . this is . . ." She nibbled on her lower lip, a deep V forming between her brows. "It's raw and passionate. I don't know anything about the streets of Chicago, but this boy . . ." She lifted her eyes to him again. "How did you come up with this story? You *have* to make this into a movie."

"Says my very biased fiancée."

"Zane, if it sucked I wouldn't encourage you to share it with anyone else." She hooked her finger into his belt loop. "But it's incredible. I don't know how you get scripts made into movies, but can you show it to your director or something?"

"I'm on the fence with showing it to anyone in the industry, and honestly, I want to be the one to produce it if I do decide to go in that direction." He'd been wrestling with this since the spring and still didn't have enough faith in his writing to do anything with it. But her support gave him a modicum of hope that it really didn't suck.

Her eyes bloomed wide. "That's awesome. You should totally do it."

"It's a little more complicated than that."

She began wiping down the counter. He grabbed a washcloth and helped, speaking in hushed tones so the customers didn't hear him.

"Right now I'm on top of my game, babe. But you've heard the stories about actors who try to become producers or directors, and when their film flops, it overshadows everything else."

She stopped wiping down the counter, her eyes flat, her mouth pressed into a firm line. "Zane Walker, you walked out of Podunk Sweetwater with zero experience and made your way to the top of the action-hero list, and you're going to let something like what *could* happen stop you from doing something bigger?" She smirked. "Guess you're not the man I thought you were."

He sidled up to her, gathering her close, and guided her to the pastry display, blocking the customers' view of them. "I think I proved what kind of man I am last night." He slid his hands to her butt and squeezed, earning an adorable *squeak* from Willow. "I'd be happy to show you right here and now that I'm far more of a man than you ever imagined."

"What if I say okay?"

He bit her earlobe, and she made an enticing sound of appreciation. "Then I'll kick out these customers and take you into the back room, strip you bare, and make you come so many times you won't remember your name."

Her breath rushed from her lungs. "You're so bad," she whispered, tightening her hands on his waist. "I like it a lot, but seriously, you need to show the screenplay to Sam Shearson or you're never getting any again."

He drew back, gazing into her amused eyes. "Who the heck is Sam Shearson, and why does he own the rights to our bedroom activity?"

"He won an Academy Award in 1962 for a screenplay, and if you're afraid it's not good enough to show anyone in the industry," she explained, "he can tell you if it is or not. He's a retired fisherman, not even remotely in your business, and he comes in every morning at eight o'clock sharp."

"Wait, we have an Academy Award–winning writer in Sweetwater?" He raked a hand through his hair. "How could I not know that?"

She began wiping down the counter again. "Because he's eighty-five years old and you were busy being a kid when you lived here. I didn't meet him until I opened the bakery." A dreamy look came over her. "He's a total banana nut muffin."

"Um . . . ?"

"Oh." She laughed softly. "You know how people say that if you have a dog, at some point you start to resemble them?"

"I guess . . ."

"Well, you'd be surprised how much people resemble the foods they order. Every morning Sam orders a banana nut muffin, and let me tell you, he is exactly *that*. He's been around forever, he's stable—banana nut muffin recipes rarely vary by much—and he's substantial. You know, smart and interesting to talk to, as opposed to, say, a date roll. If you see someone order a date roll, run like hell."

She cocked her head like she'd just made perfect sense, and he couldn't help but think she had it all figured out and he was the one grasping at straws.

"Sam's here every morning like clockwork, so make sure you're here tomorrow at eight a.m. sharp or no nookie for you."

He leaned in and kissed her. "You're a pushy woman. Do you know how much I adore you?"

"We'll see how much tomorrow morning. Oh, I forgot to tell you. I think I picked up a new wedding cake order. I have a tasting scheduled next week, and I got the menus from Payton. Gluten free, sugar free, nut free. No citrus, no red dye, no white flour. Not my favorite, but I'll make it happen. I'm going to send her a box of my pastries so she knows what I'm capable of when not hamstrung by dietary issues. Thank you for arranging the catering. I really do appreciate it."

The bell above the door sounded, and a young woman with two adorable blond-haired little girls walked in. Excitement rose in Willow's voice. "How are my favorite marble and chocolate chip cookie girls?"

"Willow!" The girls ran toward the counter as Willow came around and crouched with open arms. Both girls slammed into her, hugging her tightly as she laughed.

"I have gone a whole eight days without seeing you." Willow's eyes shimmered with delight. "Where have you been hiding?"

"We went to see Uncle Buck in Washington," the taller of the two girls said. "He's getting married."

"Is he, now?"

The girls nodded vehemently as Willow rose to her feet and hugged the girls' mother.

"And I hear congratulations are in order for you, too," the woman said.

Willow flashed a look of surprise at Zane. *Get used to it, baby, because this is really happening.*

"Thank you," Willow said. "I'm still not used to the idea that everyone knows about it. We only got engaged this past weekend. But I guess that goes with the territory of being engaged to Zane." She stole another glance at him, inciting the heat of a laser beam.

Oh yeah, he'd be meeting Sam Shearson tomorrow. He'd do anything she wanted him to.

The girls reached for Willow's hands, and she knelt again, putting her arms around them. Zane's heart thudded a little harder. He hadn't spent much time thinking beyond winning Willow over, but he needed to. Willow's life was here, with the business she'd built and the people who loved her. If he wanted Willow, he had to do more than earn her trust. He had to be willing to come back to Sweetwater for good.

# CHAPTER FIFTEEN

WILLOW HAD BEEN waking up at four thirty in the morning for years without issue, but now, as she absently slapped the nightstand in search of her phone to turn off her alarm, a deliciously tempting man shifted on top of her and began kissing her neck.

"I'm coming with you," Zane said between shivery kisses.

"You always come with me. You're the double-rainbow king. The mutual-orgasm master. The postman who always rings twice . . ."

He laughed against her neck and nipped at her skin. "I meant to the bakery, but I'm totally up for a game of Willow-go-round."

She wrapped her arms around him, surprised at how quickly she'd gotten used to sharing her bed—and her apartment. "I thought having you around all the time would be annoying since, well, you know, you kind of bullied your way into my life. But there *are* benefits to having a hot guy at my disposal."

He grinned down at her. "Bullied?"

"Tricked? Coerced?"

"I think *reentered* is better." He nudged her legs open, teasing her with the head of the world's most talented pleasure wand.

"Like *you're* trying to *reenter* my body?" She gave his ass a smack.

"Now that you mention it, that does sound like a good idea." He kissed her cheeks, forehead, chin, the corners of her lips . . .

Everywhere except her panting mouth. If he didn't kiss her mouth soon, she might combust. She mentally debated if she could be late to work without screwing up her entire morning. He dragged his tongue along the ridge of her jaw. *Oh yeah, the muffins can wait.*

She leaned up to trap his mouth, and he pulled back with a devilish grin. "You think I'm *hot.*"

She laughed. "This bed is too small for you, me, and your ego."

He grabbed her hips with both hands and held them down. His eyes turned fierce and demanding, and her entire body ignited.

"You love my big ego."

She reached for a condom from the box they'd torn open last night and tossed a handful on the bed. "I have five minutes."

He grabbed a condom and reared up to sheath himself.

"What if I want to play for ten minutes?" he asked with a smirk.

"We played for hours last night." She pointed to the area beneath her eyes. "See these bags? They're called Z-bags, and don't you dare make any *tea bagging* jokes."

He laughed as he settled over her. "You want it fast and dirty or sweet and sensual?" He slicked his tongue along her lower lip.

"Z—" she pleaded. "*Five* minutes."

He pushed the head of his cock inside her and stilled, dipping his head to tease her nipple. "Five minutes is not nearly enough."

Her sex clenched around him, and she lifted her hips. He pushed them down to the mattress without missing a beat with his magnificent tongue. He grazed his teeth over her nipple, sending darts of exquisite pain to her core.

"Zane," she panted out, and he began rocking the broad head of his cock in and out, ever so slowly, driving her out of her flipping mind.

He captured her mouth, kissing her roughly as his slow tease continued. His hands pressed harder, his kiss intensified, and she heard herself whimper. Five minutes would never be enough. A week would never be enough. Loving Zane Walker would take a lifetime. *And then some.*

"I love you, baby," he whispered against her lips. "Tell me you love me. I need to hear it."

"I love you. I've always been in love with you," she answered, but she knew he felt the part of her that was holding back.

He touched his forehead to hers. "I'll take it, and I'll love you so hard you won't be able to remember why you were scared of me in the first place."

"I don't need you to love me hard or to buy me ten dozen roses. I just need you, Zane. Plain and simple. I need to know that the Zane I love right this second is the same man who will fly back to California in a few weeks."

"I can't promise you that."

Her heart dropped to the pit of her stomach.

"My love for you has grown every moment since I told you how I felt, and it's going to get even bigger." He touched his lips to hers. "Deeper," he whispered, trailing kisses over her mouth. "So much so, I'll need all the seats on the plane just to bring it along."

His mouth came coaxingly down over hers, and emotions swamped her. She disappeared into the sensual, sweet tenderness of the kiss, and when he thrust forward, filling her completely in one powerful motion, her body shuddered in ecstasy.

A few hours and two orgasms later, Willow was wrapping up a scone for the last of the morning rush. Zane had come down with her at five thirty and helped her with an hour of baking before his jitteriness had driven her crazy and she'd sent him out of the kitchen. He was tied in knots over sharing his screenplay with Sam. She hadn't had a chance to read the whole thing, but she couldn't imagine anyone thinking it was anything short of stellar.

"Here you go, sweetie. Have a great day." She handed the bakery bag to her customer and poured a fresh cup of coffee for Zane.

He looked up from the table where he was poring over his screenplay. He'd run his hand through his hair so many times it stood on end. Willow set down the coffee and finger-combed his hair.

"I love the just-romped look," she teased. "But maybe a little less wild will go over better with Sam."

"Thanks, babe." He glanced at his watch for the millionth time. "He'll be here in five minutes."

"I don't want to push myself on him," Zane said.

"Zane Walker." She put her hand on his forehead. "Pushiness is your middle name. Are you feeling feverish?"

He pulled her in for a kiss. "Just for you."

"I get off work in a few hours. But my fiancé might kick your ass if he finds out you're hitting on me. We'd have to be *very* covert."

His eyes narrowed, and she laughed.

"Really?" She sank down to the chair beside him. "You're jealous of yourself?"

"Just nervous, baby."

"I can see how much this means to you, but you have nothing to worry about. From what I read, it's an amazing story." She sat back and crossed her arms, taking in his dark T-shirt, his golden tan, and his knee bouncing like a jackhammer under the table. She leaned in closer and lowered her voice. "You weren't even this nervous your first time."

His hand coasted through his hair again. "I was, but you needed me to be confident. And I trusted you, Wills. I had read enough about sex and watched enough porn to know I'd be pretty good at it. This is totally different."

"You researched sex?" That shouldn't surprise her, but it did.

"Think I wanted to screw up *your* first time? No way. You trusted me, and that meant the world to me."

"Aw, Z. That's so romantic."

He scoffed. "I also jerked off twice before I met you so I'd last longer. Not so romantic, sweetheart. A necessity."

Laughter burst from her lungs. "Seriously? That's . . . *oh my God.* Do all guys do that? Do you do that *now?* Geez, what other things is the male race hiding from us?"

He was laughing as Sam Shearson shuffled past the front window.

"Here he is now." Willow squeezed Zane's hand. "You'll love him."

ZANE TOOK IN the large elderly man entering the bakery. His checkered button-down shirt didn't quite go with his cargo shorts. Dark knee-high socks and black orthopedic sneakers rounded out his quirky outfit. Wrinkles mapped his deeply tanned skin like rivers coursing around a thin-lipped mouth and slightly hooked nose. Smiling eyes surveyed the bakery from behind wire-framed glasses resting on the type of ears mothers grew their children's hair long to hide.

Sam stuck a finger up toward the ceiling. "One banana nut muffin, a cuppa coffee, and a hug for my newly engaged friend." He opened his arms, and Willow walked in, embracing the man as if he were family.

"Aw, thank you, Sam." She glanced over her shoulder at Zane, and Zane's nerves went haywire. She took Sam's hand and led him to the table as Zane rose to his feet.

"Sam, this is my fiancé, Zane Walker. Zane, this is Sam Shearson."

Sam had a good two inches on him and probably thirty pounds. A fluff of white hair circled his bald crown, and Zane couldn't help but notice several fine white scars on his hands and forearms. The marks of a fisherman.

"I've heard a lot about you. It's a pleasure to meet you." Zane held a hand out in greeting.

Sam pushed his hand away. "Get on in here."

He tugged Zane into a tight embrace, slapping him on the back harder than expected. "You hurt my Willow, and I'll take you out on my boat and drown you in that lake. Got it?"

"Sam. That's illegal," Willow teased.

"Don't you worry your pretty little head." Sam pulled out a chair at Zane's table. "I'll take him out into the ocean. Ocean floors don't tell your secrets. You don't mind if I sit and chat with your gentleman friend, do you, Willow?"

Willow raised her brows. "I'll get your breakfast, but be good to him, Sam."

Sam waved her away and set a serious glare on Zane, then dropped his eyes to the empty chair by Zane's side.

Zane sat, feeling like he was about to get reamed. "Don't worry. I don't plan to hurt her."

Sam's eyes roved over his face. "No, son. I don't expect you do. But hurt comes in many forms, and I've read the papers." He slapped the newspaper down on the table so hard, coffee splashed from Zane's mug. "Not that I believe all the garbage. You Hollywood types got no privacy. It's not like it was in my day. Hell, I'd go out on the fishing boat before dawn and be gone until dark. Come back stinking so bad no woman wanted to be anywhere near me. No expensive colognes for me. No, sir." He pointed at Zane, leaning forward and lowering his voice. "I don't care what the papers say. I know enough about you from when you lived here."

*Aw, Christ.* What the hell did that mean?

Willow brought Sam's coffee and muffin, along with a fork and knife. "You guys let me know if I can get you anything else." She headed back to the counter and gave Zane a thumbs-up.

Zane hung on Sam's next breath as the old man lifted the coffee to his lips.

"Mm. Willow makes a mean cup of coffee." Before Zane could respond, Sam said, "Star quarterback, on the track team, the homecoming parade. You were the boy whose parents lived on the other end of town. The *scared* boy."

"Excuse me?" Zane felt like he was sitting at the bottom of a valley and all his childhood fears were about to come crashing down around him.

Sam proceeded to cut his muffin into bite-size pieces, working in silence. If it weren't for the kind smile on his lips, Zane would think he was purposefully dragging out his misery.

He took a bite of the muffin and pointed the empty fork at Zane. "I know a thing or two about being scared. Can't be afraid out on the high seas. Mother Nature will beat that fear out of you quicker than you can drop a fishing line."

Zane raked a hand through his hair, unsure what to make of the old man.

"You ever fish?" Sam asked.

"Sure."

"Then you know when you hook a live one, every muscle comes to life. Adrenaline surges through your veins, and you hold your breath, or curse, or pray that you'll be able to reel her in. And when you do, you finally breathe like you've never breathed before." He took another bite, sipped his coffee, taking his sweet time. His eyes never left Zane's. "You were stuck in that middle ground for a while. Scared but ready to bolt. And then you made it. Everyone in Sweetwater followed Zane Walker's success. You were the talk of the town for the first few years after you left. I couldn't walk into the post office without hearing a story or two."

Zane wondered if that was why his parents had moved away.

"So tell me," Sam said. "Can you breathe now, son?"

A laugh escaped before Zane could stop it. Now he knew why Willow loved this man. He had successfully dragged Zane through an emotional roller coaster in less than five minutes and completely disarmed him with the unexpected question.

"That's a hell of a question."

Sam popped another piece of muffin in his mouth. "Yes. Yes, it is." His eyes dropped to Zane's screenplay, lying faceup on the table. "*Beneath It All.* That yours?"

At least he'd let him off the hook with the first question. Only now he felt like one of the fans begging for his autograph. He didn't like being the guy who wanted something from a stranger, and Sam was too nice a guy to be used like this. Zane decided not to ask for his help after all. "Yes."

"Good story? Turning it into a movie?"

He shrugged. "I hope so."

"I wrote a story once."

"Willow told me that you won an Academy Award."

Sam finished his muffin and coffee and rose to his feet without acknowledging Zane's comment.

"All done?" Willow came out from behind the counter, wiping her hands on her jeans. She gave Zane a concerned look, and he shook his head, indicating for her not to say anything.

Sam handed her a wad of cash. "Delicious as always. Thank you."

"You're welcome, Sam. As always."

"Walk with me, Zane," Sam said.

"Sure." He folded his screenplay and stuck it in his back pocket. Willow gave him a curious look. He hugged her and whispered, "It's all good."

Zane pushed the bakery door open for Sam, inhaling the crisp mountain air. Sunlight glistened off the lake across the street. He was glad they no longer needed security at Willow's door. "You lead, I'll follow."

"You are no follower," Sam said, surprising him.

Bridgette was setting up a display in front of the flower shop. "Hi, guys. Pretty day today."

"Sure is, sweetheart," Sam said. "How's that boy of yours?"

Bridgette's eyes lit up, as they always did when she spoke of her son. "Brilliant, bossy, and infuriating. Unfortunately, I think at five he's already well on his way to manhood."

Sam and Zane both laughed.

"That's my boy," Sam said, and continued walking at a slow pace.

They walked in silence and turned at the corner. It was still early summer, with a nice morning breeze, and many of the shop owners had their doors propped open.

"It was 1960," Sam said out of the blue.

"Excuse me?"

"When the whole award thing got under way. Hell of a fluke, too. We'd docked the boat in San Diego and hit a local bar. I'm sitting there drinking my beer, and the guy next to me is talking to the bartender. It was pretty dark, and I was dead tired, but the guy had a gorgeous, deep voice, and it was the kind of voice you don't forget. Well, I waited until he was done talking, and I said, 'I'm sure this will sound crazy, but you sound just like Orson Welles.'" Sam turned left at the next corner. "The guy picks up his drink and says, 'That's because I am Orson Welles, and this voice has made me a hell of a lot of money.'"

"No way." It wasn't the most eloquent of responses, but it was too late for Zane to take it back.

"That's exactly what I said. We got to talking, and I told him about this little tale I'd written. To make a long story short, he said to send it to him. I did, you know, expecting nothing. And a few weeks later I got a phone call from him. The whole thing was crazy. But sure enough, he got it made into a film. *Winter Fear.* You ever see it?"

"No, I'm sorry," Zane admitted, wishing he had. "Were there more opportunities that followed? Did you ever write anything else?"

Sam waved a hand dismissively as they turned another corner, heading toward the lake again. "Oh, opportunities were offered, but happiness isn't found by taking every opportunity. It's choosing the *right* opportunities. I didn't *mean* to write that story. It came to me, I wrote it, and that was it. Strangest thing, too. I was horrible in school. Why do you think I became a fisherman? My father had taught me a trade, and thank goodness he did. Oh, I bitched a blue streak when I was younger. I wanted to hang out with my friends over the summers, but you didn't tell my father no." He laughed under his breath. "No, sir. Back then you got the belt. Not like nowadays, when kids curse at their parents."

Zane knew all about being horrible in school. "That's quite an accomplishment."

"Dumb luck. That's what it was. But I made a few good friends over that time." They reached Main Street and turned toward Willow's bakery. Sam stopped in front of the hardware store. "Here we are. Get that door for me, will you, please, son?"

Zane pulled open the door. "Why did we walk around the block when we could have walked two doors down?"

"A man's got to have a purpose at eighty-five," he said as they entered the store, "or he won't make it to eighty-six." He went straight to the aisle with nails and picked up three, three-inch nails.

"They sell them in boxes." Zane reached for a box.

"I don't need a box. I need to fix a loose board on my deck."

"You may need more than three nails, and then you'll have to walk back here."

Sam smiled and headed up to the cash register with his three nails in hand. "Like I said. At my age a man's got to have a purpose." He paid for the nails, and when they left the store, Sam stood on the sidewalk looking out over the lake. "What's your purpose, Zane?"

"That's a tough question." His goals were clear—to do whatever it took to win Willow over once and for all, to be the best man he could be for her, and to get up the guts to bring his screenplay to the big screen, but his purpose? That was much more difficult to define.

"Goals and purpose are two very different things. Your goal might rely on others, but your purpose? That's all you, son. And I guarantee, when you figure that out, the rest will follow." He checked his watch. "It's time for me to head down to the library. Thank you."

"For what?"

"For giving me a purpose to reach my goal," Sam said. "I made it around another block. That's a good day in my book."

Zane watched him stroll away and called after him, "Hey, Sam. How does a deep-sea fisherman from San Diego end up in Sweetwater?"

A smile crept across the elderly man's face. "My right opportunity came in the form of Ruthie McGee, the sweetest woman to ever come out of Sweetwater. That is, until your Willow came around."

Emotions bubbled up inside him. "My girl is something, all right."

"So are you, Zane. You're not that scared kid anymore. If you believe in that story in your pocket, you'll find a way to bring it to life. But I'm not telling you anything you didn't figure out a long time ago."

# CHAPTER SIXTEEN

"LOOK WHO WANDERED into my shop." Bridgette came through the arched doorway from her flower shop after closing Thursday afternoon with Aurelia Stark, looking just as fresh and beautiful as she had first thing that morning.

Willow wiped her hands on her shorts, which were stained with flour, frosting, and grease from trying to repair her oven. "Girls, you're right on time. My oven went wonky again, and the cupcakes came out funky. We have no choice but to eat them." She locked the door to the bakery and hugged Aurelia. Her long, naturally wavy brown hair fell to the middle of her back. She was as petite in height as Piper, but curvy like Willow, and at twenty-seven she still wore some of the same clothes she'd worn when she was eighteen—today it was jeans with holes in the knees, white Converse, and a simple white tank top. And somehow she managed to look like a million bucks.

"You look incredible. Whatever you've done, it suits you."

"Long story." Aurelia made a beeline for the kitchen.

Willow and Bridgette exchanged a concerned glance.

"I've been texting you all week. What's going on?" Willow grabbed plates from a cabinet and slid them across the counter.

"My phone is having issues." Aurelia took a big bite of cupcake and set two more on the plates for the girls.

"Bummer. What happened?" Bridgette nibbled on her cupcake.

"I think it has something to do with being thrown at a moving car."

Willow nearly choked on her cupcake. Aurelia's phone always took the brunt of her bad days.

"I know, right?" Aurelia stuffed more cupcake in her mouth. She glanced at Willow's ring, and her eyes nearly popped out of her head. "Holy crap. So it's really true? You and Zane? You guys *own* the Internet right now. They're running the pictures of you two in Lake George with different headings every day."

*True and becoming more real every day.* Willow had made a point of avoiding the Internet since she and Zane had gotten together. She didn't need to see what she already knew, and the Internet cheapened everything. Between gathering recipes for the set breakfasts, keeping up with the bakery orders, and Zane preparing for his filming and working on his screenplay, which he hadn't stopped tweaking since he met Sam, the past few days had flown by. And the nights? They'd made love into the wee hours of the mornings. Willow was running on pure adrenaline, or as her mother had said when she'd come by that morning, she was *living on love*. Willow couldn't deny the way her heart soared every time she and Zane were together, or that he hadn't ogled a single woman since he'd made his feelings toward her clear. Or the way his laugh made her stomach flutter, his kisses turned her inside out, and seeing his stuff in her apartment made her never want him to leave.

"It's really true," Willow finally answered. She and Aurelia had been close in high school, but Willow realized that while she'd clued her in on other meaningless crushes throughout those years, she'd never told her about her crush on Zane.

"Wow. So does that mean you're moving to California? What about the bakery? Oh my God, you can't move that far away. Your mom would go crazy." Aurelia spoke a mile a minute, and she grabbed Bridgette's hand. "What about Bridge? No. You can't do it, Willow. You can't leave Sweetwater."

"Oh my gosh, Aurelia!" *We aren't even really engaged.* "We haven't even set a wedding date." Willow had been trying *not* to think about how all those things would play out. She couldn't expect Zane to move to Sweetwater, but she wouldn't want to move away from everyone she knew and loved, and her business. She was getting *way* ahead of herself. He hadn't proposed to her, no matter how much Zane wanted it to be real. Or how much she fantasized about it. He'd handed her a gaudy ring under a cloud of trickery. They were only playing house. That was the bottom line. She drew in a deep breath, feeling strangely relieved and sad at once.

"So where is he?" Aurelia asked. "He starts filming next week, right? Is he out rehearsing?"

"He's been rehearsing like a maniac. He finally took a break and went to hang out with Ben."

"How is Benny boy? Believe it or not, I miss that pain in the ass." Aurelia and Ben had a love-hate relationship. She finished her cupcake and grabbed another. "You meant it when you said I could eat these, right?"

"Ben's great. Still the luckiest man on the face of the earth where investing is concerned, and yes. Eat all you want. Please." Willow was used to Aurelia bouncing between topics. She'd done it her whole life.

"Can we *please* get back to the phone throwing?" Bridgette pleaded. "I have to pick up Louie soon. Harley bought him a Spider-Man bike, and he's giving it to him tonight."

"Have you nailed that big, sexy hunk yet?" Aurelia asked.

"*Tsk!* No. He's just a friend." Bridgette bit into her cupcake. "Besides, I think he has the hots for Piper."

Willow's ears perked up. "Seriously?"

Bridgette nodded. "He's always asking about her."

"You guys," Aurelia said conspiratorially. "They used to call him the *muff marauder*. The guy is packing major heat."

"What?" Bridgette squealed. "Muff marauder? I've never heard that."

"Oh *yes*. Heaven Love made out with him when she was in twelfth grade." Aurelia turned her arm over and ran her finger from wrist to elbow.

Bridgette's eyes widened, and she inhaled her cupcake.

Willow laughed. "Oh my."

"No shit, right?" Aurelia agreed.

"You guys are pigs," Bridgette teased.

"Hey, I'm being serious," Aurelia said. "It's not my fault he's blessed with a godlike penis. Zane, too. Don't you remember Frances whatshername saying he was hung like a horse?"

Willow held her hands up. "Okay. Stop. I can't talk about my man's manhood." She scooped frosting from a cupcake and sucked it off her finger, trying to drown the image of Zane with any other woman.

"That's confirmation right there," Aurelia said. "And, Bridge. Jesus, girlfriend. Go get laid already."

"Don't bother, Aurelia," Willow cautioned her. "Half the single men in town would give anything to take her out, and Bridge acts oblivious to them all."

"I'm not oblivious," Bridgette insisted. "You see things that aren't there. But enough about that. What happened with Kent?" Kent was Aurelia's on-again, off-again boyfriend.

Aurelia plunked down on a chair with a loud sigh. "First of all, he had a small pecker. Not that I really care that much about it, but it should have tipped me off. Guys with small dicks have all sorts of crazy shit in their head. They're always trying to prove their manhood. I finally had enough of his nonsense. He grated on my last nerve, and I ended it. The phone throwing was just a momentary lapse in judgment." She pulled her phone from her pocket and showed them the shattered screen. "I pretty much just carry it like a security blanket.

You know, to remind myself to stay away from men. Or at least guys with small peckers."

"Lordy." Bridgette hugged Aurelia. "I'm so sorry. What can we do to help?"

Aurelia shrugged. "Nothing. I'm thinking about moving back here and starting over. Clean slate and all that."

"Really?" Willow's mind zoomed ahead twelve steps. "Would you consider reopening the bookstore full-time?"

"I'm not sure of anything right now. Since my grandfather was put into a year-round care facility and my grandmother decided she won't be coming back, we need to give Mick Bad, the attorney who bought the bookstore, a decision one way or another. You know his apartment is above the store, and I'm sure he'd like to have that space to actually live in. I don't know what to do. I've worked at Pages since college, and I love it. But I can't be around Kent. He makes me want to throw more than my phone." Pages was the largest bookstore chain on the East Coast, and Aurelia worked in their flagship store in New York City.

"I have an idea I've been tossing around," Willow said.

"I know all about Willow's fantastic plan, which I love, by the way. I'm going to take off and pick up Louie so we don't miss Harley." Bridgette wrinkled her nose. "Who, thanks to you guys, I won't be able to look at again without wondering about the muff marauder. Ew. Geez. This should be fun."

Willow and Aurelia laughed.

"Sorry, Bridge," Aurelia said. "After you put your little guy to sleep, do some recon and report back. I want details."

Bridgette shook her head on the way out the back door.

"She's so cute it kills me. If I move back here, my first job is going to be to make sure she gets some action." Aurelia folded her arms on the counter and rested her head on them. "What should I do, Willow? What's your idea?"

"Selfishly, I wish you'd come back to Sweetwater and consider going into business with me." She watched confusion setting into Aurelia's features. "Think about it." Willow waved her hand in an arc, as if she were presenting something. "Books and Bites, or Pages and Pies, or Sweetie Pies and Great Reads."

"I know nothing about baking, and my family doesn't own the bookstore anymore. Mick's been nice enough to let me run it when I'm in town, but it's not *mine*."

"I know. That's why I think we should consider buying it back from him."

Aurelia sat upright. "You're serious?"

"Totally." Hope swelled inside her.

"But what about you and Zane? What if you get married and move away? I can't run a bakery."

"I know that, too," Willow conceded. "I don't have all the answers. It's just something I'm kicking around." *I don't have any answers.*

"I can't do anything yet anyway, no matter how much I want to. I have to go back this weekend and get my head together. If I decide to move, I have to give notice at Pages, deal with my apartment lease, and deal with *tiny pecker* once and for all. *Ugh.* I wish I could just crawl up in the corner with the rest of those cupcakes and go into a sugar coma."

Willow swallowed hard. A sugar coma sounded just about perfect. If anyone needed to get her head on straight, it was Willow. She was wearing a rented ring from the man she had no doubt she was in love with, but how could their lives ever mesh? Their worlds were on opposite sides of the country. Could they ever be more than just a two-week fantasy?

Her phone vibrated with a text, and Zane's name flashed on the screen, chasing her anxiety deeper into her chest. *I'll pick you up at seven. Can you pack a picnic?*

"Romeo?" Aurelia asked.

"Yeah," she said a little breathlessly. *A picnic.* Her big, cocky, smart-ass actor wanted to take her on a *picnic.* She'd never stood a chance around him. Not all those years ago and definitely not now.

"WHY DO I have to be blindfolded?" Willow clung to Zane's arm as he helped her from the car. "I mean, in the bedroom, sure, but on a picnic? Did you become a cult member while you were out today? Are you taking me to a secret ritual? Because if you are, I'd like to eat before I'm burned at the stake. No one should ever die hungry."

Zane laughed and gathered her in his arms. "Do you have any idea how happy you make me? I love your sense of humor." He kissed her lips. "And I love this sexy little picnic dress." He ran his hand up her thigh and kissed her again. "Knowing I can bring the blindfold into the bedroom is just the frosting on the cake."

Her lips curved up in a seductive smile. "You can bring frosting into the bedroom, too."

"That's been on my list ever since you made me a birthday cake when I was seventeen." He grabbed the picnic basket from the car and wound an arm around her waist, guiding her through the gates of the airfield. He'd been too wrapped up in preparing for his role and, thanks to Willow's encouragement and Sam's nudge in the right direction, polishing his screenplay. He hadn't had nearly enough time to do special things for Willow. He knew their lives were only going to get busier, and he was going to make damn sure that no matter how crazy their schedules got, Willow knew that *she* was his priority.

"Where are we? It feels . . . weird. I don't hear the water."

"You're very inquisitive." He nodded a greeting to the pilot of his private plane. "Okay, Wills, we're going up a number of steps. I've got you." He guided her left hand to the metal railing.

"That's cold. You're very mysterious."

Chuckling, he helped her into the plane and led her to a seat. She wiggled her butt, settling into the plush leather. His eyes followed the hem of her skirt as it bunched up around her thighs.

"This is super comfy."

He leaned over, speaking in a low voice even though they were alone. The pilot was preparing the plane for takeoff. "You'd better stop wiggling like that. Blindfolded with the world's most gorgeous gams there for the taking is not a power position."

"Can anyone see us?" she whispered.

"Nope. It's just us, sweet girl."

She curled her fingers around the arms of the chair, trapped her lower lip between her teeth, and spread her legs. His cock came to a full salute.

"I think you're wrong, Z." Her voice was liquid heat. "Very, *very* wrong." She crossed one gorgeous leg over the other.

He groaned, taking the seat beside her, and slid his hand between her thighs. "Surely you don't think a little leg crossing will keep me from making you come, do you?"

She grabbed his hand, keeping him from moving any higher. "Tell me where we're going and maybe I'll let you."

He waited for the engines to rumble to life. She curled her fingers around his hand.

"Zane?"

Fear threaded through her voice, spurring him into action. He took her hands in his and kissed her knuckles. "I've got you, baby. You're okay."

The plane started down the runway, and she began to tremble. Panic showed in her erratic breathing. "Zane?"

He pressed his cheek to hers, holding her around her shoulders. "I've got you, sweetheart. I promise you're safe." The nose of the plane lifted, and she made a frightened sound. He took off the blindfold, and her eyes were squeezed shut.

"Baby, haven't you ever flown before?"

She shook her head, her fingernails digging into his hand. "You *know* how rarely I leave Sweetwater. Have I ever said, 'Hey, I'm flying off to wherever'?" She didn't wait for an answer. "No! I haven't. Why do you have to do things so *big*? I thought we were going on a picnic." Her voice escalated. "Please take me back, *please*."

*Shit!* This was not the reaction he'd hoped for. Framing her face in his hands, he said, "Open your eyes, Wills. Focus on me."

She shook her head.

"Willow, I promise you this will be worth it." *I frigging hope it will.* "Look at me, baby. *Now*."

Her mouth pinched tight, and she opened her eyes. The fear in them nearly brought him to his knees. "Good, baby. Just keep looking at me. You're fine."

"This isn't a *picnic*." Her voice escalated.

He brushed his thumb over her cheek. "It will be." The plane veered to the right, and she grabbed at him.

"Zane? He's going to crash. He's going down!"

"No, Wills. He's turning. This is my plane, my pilot. I promise you the plane is in excellent condition, and my pilot is the best there is."

"You're all set." The pilot's voice called her attention up to the front of the plane.

"I'm going to reach over and open the shade, okay?"

She nodded, clutching one of his hands tightly as he opened the shade and the lights of Sweetwater came into view.

"Sweetwater, baby. That's your little slice of heaven right there."

She leaned over, fingernails carving half-moons into his skin. But he didn't care. The light rising in her eyes was worth every bit of the sting.

"Oh my gosh. It's so beautiful." She laughed, and tears he knew she'd been holding back trickled down her cheek.

He wiped them away, exhaling a relieved breath. "Sit by the window, baby."

She shook her head. "Too nervous to move. You stay there."

He moved the arm of the chair and pulled her against him, kissing her cheek as she gazed out the window. "See the lights of the chapel? And the dock?"

"Look!" She pointed at boats in the distance, the tips of their sails lit up like stars.

"In a few days, Hollywood is going to crash into Sweetwater, and I'll be working sixteen hours a day. When it feels overwhelming, I want you to think of this moment. This view of Sweetwater. Not the temporary craziness."

Tension formed around her eyes. He took her in a languid kiss, letting her know he was right there with her. "Don't worry, baby. Nothing will change between us. I promise you that." He pointed out the window to distract her from the reality he'd just mentioned. "Can you spot your apartment?"

Her eyes trailed over the landscape, while his landed on the twinkling red lights he and Piper had hung from Willow's balcony. They'd wound red lights around a wooden sign in the form of "W+Z." Piper had been much more accepting of him since Louie's birthday party, and he was glad for it. Of course, she'd given him hell about not having his own tools. Clearly another trip to the hardware store was in order.

"Z." Her beautiful green eyes met his, clear and full of love.

"I know I do everything big, and you think you're a small-town girl. But you're *my* small-town girl, Wills, and I don't ever want you to miss out on anything."

Fresh tears streamed down her cheeks, and a soft laugh escaped as she touched her lips to his. "I love you, Zane. I seriously love you so much I ache with it."

# CHAPTER SEVENTEEN

EXCITEMENT AND UNCERTAINTY rolled in with the clouds Sunday morning, and by midafternoon it felt like the whole town was holding its breath to see what would happen when Hollywood and Sweetwater collided. The first trucks arrived in the late afternoon, followed by a small bus and a few nondescript cars, each of which pulled onto the fairgrounds. Not into the parking lot, but onto the grass. "The crew"—that's how Zane referred to them. The underlings who were tasked with showing up early to erect sets and prepare for the actors, directors, and other important people whose titles alone gave Willow an unsettled feeling in the pit of her stomach. She drew upon the midair picnic she and Zane had enjoyed the other night. *When it feels overwhelming, I want you to think of this moment.* It seemed their relationship was made up of moments she never wanted to forget.

Zane had been with the crew most of the afternoon, while Willow, along with half the town's residents, had watched from afar as trailers pulled onto the lot, tents were erected, and a handful of people wearing headsets and carrying clipboards traipsed through the town "spotting locations."

Willow locked the door to the bakery and sank down to a chair beside Talia, who had come by to hang out while she graded papers. "At least you and Zane won't be the talk of the town anymore. I swear

I fielded more questions in my classes about what Zane was really like than I did about the actual lessons. Now people will be gossiping about the movie instead."

"True. Although I have to admit, Zane did a great job of keeping the onlookers at bay."

Talia set down her pen and studied Willow. Of all her sisters, Talia was the one who took the most time to tend to her appearance. Her thick, dark brows were perfectly shaped, like Liz Taylor's, which made her eyes *pop*. Her makeup was flawless, and Willow knew she threw it on in a matter of seconds, like she had been a makeup artist in a previous life. A *brilliant* makeup artist, given her genius IQ. Talia was taller than Willow and their other sisters. At five nine, the girl who had once been as lanky as an asparagus stalk had turned into one of those women who could wear anything, though she almost always leaned toward the professional side, whereas Willow preferred comfort over anything else.

"He's really changed, hasn't he?" Talia asked.

Willow smiled. She'd been thinking the same thing last night when she and Zane had taken a walk around the lake.

"I think it's less about changing and maybe more about finding comfort in being himself again. His *real* self. Have you ever felt like you've known someone your whole life, truly *knew* them, but you were the only one who did? Zane is exactly the guy I've always known he was." She put her hand over her heart. "Here, I mean. Not when we've seen him over the years when he was snarky and putting on a show."

Talia leaned across the table with a curious expression. "What was it like? When you and Zane first realized you wanted to see if this would work. What was that like? I keep trying to picture it, but you've always been so . . . I don't know. Careful around him? Sassy toward him? Those two things conflict, but you seemed to be both around Zane."

Leave it to her astute sister to ask the one question that could nail Willow to the wall with her lie. A string of guilt wound around her neck at the prospect of deceiving Talia again.

"It was maddening, exciting, and scary as hell." *Wow, that wasn't a lie.* Talia's eyes narrowed as she sat back. "I don't think I could do it."

"Be with Zane? I hope not, considering he's with me," Willow teased. Talia was careful with the men she dated. She and Willow had never shared secrets the way Bridgette and Willow did. Willow and her other sisters had tried to pry details from Talia after her dates, but she was tighter-lipped than a zipper.

Talia laughed. "No. Be with someone with that public of a wild past. I mean, I love Zane. You know that. But I remember him as the funny kid who hung out with Ben, which makes it easier to look past all the other stuff."

"You know what, T? I can honestly say that I've never been with any man who makes me smile and quiver and laugh and cry—in a good way, of course—as much as Zane. I'm terrified of what will happen when he goes back to California, but I'm just as afraid of what will happen if he doesn't. He could resent me if he moves away from the place he's lived for so long. But the media would drive me crazy if I moved there, and I'm afraid of gorgeous fans pawing at him all the time. I've never been a jealous person, but with him, it's hard not to be." She sighed. "Believe me, I know there's a lot to be afraid of. But there's so much goodness. I wake up and see the man I never realized was one of my best friends. Nothing beats that."

"Well, we all knew that. Before you opened the bakery, you texted him to ask his opinion."

"Yeah," she said absently. "See? I never really thought of us like that. Zane was just . . ." *The boy I fell in love with and could never let go of.* "*Zane.* But now I see our relationship more clearly. And even though there's all that scary stuff floating around, I trust him. I *really*, truly trust him. He looks at me like he wants to disappear into me. I don't know where we'll end up, or if I'll slaughter Remi Divine the first time they kiss, but I know I want to be with him."

"Geez. That's a whole different level of things I could never do."

Willow shrugged, though her insides were twisting into pretzels. "I knew he was an actor when we got involved. What kind of person would I be if I got jealous of his costars?" She pushed to her feet and went to the pastry display. "Seriously. So what if Remi is gorgeous, and rich, and going to thrust her tongue down his throat?" She took out a tray of Loverboys and shoved one in her mouth. She held it up, offering Talia one.

"No, thanks, but I can see how well you're handling the idea."

"Hey, whatever it takes, right?" She returned to the table with a glass of water and her pastry. "I'm meeting Zane and his assistant, Patch, at Dutch's for drinks and dinner in a little while. Want to go? I asked Bridge to go with me, but she couldn't."

Zane had texted earlier to say he and Patch were in his trailer in case she needed him, which she'd found very thoughtful. Apparently all the A-listers needed their own trailers, despite the fact that Zane was staying at Willow's apartment just down the block. She guessed that made sense, so he had a place to go between scenes, though it still seemed like an excessive and unnecessary expense to her. Then again, what did she know about the movie business? She was having a hard time reconciling the guy who had made a point of being in the bakery yesterday morning at eight o'clock sharp just to take a walk with Sam so he could check the decking on Sam's house, which Sam had mentioned was in need of repair, with an A-list actor who needed special accommodations. Zane had once again become Z, the guy she'd fallen for years ago, only now he'd recaptured her heart with a vengeance.

Talia gathered her things. "I don't think so, sorry. I have a lot of papers to grade." She leaned down and kissed Willow's cheeks. "I'm happy for you."

"Thanks. I wish you'd reconsider joining us. Maybe you'll meet someone nice."

Talia wrinkled her nose. "You know I don't love bars. Good luck catering tomorrow."

After Talia left, Willow double-checked the ingredients and recipes for the next morning, finished cleaning up, and finally went upstairs to shower and change.

An hour later she stood at the entrance of Harley Dutch's pub, feeling ridiculously nervous. She'd taken far too long to choose an outfit, even though she knew Zane wouldn't care what she wore. She looked down at her black skinny jeans, blousy white spaghetti-strap top, and flirty, strappy red heels. She was overdressed for Dutch's Pub and overdressed for *her*. But after her conversation with Talia, she felt the need to measure up. She hated that feeling, but she'd be damned if she'd sit in the pub wishing she'd dressed sexier when women were ogling her man.

"You just going to stand there looking pretty, or are you going in?" Piper reached for the door.

Willow startled. "Where did you come from?"

"Well, you see, baby sister, when two people love each other—"

"You're such a pain." She followed Piper into the dimly lit bar. Music filled the air, and the scent of alcohol and relief from the end of a long day surrounded them.

"A pain that's saving your butt. Bridgette called and said you were nervous about showing up by yourself." Piper flashed a cheesy smile. "I'm never nervous. I've got your back. I even put on respectable clothes."

"Oh my God, I love you," Willow whispered, quickly glancing at Piper's off-the-shoulder white top and tight jeans with fashionable worn spots on the thighs and knees. "You look amazing. I wish I didn't have to wear a bra. You're so lucky, and I am *way* too nervous." Standing just inside the door, she fidgeted with the neckline of her blouse. "Is this too low-cut?"

Piper laughed. "Don't you think it's funny that we wish we had each other's bodies? You're gorgeous, and your man apparently thinks so, too." She nodded toward Zane, heading in their direction with a proprietary look in his eyes.

"God, Pipe. My heart is going crazy over him."

"Please don't drool," Piper said. "It's embarrassing."

"Hey, Piper," Zane said as he slid a hand around Willow's waist. "Thanks for your help with the lights the other day."

"No prob." Piper glanced at Patch. "Who's that tatted-up morsel over there?"

"That's Patch. Zane's assistant," Willow explained.

"Damn." Piper ran her fingers through her hair. "Scruffy, tatted, with a face like chiseled granite, and only in town temporarily. He might be the perfect man. Mind if I take your seat at the bar, Zane? You do owe me one."

She was already on her way to the bar when Zane said, "Who am I to stand in your way?"

He leaned down for a kiss and wrapped his arms around Willow's waist, giving her his full attention. "Hey, beautiful. I missed you today."

"I missed you, too. Piper helped you?"

"She made the wooden sign hanging from your balcony and helped me string the lights. She was pretty cool. I think I'm growing on her." He eyed the people around them. "Every man in here is checking you out in those sexy heels and skintight pants. It should be illegal to look that sinful."

She laughed, but inside she was gobbling up his praise. "Hardly. They're probably checking *you* out. Buy me a drink before Piper scares Patch away."

"Congratulations, soon-to-be Mrs. Walker." Patch stepped from the stool and hugged Willow. He was as tall as Zane, with colorful tattoo sleeves, a few days' scruff, and shaggy brown hair. With his low-riding jeans and gray T-shirt, he looked like he'd just climbed off his motorcycle or belonged in a hipster café.

"Yeah, about that." She lowered her voice so Piper wouldn't hear her, although her sister was busy talking with Harley. "I have a bone to pick with you, *Patrick Carter.*"

Patch sat on the stool between her and Piper.

"I'm going to run to the men's room while you two catch up." Zane gave her a chaste kiss and headed for the rear of the bar.

"Hey," Patch said, holding his hands up, "I only do what I'm told by the big man. But for the record"—he leaned closer—"when he came up with this crazy scheme, I suggested he ask someone else because you two are such good friends. But Zane would have no part of it. I guess it all worked out for the best."

"Wait. What do you mean he came up with it? What about all that stuff about cleaning up his rep and the focus group?" She stole another glance at Piper. Harley was leaning across the bar, saying something for Piper's ears only, and Willow wondered if what Bridgette had said was true.

"That's true. They wanted him to act like he had a long-term girl-friend, lie low on the social scene. But the whole"—he lowered his voice to a whisper—"fake fiancée thing was his idea."

"I'm so confused." She wasn't sure if she should be flattered that Zane only wanted her, or hurt that he'd led her to believe this ruse was a necessity.

Patch turned his back to Piper and spoke fast. "He needed to clean up his rep, but he refused to spend any length of time with any woman but you. There was never any question, Willow. It was you or no one, which makes perfect sense. I mean, whose picture does he have in his bedroom?"

Her mouth dropped open. Her picture was in his bedroom? Just like in the story he'd told her about their fake trip to Washington.

"You didn't know?"

She shook her head. "I bet all those other girls *loved* that."

"What are you talking about? It's like we're talking about two different guys. He never takes women to his house." His eyes widened. "Wait. I assumed you'd been there. No?"

"I hadn't even been on a plane until the other night. Besides, I'd probably get lost in his mansion."

Patch laughed. "If he had one, maybe. He could own five mansions, but he lives in a modest three-bedroom home tucked away from everything."

He glanced over her shoulder just as she felt Zane's hand land on it. She bristled, and hated herself for it. Her head was spinning, and not just because of what she'd learned about the fake engagement or the photograph, but also because the impression she'd had of Zane had been all wrong. They needed to talk, but she couldn't exactly drag him away from Patch.

"Is this guy bugging you, babe?" Zane kissed her cheek and climbed onto the stool beside her.

Willow managed a smile. "No. I'm good." She leaned over the bar. "Harley? Can I get a whiskey? Neat?"

"Uh-oh." Piper leaned around Patch. "What's wrong?"

"Nothing. I'm just thirsty."

Piper and Zane exchanged a disbelieving look.

Harley puffed out his massive chest and set her drink across the bar, eyeing Patch and Zane. "Everything cool here, Willow?"

*If by "cool" you mean I feel like I've been shaken up and uncorked. Yeah. Totally cool.* "Yes, thank you."

"NOW I'M IN a quandary." Piper's eyes moved between Willow and Patch, making Zane's gut clench. "I've got this hot guy sitting next to me who should be buying me a drink. But based on the fact that my sister has just downed her I'm-so-pissed-or-confused-I-can't-see-straight drink, I'm thinking I might need to deck you. Which would be a total shame, given that you have *such* a handsome face."

*What did I miss?* "All right. What the hell's going on? Patch? Willow? Someone's going to give me the lowdown."

"There is no *lowdown*." Willow slid off the stool and took his hand. "I was nervous about seeing you kiss your leading lady, and the drink took the edge off. Now dance with me so Patch can buy Piper a drink."

She dragged him to the dance floor and wound her arms around his neck, but he could feel tension in her body.

"Wills, what just happened?"

"I'm not sure, so dance with me to keep me from overreacting." She smiled up at him, but it wasn't his girl's smile. It was a troubled smile, and it reached into his gut and fisted around his insides even as her lush curves moved against him, creating sensation overload on both ends of the spectrum.

"You're killing me here. Did Patch say or do something inappropriate?" Patch had worked for Zane for the past six years, and he trusted him explicitly.

"No." She rested her face on his chest.

That should be enough to take away the worry, but it wasn't. "Sweetheart, look at me."

She lifted her beautiful green eyes, and it was all right there, clear as day. Hurt and confusion. He took her hand and stalked toward the bar.

"Patch, are you okay to find your way back?"

"I'll make sure he gets home okay," Piper offered.

Harley glared at Patch. "I can give him directions."

Piper rolled her eyes.

She was a big girl and could deal with *that* situation. Zane needed to get to the bottom of whatever was bothering Willow. He cut a path through the crowd and pushed out the door. The brisk night air heightened his senses.

"Talk to me, Wills."

A breeze swept off the water, and she pushed her body closer to his like a heat-seeking missile. He wrapped an arm around her shoulder. A quick sweep of the parking lot told him she'd walked to Dutch's. He headed up the hill, away from the marina.

"I'm not sure where to start." She shoved her hands in the front pockets of her jeans.

"How about with whatever ticked you off, because you're sending me mixed signals and we don't do mixed signals. We do black-and-white. No matter how messed up whatever it is gets, we talk about shit."

She pulled away, and he grabbed her hand, lacing it with his, and tugged her back to his side.

"You don't get to pull away when I have no idea what I did wrong."

She stopped walking and glared at him. "You told me the focus group demanded this whole thing."

"Yeah, and?"

"And they didn't. Patch told me, Zane."

"What are you talking about? Patch knows they said I had to clean up my rep. He must have been messing with you, but I don't know why he would."

She tugged her hand free, and he snatched it back.

"I lost you once over miscommunication. I'm not losing you again over bullshit, Willow."

"You're not *losing* me." She stormed up the road. "I just want to understand."

"Help me out here, Wills. Give it to me piece by piece, okay? The focus group said I had to clean up my reputation. That's one hundred percent true. I came up with this plan to stage an engagement—"

"*You* came up with it. With *me*," she huffed.

"Yes. With *you*. We're on the same page. What's next?"

"*Ugh!*"

He hauled her against him. Her jaw was tight, her brows pulled together, and he was afraid to let her go. "Willow, baby. I have loved you since you first stormed off in a huff. You were fifteen when you learned to do that hip-jaunt-scowl thing you do. I knew then that I wanted that sweet side of you and the fierce, determined, demanding side. I wanted all of you then, and I want it even more now. So if you think I'll give up because you get angry, you're wrong. I don't care how rough things get, or how many times I look like I'm thickheaded. Because I *am* thickheaded. I'm not giving up on us, so please, spell this out for me."

Her eyes warmed. *Thank fucking God.*

"Why didn't you tell me that you thought up the fake engagement?"

"I told you they demanded I clean up my act."

"The. Fake. Engagement. *Specifically.*"

"The . . ." *Holy shit.* Had he omitted that he'd come up with the idea? "It wasn't intentional. I never said the focus group came up with the fake engagement, did I? I'm a lot of things, but since we said we would be one hundred percent honest with each other, I haven't lied. And I'm not lying now."

Her shoulders dropped, and she sighed.

"Think about it, Wills. Did I ever say they demanded anything other than that I had to clean up my rep? Because if I did, I deserve to be reamed. And maybe I do anyway for being so focused on getting you to agree that I forgot to mention that part. Or for being so wrapped up in trying to win you over ever since, that I never clarified. But I promise you that I didn't purposefully keep it from you. Why would I do that?"

"Patch said you told him that if I wouldn't do it, you wouldn't go through with it," she said less angrily.

He reached for her hand. "May I?"

"Yes, of course."

He took her hand, and they headed down Main Street. "What Patch said is true. I couldn't stand the thought of spending day after day with anyone else."

She stopped and toed off her sandals. "These things kill my feet."

"You don't need them. You could be barefoot and wearing rags and you'd still be the most beautiful woman on earth." He picked up her sandals and pressed his lips to her cheek. "I'm sorry, baby. I didn't mean to mislead you."

"Z, I don't want to worry that you're tricking me. You're too good at it."

He pulled her against his side as they walked past the hardware store. "And I don't want to worry about losing you, which is why I will never trick you again. I love you, Wills. I wasn't trying to deceive you. Well, at first, the whole cupcake gig was a trick, but not this. This was a mistake."

"Can we keep walking?"

"Until the cows come home." He didn't care that he had to be on set at seven in the morning, or that he needed to study his lines one more time. All of that was meaningless if he lost Willow. "I promise I'll pay closer attention to everything I say."

"I know it wasn't intentional," she said softly, looking at the engagement ring with a thoughtful expression. "But it still hurts to think any amount of this was a trick. I kind of want to be the girl you wanted all along."

He felt flayed open knowing he'd caused that pain, and Sam's question rang through his mind. *What's your purpose?* She was right there beside him, and in that moment his world shifted, as did his goal.

"You are that girl, Wills. You're my *only* girl. You know the truth, baby. If you hadn't agreed, I wouldn't have done a damn thing to clean up my rep. Remember at the resort when you needed the tequila to get the courage to kiss me? Maybe this ruse was what we both needed to let go of everything else. We're right for each other. We're each other's *only* one. We always have been."

They walked in silence for a few minutes, and when they reached the fairgrounds, they crossed the street and sat on the bench overlooking the lake and all the tents and trailers. He'd entrenched himself in reality with Willow, and it was a struggle to muster the desire to dive back into acting again. For the first time since he'd left Sweetwater all those years ago, he felt grounded and *happy*. Truly, deeply happy. He didn't want anything to come between him and Willow, least of all a mistake of omission.

Willow rested her head on his shoulder, and the broken pieces of his heart began to heal.

"It looks like a campground," she said softly. "Are the actual sets more glamorous?"

"No. There's nothing glamorous about a film set. It's like any other job, where a bunch of people are trying to make things operate as expected. It's stressful. There are always too many people giving directions, and I'll spend a lot of my time in the trailer just waiting to be called to the set." He looked around, feeling the same way he knew Willow did. Like their quaint small town had been overrun by outsiders.

"It all starts tomorrow, Wills. Sixteen-hour days, overinflated egos, and the pressure to be what everyone out there wants to see."

"Don't forget *kissing Remi Divine*."

His chest constricted. The arc of her voice told him she was teasing, but he was already dreading kissing another woman, whether it was a fictional kiss or not.

He took Willow's face in his hands and gazed into her eyes. "How did this happen?"

"What?"

"How did I fall so hopelessly in love with you that even the thought of having my mouth on someone else pisses me off?"

Her lips curved up in a sweet smile. "Don't give me lines, Z."

"No lines, baby. I promised only truths, remember?" He rose to his feet and brought her up with him.

She put her arms around his neck and went up on her toes. "Maybe I should wear out your mouth so you can't kiss her."

He lowered his mouth to hers in a kiss hot enough to join metal. "Home, baby," he said between kisses, loving the way the word *home* felt so right. "I need to be closer to you."

They kissed as they ran across the cobblestone street. Laughed as they stumbled up the back steps to her apartment, stopping only to deepen their kisses. They tore off their clothes on the way to the bedroom and tumbled down to the bed, breathless and greedy. He claimed her mouth again, fumbling blindly for a condom in his refusal to break their connection.

"Hurry," she said against his lips.

He reluctantly broke away to sheath himself.

Trailing her delicate fingers up the outsides of his thighs with a sexy smile on her lips and love in her eyes, she said, "I love that there was only me."

He laced their hands together as he came down over her and kissed her again. Their bodies fit together like each was the only person on earth who could complete the other, moving in perfect harmony. They gazed into each other's eyes, and years of love wound around them, bringing the truth once again.

"I love that there will only ever be you."

Willow was his.

Willow was *home*.

# CHAPTER EIGHTEEN

"WHAT CAN WE do to help?" Willow's mother stood in the middle of Sweetie Pie Bakery's kitchen with her hands on her hips and a determined look in her eyes at six thirty Monday morning. Beside her, Talia, Piper, dressed in her "good" jeans, and Bridgette, who had brought three floral centerpieces "to spruce up the tables," stood ready to help.

Willow's cavalry had arrived to help on what she hadn't realized would be the most nerve-racking day of her life. She usually only needed help with bigger catering jobs, but she was beside herself with gratitude. Even her father had pitched in by babysitting Louie today. The funny thing was, she hadn't realized she needed help. She'd been baking since four o'clock, and she was fully prepared for catering the set. But she hadn't counted on the sudden and all-consuming worry about meeting people from Zane's world. Luckily, her family knew her better than she knew herself. "T, don't you have to teach today?"

Talia shook her head, her efficient ponytail swinging from side to side. "I got Cam to cover for me. Besides, who knows? I might meet someone nice, right?"

"Someone *not* tatted up," Piper chimed in.

Willow's eyes widened.

"No, nothing happened with Patch," Piper said with an exasperated sigh. "Harley got all up in my face about how I'd end up on one of those gossip websites and how I was better than that. I'm going to have to knock that man down a notch. He's always blocking me from having fun. Guys are afraid of him because he's big and bossy."

Bridgette slid Willow an *I told you so* look, but Willow was too nervous to worry about Piper and her man issues. She had worries of her own—like meeting Remi Divine.

The kitchen door blew open, and Ben burst into the room. "Oh, good, you're still here. What can I do? I'll go get your van if you give me the keys."

"Benny, that's so nice of you." Their mother grabbed the keys from the hook on the wall and tossed them to Ben.

"Hold on." Piper held her hands up. "Why are you *really* here? Does this have anything to do with Remi Divine?"

Ben feigned an irritated wince. "I'm shocked that you would think I'd pretend to want to help my sister just to see the most gorgeous actress on the planet."

Aurelia poked her head in the door. "Wow, looks like a family meeting. I was just coming by to say goodbye before I left tow—" Her eyes landed on Ben.

"Aurelia," Ben said too sharply for the look of pleasant surprise on his face. "I didn't know you were in town."

She narrowed her eyes and hiked a thumb over her shoulder. "I'm leaving. I . . . um . . ." She peered around him with a flush on her cheeks. "Willow. I . . . What we talked about? I'm in. I *think*. Depending on your living situation. And mine. We'll talk." She stood up a little taller, her eyes darting to each of the girls and their mother and avoiding Ben altogether. "Okay. I'm out of here. Love you guys." Just as quickly as she'd arrived, she was gone.

"Wow," Ben said. "She looks great."

Their mother nudged him out the door. "Go get that van, honey. Willow can't be late." As soon as Ben was out of earshot, she turned to the girls with wide eyes and a gaping mouth. "What have I missed between those two?"

"No idea," Willow admitted.

"Ben's just horny," Piper said. "Come on. Let's get this show on the road."

Ben brought the van around, and they loaded it up, driving the van and Ben's car over to the set.

"I shouldn't be this nervous," Willow complained as they parked by the craft services tent. *But somewhere on this set is my man, and he's probably got Remi Divine draped all over him.* She had no idea what Zane and Remi's scenes called for other than a fade-to-black love scene Zane had mentioned, but it didn't matter. All the actors and actresses were Hollywood stars, and she suddenly felt very small-town, which had never bothered her before. And that made her even more nervous *and* annoyed.

"They're just people," she said more to herself than anyone else. "Sheesh. I really need to pull my head out of my butt."

"Right," Bridgette said. "So what if they've been in *People* and *Vogue* and are regulars on the red carpet."

"Not helping, Bridge," Talia said.

A pretty redhead wearing shorts and a tank top and carrying an iPad greeted Willow as she stepped from the van. "Willow?"

Shorts and a tank top? A friendly smile? Willow liked her already. "Yes."

The smiling woman thrust a hand out and shook Willow's hand. "I'm Payton. It's *so* great to finally meet you in person. Those Loverboys you sent were amazing." She looked over the others. "Wow, you have quite a large staff."

"They're not my staff. They're my really helpful family members," Willow said with a proud smile. She introduced everyone, and of course Ben cornered Payton in conversation about God only knew what.

"What's up with Ben today?" Talia whispered.

"I think he's wearing that new cologne I made him," their mother answered. "It's got a love potion in it. I think it's working."

Willow laughed. "Right, Mom. It couldn't be that he's a good-looking single guy on the prowl."

Her mother waved her hand. "Frosting on the cake, princess. Every bit helps, and Benny's getting up there in age."

They all laughed. He was almost thirty.

Payton's cell phone rang, and she stepped away from Ben, who joined the girls by the van again.

After Payton's call, she came to Willow's side. "I have to run some coffee over to the set, but Zane asked me to show you around this morning, so I'll be back. I've never seen him so happy. Congratulations on your engagement." She handed her an ID badge on a long lanyard. "This will keep security off your back."

Willow slipped the lanyard over her head and smiled at her family as Payton drove away in a golf cart. "I feel very official. Let's get moving before people get hungry."

Willow wasn't sure what she'd expected, but as she took in the people hustling around the grounds dressed like they *belonged* in Sweetwater, it wasn't *that*. Jeans and shorts appeared to be today's fashion statement, which meant she was overdressed in her favorite light-blue summer dress. That helped bring down her anxiety a notch while she and her family carried their supplies into the craft services tent, which was another reassuring surprise. Even though Zane had told her that there was nothing glamorous about a film set, she'd thought he was just downplaying it to ease her mind. But the craft services area was nothing more than a big white tent with long tables set up in a U shape, and a few card tables with chairs scattered about. It was all very casual.

They paired up and spread the pink Sweetie Pie tablecloths she'd brought over each of the tables. Ben and Talia took care of setting up the beverages, while Piper and her mother set out silverware and her special catering china. Bridgette and Willow laid out the food and placed the centerpieces on the tables. They made a great team, the six of them, and just having her family around, listening to them tease one another and work so hard on her behalf eased Willow's tension.

She stood back after everything was set up and took it all in.

"I've never seen so many gluten-free, refined-sugar-free, nut-free, white-flour-free treats in one place." Her mother put her arm around her. "You did a wonderful job, as always, baby girl."

"Thanks, Mom. How come when I cater weddings you guys don't show up like this unless I ask for help?"

Her mother took Willow's left hand in hers, lifting her ring into view. "When you cater weddings, Zane doesn't call and ask us to help ease your stress. That man loves you something fierce, Willow."

"He did that?" How had he known she'd need their support when she hadn't known it herself?

"He did indeed. We all know how you like to handle things on your own." She dropped Willow's hand. "But I have to admit, I like knowing he's watching out for your emotional well-being."

"Yeah. I do, too." *Zane's showing me how much he loves me every day, just like Dad did for you.* "You know what? I feel good about this. You guys don't have to stick around all morning. I've got this."

"Maybe I should stick around," Ben offered. "Just in case—"

"Remi Divine shows up?" Piper interjected. "Nope. Come on, big brother. Drive me back so I can get to my job site and get some work done."

After her family left, various crew members popped into the tent. Some introduced themselves with casual politeness, filled their plates, and took off, obviously on a dead run, while others stuck around to chat.

"How's it going?" Payton asked when she returned.

"Great. No complaints so far. Everyone is really nice, too."

Payton grabbed a muffin and a napkin. "You won't get the attitudes that everyone else does. You're feeding the animals. They need you."

Willow felt her eyes widen.

"I'm kidding." Payton waved a dark-haired girl into the tent. "Keisha, this is Willow. Can you man the food while I show her around?"

"Absolutely." Keisha smiled at Willow and headed into the tent as they walked out.

"The actors aren't that bad. I mean, some have their diva moments, but in general if they're cranky, it's because they're stressed," Payton said as they walked over to a golf cart. "Have you ever been on a movie set before?"

"No. Where are they actually filming? It looks like it's just tents and trailers."

"They'll be all over town, but right now they're filming by the water tower. I'll drive you by Zane's trailer so you know where to find him when he's not filming." She drove parallel to the water, passing a group of work trucks and a number of tents. A line of trailers came into view.

"How many movies have you worked on with Zane?" Willow asked.

"Three. Lots of people were surprised when he took this movie, but I wasn't."

"Why weren't you?"

Payton flashed a Cheshire-cat grin. "Oh, please! I was working on the set in Toronto when you got appendicitis and Zane took off claiming a 'family emergency.' Suddenly the guy who never even showed up late on set agreed to pay the entire crew's salary for the weekend just so he could see with his own eyes that you were okay. I have no idea how you guys kept your relationship under wraps for so long, but when he did that, I knew you had to be someone special. It makes sense that he took the role to be near you." She stopped the cart in front of a big black trailer. "This is his trailer."

*Trailer?* She was still stuck on Toronto. "I think you're confused. He said he was in the next town over." She remembered being groggy from pain medication after her surgery. She'd thought she was dreaming when he walked through the door of her hospital room. *Hey, Wills. I was in the area and thought I'd swing by. Looks like perfect timing. How're you feeling, beautiful?*

Payton laughed. "Guys say crazy things when they're in love. He probably didn't want you to know he'd gone to such trouble. Do you want to go inside the trailer?"

She shook her head, a little dizzy and feeling an overwhelming need to see Zane. She'd had appendicitis four *years* ago. *I really was the one you wanted all that time.* "Do you think we could go watch them film for a few minutes?"

Payton turned the golf cart around and headed away from the center of town.

They left the golf cart at the curb and walked across the field toward the tower, where filming was in progress. Long grass tickled Willow's legs, which was a good thing, because she was still a little numb after hearing what Zane had done. The tickling sensation kept her aware of her surroundings. She scanned the activity at the base of the tower. A crane held up some type of screen, forming a barrier to the right of the action. Giant spotlights and white panels, which she assumed were also for lighting, pointed just beyond a buffer of people. As they neared, she was able to get a better look at the action. They stopped a good distance away. Payton warned her not to cough, sneeze, or make any noise at all. A camera on wheels moved across tracks on the ground, and a few people shifted their positions, affording Willow a clear shot of Zane in a heated argument with another man. His face was a mask of anger and determination. Even from that distance she could see the cording of his muscles as he grabbed the guy by the collar and shook him hard enough that Willow gasped. She slapped her hand over her mouth, watching as Remi Divine, the woman who was destined to kiss Willow's man, trembled and cried in fear behind him.

She'd seen every one of Zane's movies several times, but she'd never thought about what it took to make the characters come to life. The man who had made love to her with tender touches and sweet whispers last night had his hands around the other man's neck, throttling him. He was totally immersed in his character, as was Remi, who began shrieking and stumbling backward. As Willow bore witness to Zane's rage and Remi's fear, she silently rooted for him. It didn't matter that this was a movie set, or that he was the hero who would, of course, win. In her head the man she adored was doing whatever it took to protect a woman, and it was the hottest, most heroic thing she'd ever seen.

Someone yelled, "Cut!" and a round of praise followed. As if Zane sensed her presence, his eyes sailed over the crew, landing on her with the heat of a thousand suns. His lips curved up, and his shoulder lifted in a shrug meant only for her. Pride and love swelled inside her, and she knew that when he finally kissed that beautiful actress, she'd be cheering him on just the same.

ZANE STOOD ON the sidewalk in front of the bakery, peering up at the illuminated W+Z lights hanging from the balcony. They'd had a late meeting after filming. It was after eleven, and he was whipped. The apartment was dark, and he wondered if their late nights had finally caught up to Willow. He headed around the corner and climbed the steps to the apartment, loving that she'd turned on that sign to welcome him home. He pushed the door open and was surprised to see candles dancing in the darkness. The scent of lilacs hung in the air.

Willow came out of the bedroom wearing a pair of sweatpants and one of Zane's T-shirts. "Hey, you," she said softly, and set the basket she was carrying on the coffee table. "I hope you don't mind that I borrowed your shirt, but I missed you, and I feel closer to you when I wear your things."

"You are a sight for sore eyes, baby." He set his bag by the door and gathered her in his arms. "My shirt has never looked so good."

She went up on her toes and kissed him. "Don't get any dirty ideas. I've got a special night planned for you." She pointed to the couch. "Take your boots off and relax."

"What's the occasion?" He removed his boots and sank down to the couch. "*Ah.* I've been on my feet all day."

"I know." She came out of the kitchen with a mug of something steamy and set it on the coffee table beside him. "Chamomile tea. It'll help relax you." She sat on the far side of the couch and pulled his legs up on her lap.

"You're pretty far away." He'd showered in his trailer when they'd finished filming, but he lifted his arm and sniffed his pit.

She laughed. "You don't smell, silly." She slithered up the side of his body and kissed him. "Even if you did, it wouldn't stop me from being close to you."

When he tried to lift her on top of him, she wiggled out of his grip.

"Uh-uh. You just worked a hundred hours. You need to be pampered."

He scoffed. "I'm a man. Men don't ever need to be pampered, unless it comes in the form of you, *naked.*"

"Why do you think I wore this outfit? Out of sight, out of mind. Can you hand me that basket, please?"

"For another kiss." He lifted the basket above his head.

She was so damn cute, moving up along the back of the couch with her legs trapped beneath his feet. She puckered up like a fish and laughed when he kissed her. He handed her the basket, and she tugged off his socks.

"Naked time?" he asked hopefully.

She rolled her eyes. "How was filming?"

"It went well, but I hate getting back this late. The highlight of my day was seeing you in the field."

She smiled as she poured lotion into her hand and began massaging his foot, flooding his body with a euphoric feeling.

"Man, Wills. That feels incredible."

"Because foot massages increase the release of hormones that create relaxation and a sense of calm. They also decrease the release of hormones that keep you stressed and tense."

"My brilliant girl, if you follow that foot up that leg, you'll find another part of my body that likes to be massaged." He raised a brow, and she massaged the arch of his foot. Her hands were incredibly soft, surprisingly strong, and utterly perfect. He closed his eyes and relaxed into the cushions.

"I loved watching you today. When I see you in movies, it looks easy. I don't know how you do it, Z. My heart was beating so hard just watching you. I wanted to run in there and jump on the guy's back to get him away from you."

He opened his eyes and watched her. Her brows were knitted in concentration as she rubbed his heel, the ball of his foot, and all the spots in between. "That's because you love me, sweet cheeks."

"Sweet cheeks? Really?"

"Do you know why I call you that?"

She shook her head.

"Because that night . . ."

She stopped rubbing his feet and looked at him.

"That night, when you were lying beneath me by the creek . . . Remember how high the moon seemed that night? And the way it cast a bluish light around us?"

She nodded, holding his foot a little tighter.

"Your cheeks were flushed, and in the moonlight you looked so sweet. You were—*are*—so beautiful, Wills. I'll never forget that night, and even if you hate it, you'll always be my *sweet cheeks*."

She relaxed back against the couch, her hands moving lovingly over his feet. "I always thought it was because of my big butt."

A laugh bubbled out before he could stop it. "Big butt? Baby, you have got the most perfect ass on the planet."

That earned him a wide grin. "I'm glad you think so, because I'm kind of stuck with it."

He sat up and pulled her into his arms, kissing her cheeks so many times she fell back laughing.

"Want me to show you how much I love your butt?"

"No!" She playfully pushed his chest, and he fell back against the cushion. She rubbed his feet again. "Did you know a quarter of your bones are located in your feet?"

"This is just like math tutoring all over again," he teased. "I'm thinking about your ass, and you're spewing academics."

They both laughed. She picked up the remote and clicked on the television and the DVD player.

"Porn?" He sat up again, and she pushed him back down.

"Drink your tea, sex maniac."

*Unforgiven* came on. His favorite movie. "Baby . . ." He sat up again, slower this time, and slid an arm around her shoulder, pulling her closer. "You remembered?"

"I remembered," she whispered. "'Hell of a thing, killing a man. You take away all he's got and all he's ever gonna have,'" she quoted from the movie he thought she'd never watched. "I used to sit at the top of the stairs and listen to the movie while you and Ben watched. But I might have to cover my eyes at the bloody gunfight with that Daggett guy."

He moved his feet off her lap and hauled her up so she was lying half on, half beside him.

"I wasn't done pampering you," she complained with an adorable pout.

"This is the only pampering I need. You by my side. Always."

He kissed that pout off her lips, and she snuggled in against him, resting her cheek on his chest as the movie began playing.

"I hate the idea of leaving next weekend without you to finish filming in LA. Think you can take a day or two off to come home with me Saturday morning before we start filming again? I know you'll have to close the bakery, but I can subsidize that. And you can come back Sunday."

She drew slow circles on his stomach for a long, silent moment. Then she lifted a sweet smile in his direction. "You don't have to subsidize anything. I want to go. I'm just nervous about LA. It seems so . . . *big*."

"You handle *big* things like a pro," he teased.

She rolled her eyes, but her smile never faltered.

"We don't even have to leave my house, Wills. I want to be with you. I want you in my space. In my world. In my *bed*, so I can hold you, and love you, and wake up with you. I'll have withdrawals if I don't see you in the morning, and that could wreak havoc with my acting."

She pressed a kiss to his chest and laughed. "Is it true that you don't bring women to your house?"

"I see Patch has a really big mouth."

"And you have a picture of me in your bedroom?"

"Yes." He feigned exasperation. "But if you want to know which one, you have to come back to LA with me."

She rested against his chest again without answering. Many minutes later she said, "Of course I'll come," and he finally felt like he could breathe again.

She fell asleep before the gruesome scene she'd hoped to miss, and Zane lay awake for a long while after the movie ended, wishing they were filming the entire movie in Sweetwater. How could he ever have thought it would be easy to walk away from Willow when they were done filming? A fake engagement to the woman he'd always wanted had been his most brilliant idea and his worst.

They never should have lied to her family. The guilt was killing him, and even though Willow had come clean to Bridgette, he knew it had to be eating away at her to have lied to the others. When he'd called them about being there to support Willow the first day on the set, they'd been eager to help, and it had driven that guilt even deeper. He needed to rectify that situation in a way that wouldn't come back on Willow.

He pressed his lips to the top of her head and pulled the throw blanket from the back of the couch over her. "I'll fix this, baby. I'll fix everything."

# CHAPTER NINETEEN

IT WAS BOUND to happen at some point. Willow hadn't known when or how, but she'd assumed she'd eventually meet Remi Divine. She just hadn't expected it to be Tuesday evening at eight o'clock while she was sitting on the steps of Zane's trailer in a pair of shorts and one of his T-shirts tied at the waist like an eighties girl at a creek party, drinking a Kinky Pink cocktail and eating all the frosting off a dozen cupcakes. With her *fingers*. She smiled up at the Natalie Portman lookalike, who was even more gorgeous in person than on the big screen.

"Hi." *Did that sound too perky? Not perky enough? Like I'm as lame as a drunken duck at the moment?* She'd had a hell of a day at the bakery. The oven that had been on its last leg had died, leaving her with one, which was fine most days but would cause a crunch with her next big event. She'd called the distributor, but the model she wanted couldn't be installed for another four weeks. She pushed to her feet and held out a hand.

Remi, who was in full makeup with her hair tied back in some kind of complicated knot and wearing a cute little silky robe and heels, glanced down at Willow's hand with a disgusted expression.

*Oh shit.* Willow realized she'd been sucking frosting off her index finger when Remi had approached, and quickly pulled back her hand, wiping it on her back pocket. "Sorry! Um, hi. I'm—"

Remi lifted her adorable and slightly pointy chin, and in a voice as rich as dark chocolate said, "I know who you are. Willow Dalton. Zane's *fiancée*." She said *fiancée* as if it were a dirty word.

Willow's stomach sank, but she wasn't about to let a snooty actress make her feel bad about herself or how she felt about Zane. She lifted her own perfect chin and squared her shoulders, meeting Remi's serious gaze. Jesus, did the woman even know how to smile, or was that a trick of the camera? She emitted sweetness like syrup on pancakes on the big screen.

"Yes, that's right." Willow held out her left hand, flashing the gaudy ring, which earned an appreciative "Hm" from Remi.

"You're waiting for him." It wasn't a question. She walked with the grace of a swan and the coolness of a movie star to the steps of the trailer and sat her tiny ass down, patting the space beside her.

Fighting the urge to roll her eyes, Willow sat next to her. "I'd offer you a drink, but all I have are these." She held up the six-pack. "Kinky Pink, 'an irresistible combo of mango, passion fruit, and blood orange flavors that's so good it's naughty.'"

Remi arched a thinly manicured brow.

"That's . . . It's their tagline. Sorry, my small-townness is showing."

A smile split Remi's properly painted lips, and a soft laugh escaped.

"Cool. You *do* know how to smile." Willow's eyes nearly bugged out of her head, and she felt her cheeks burn so hot she thought they might actually release steam. "I'm sorry. That just slipped out. Oh my God. I'm sorry. I just—"

"I think I will have that drink, thank you." Remi reached across her and grabbed a bottle. "Do you share your cupcakes, or are those for your fingers only?"

Willow was stunned into silence.

"Hm? I'm going to take that as sharing, because I'm frigging starved." Remi grabbed a cupcake and licked the frosting right off. "You can breathe now. I'm a normal person."

The breath Willow hadn't realized she'd been holding rushed from her lungs.

"I was just trying to see if you were like the usual fangirls who knock around with the actors. The two of you are all over the Internet. The *newest, hottest* couple. At least they've kept the bloodhounds away from the set." She looked down at the drink and the cupcake and handed the bottle to Willow. "Can you please help me open this while you find your voice? If I ruin my nails, I have to sit in the chair for another half hour."

Willow uncapped the bottle and handed it back to Remi, taking a long swig of her own, feeling like she had just been whirled in a blender and the world was still spinning.

Remi lifted her cupcake like she was toasting and took a drink. "I'll pay for this tomorrow. Can't afford the extra pounds." She rolled her eyes and bit into the cupcake. "Oh my Lord. This is the *bomb!*"

Willow smiled. Baked items were the ultimate equalizer. "Thank you. I haven't seen you at the craft services tent in the mornings."

"The camera is very unforgiving. I don't eat much while filming, but after the day I had, I need this. I'm not on camera again until late tomorrow, so I have time to get it out of my system, detox and *de*hydrate again. Tricks of the trade."

"Sounds fun," Willow teased, feeling more like herself again. "Anytime you need a good sugar fix, hit me up. My bakery, Sweetie Pie, is right down the street."

"Thanks. But do you deliver outside Sweetwater to other rural New York locations or Cape Cod? Because when I'm not filming, that's where I am. As my alter ego, of course, and I rarely leave my house." She took another swig of her drink and eyed the bottle. "This is awesome, too. I've never had it."

"It's cheap and fruity. I'm not surprised." Oh, damn, was she going to put her foot in her mouth all night? "I'm sorry. I'm still a little rattled to be sitting here with *Remi Divine*. And yes, I will deliver wherever you are, under whatever name you use."

Remi smiled and took another swig of her drink. "Probably just as rattled as I am to be sitting with you."

*"Please."* Willow laughed and grabbed a cupcake.

"It's just as nerve-racking for actors as it is for people outside the industry. Will I be hated because of my looks or celebrity, or worse, will people like me only for those reasons? Zane must have told you that."

"Zane and I don't actually talk about the industry very much. I've known him since we were kids. So to me, he's just funny, sweet, smart, and *smart-ass* Zane. I haven't thought about those things. That has to be tough." Gazing down at the blue frosting on the cupcake, she remembered waking up in his arms on the couch that morning and realized that what she'd said wasn't true.

"Actually, Zane's much more to me than *just* anything," Willow clarified. "I don't mean to negate his acting, because clearly he's incredible at his job. But I love the man he is, and it wouldn't matter what he did for a living."

Remi sighed. "I envy you. As I said, I never know if a guy likes me for me or for who they think I am." She finished her drink and grabbed another.

"I can see how that would be frustrating."

"I have to kiss your fiancé," Remi said softly. "I figured you'd pretty much hate me because of that."

"So did I." Willow laughed. "But you're not exactly hateable, and kissing you *is* his job."

"So, you're not jealous?"

"Wicked jealous. And so freaking *more* jealous now that I've met you. I mean, if you could ugly it up a bit, that would be good." Willow waved her hand toward Remi's robe. "And maybe wear a snowsuit or something."

Remi laughed.

"I could pull a few of your teeth with pliers. That would help, too."

Remi covered her mouth. "My teeth?"

"You don't really need them anyway." Willow took another drink and smiled at Remi. "I'm female, so yeah, I'm jealous. But I want you to nail that scene and show the world how amazing the two of you are. And now I'm going to change the subject, because I have to picture something other than you two in a lip-lock or I'll lose my mind."

"Just so you know, I hate kissing scenes. Truly hate them. I've had nightmares about him pulling away and saying I suck at kissing. So, *yes*, please change the subject. *Quickly.*"

"You have not!"

"*Have to.* Subject change, please."

Laughing, Willow asked the first thing that came to mind. "How did you get into acting?"

"It's a weird story." Remi took off her heels and stretched her toes. "My brother had a friend who said his uncle was in the industry back in the day and well connected. He said he could get me into the business. It all happened so fast. We met at a party, and the next day he brought me to meet his uncle, who took me to meet his colleagues. It turned out he was a fluffer, and . . . oh my Lord. You can imagine what my reaction was."

"At least you had an *in*. What's a fluffer?" She popped the rest of her cupcake into her mouth.

Remi swayed a little. "I'm such a lightweight. I'm already buzzed." She lowered her voice and said, "A fluffer is the person who, before Viagra, kept male porn stars aroused."

Willow choked on her cupcake, coughing and spewing crumbs all over Remi's robe. Remi burst into laughter and patted her on the back so hard they both tumbled off the stairs and spilled their drinks.

"Oh my God! A fluffer!" More laughter burst from Willow's lungs, causing Remi to laugh harder. "And his *uncle*? A guy? Was it gay porn?"

Remi squealed. "I don't know! Can you imagine? 'Excuse me, sir,'" Remi said between laughs. "'May I *fluff* you now?'"

Willow roared and grabbed Remi's arm. "What did you *do*?"

"I screamed something like, 'I'm not doing that!' and ran out of the room." She laughed again. "It was awful. I hid in my room for a month afterward. And when my brother found out"—she breathed deeply, regaining control—"first he beat the crap out of his friend's uncle. Then he made it his goal to get me into real movies." Her voice became serious and thoughtful. "I owe everything good in my life to Aiden, actually. He's the kindest, most determined man I know, and I'm lucky to have him as my brother. He's twelve years older than me. He raised me, and he manages my career now, but he also owns all sorts of businesses."

Hearing Remi had been raised by her brother sobered Willow up. She'd like to say she was sorry if they had lost their parents and hug her, just because her heart was aching for her and everyone needed hugs. But she didn't know Remi well enough to do either of those things, so she said, "Sounds like he'd get along well with my brother, Ben. He's a venture capitalist and just as protective of me and my three sisters. Too bad Aiden's not around. We could all have dinner one night."

"You're so lucky. I wish I had sisters," Remi said with a sad look in her eyes. "Sometimes this life can get really lonely."

"Aw, Remi. You can be our honorary sister." Willow couldn't resist reaching out and hugging her. Remi embraced her for a moment longer, and tighter, than she'd expected, making her glad she'd done it.

"Aiden's coming Friday to see the last day of filming," she said, fussing nervously with her robe, as if the hug had taken her by surprise, too. "He always tries to catch a day or two when his schedule allows. Maybe if you and Zane and Ben are up for it, we could have dinner then? You can bring your sisters."

Thinking of how great it would be for Bridgette to meet a nice, responsible guy, she said, "We can be a little overwhelming as a group. Maybe I'll bring just one."

*ONLY A FEW more days*, Zane reminded himself as he headed for his trailer late Tuesday night. They'd had to film the last scene eight times because the other actor kept messing up his lines. It had been a long, grueling day, and Zane couldn't blame him. The guy was sidetracked with thoughts of his wife wanting a divorce. The whole situation sucked, and on top of that, Zane thought they'd both made a mistake by taking this film. Acting in a romantic suspense role was incredibly different from acting in action movies. The scenes moved too slowly, every step felt measured, every breath overdramatized, whereas in action, there was barely time to think before he had to take someone down or blow through a building.

The lights were on in his trailer, which could only mean one thing. Willow was waiting for him. Patch had already taken off for the evening to meet Piper for drinks, and no one else had a key. He smiled to himself. He'd called her father today and planned to stop by after filming tomorrow, while Willow was holding a tasting for a potential new client. Filming was scheduled to end early, which should give them plenty of time to talk.

He pulled open the trailer door and stepped inside. It smelled like Willow, and his body pulsed to life.

She looked up from where she was lying on her stomach on the couch, and a smile lit up her glassy eyes. Her cheeks were pink, her legs were bent at the knees, her feet crossed at the ankles. A half-empty bottle of Kinky Pink sat on the floor, and he noticed five other empties on the table.

"Z, this is a love story," she said with the slow speech of too much alcohol as he sat down beside her.

He noticed his screenplay lying open in front of her, and his chest constricted.

"I thought it was about a lost boy who finds his way in a gritty city against all odds. But it's so much more. This is about family and friendship, and . . ." She flipped through the pages as she sat up. "I'm not done yet, but this part where he and his brother climb the water tower when he's thinking about running away? That made my heart break. And the way he talks about that girl? Oh my gosh, Zane. I hope they get together. Do they?"

She was so freaking cute he pulled her onto his lap. "Yes, they get together."

"Thank goodness, because I was worried that when he finally gets his life together he moves on without her."

"Have you gotten to her date yet?"

"She goes on a date?" she said excitedly. "With him?"

He pushed his hand beneath her hair, rubbing her shoulders. "Are you tipsy?"

"Maybe. Did I tell you my oven broke? And they can't bring a new one for four weeks."

"Oh no, babe. Four weeks? Can't you pull some strings?"

She shook her head. "Nope. I'm a mere mortal."

"Well, I'm not. Let me see what I can do." He made a mental note to check into it.

Her eyes widened, and she gasped. "I met Remi! We're having dinner with her Friday night."

He laughed at her non sequitur. *Gotta love tipsy Willow.* "Sounds great. She seems like a nice person."

"Super nice. Do you know what a fluffer is? In porn, I mean?"

"Um. Is this the type of trick question girls ask to turn around on guys? Like if I say I do, then you get mad because I've probably watched porn?"

She grabbed his face. "No. I assume you've watched porn. But *no one* is *fluffing* you, got it?"

He rocked his hips beneath her. "You're all I want or need, baby."

"Good. As long as we're clear."

"Perfectly clear, sweet cheeks. But you can fluff me after I shower." He pulled her T-shirt—his T-shirt, he realized—off her shoulder and kissed her there.

She wiggled her butt, fluffing him right up.

"Are you too tipsy to read a scene in the screenplay for me?" He'd decided to show the screenplay to the director, and he hoped to give it to him tomorrow. Steve Hileberg might be a hothead perfectionist, but he was without a doubt the best director in the business. Getting Steve on board with the project was the first step toward moving forward.

"No." She watched him flipping the pages. "But I don't want to skip ahead to the end."

He'd covered his muse pretty well by mixing up the locations and particulars of the story. But he knew the girl who'd taught herself calculus by reading a book would see right through it. And he wanted her to, so there was no chance for miscommunication. He folded the screenplay over and pointed to the beginning of a scene. "Just read this scene for me, okay, beautiful? I'm going to shower real quick."

She slid off his lap and pulled him down for another kiss. "I like Remi. I'm glad you have a nice costar."

"Thanks, baby. I'm glad I have *you*."

He went into the bathroom and turned on the shower, shaving at the sink as the room steamed up. He stripped out of his clothes and stepped beneath the warm spray, tipping his face up to catch the rain. His mind ran through all the possible reactions Willow might have to the scene. When Willow was in high school, one of the football players had asked her out. Zane remembered how proud she'd been. Her green eyes had twinkled with delight. She'd always thought of herself as awkward and a brainiac, but he knew better, as did half the guys in their school. But of all her luck, the asshole who had asked her out, Butch Clayborne, had proceeded to run his mouth in the locker room after football practice. He'd bragged about asking her out to "get a piece of ass," among other parts of her, which had sent fire through Zane's veins. Even in remembrance his fingers curled into fists. He'd waited for the rest of the team to clear out, and he'd grabbed the asshole by the collar and shoved him against the lockers. *You're not going out with Willow. You're not to talk to her ever again. And if I hear you so much as mention her name, I will kill you.* They hadn't come to blows, but Zane would have taken him down without thought. What he hadn't counted on was how upset Willow had been for being stood up. He hadn't told her what he'd done because she'd already felt self-conscious about her breasts, and the last thing she'd needed was to think guys believed she was only good enough for sex, when in reality it was only the scum of the earth who treated women like that. He should have told the asshole to cancel the date, but he'd been too pissed off to think straight.

He pressed his palms against the tiles, the water streaming down his back, and prayed Willow wouldn't hate him for what he'd done. The scene in the screenplay wasn't the same, but he'd left enough clues. And if she didn't get it because she was too tipsy, he'd tell her outright. But he had faith in his beautiful, brilliant girl.

When the shower door opened, he hesitated before looking over, taking one last second to throw a plea up to the powers that be. She stepped into the shower, raw hurt glittering in her eyes, slicing through him like a knife.

"Wills—"

She wrapped her arms around him and pressed her face to his chest. Her lush, naked curves molded to his body, arousing more than just his heart.

"The lunar eclipse," she said softly.

"I'm sorry, baby. I should have told you." The night the date was supposed to occur, there had been a lunar eclipse. The whole town had gone to the fairgrounds to witness it, but he'd found Willow down by the creek behind her parents' house. Her thinking spot. Two years later, that spot had become *theirs*.

Her delicate fingers trailed along his back, and she gazed up at him. "I'm glad you didn't. It would have mortified me, and there's nothing I hate more than being embarrassed. That's why you came looking for me that night. I remember. You said my mom was worried about me and you offered to go find me."

He nodded. "One day when Ben and I were playing basketball, you said you were going to the creek to read. I saw you heading for the woods a few weeks later, and Ben said that you went to the creek to think. When you didn't show up with everyone else at the fairgrounds that night, baby, I assumed you were there."

Her hands slid to his ass, holding her body firmly against him and making him hard as steel. "You really have loved me forever."

"I'm pretty sure we've determined that you've had me since I first set eyes on you."

"Do you remember the very first time you saw me?" She swayed against him and flicked her tongue over his nipple.

"I can barely think when you do that, much less retrieve a memory from so long ago."

She sucked the pebbled peak into her mouth, and he groaned, backing her up against the wall. When she clamped her teeth around the sensitive nub, he pushed her legs open with his knee and thrust the head of his arousal against her center.

"Fuck, baby." He rocked his hips, teasing her slick flesh. "I don't have a condom, and I want to make love to you so badly."

"I'm on the pill and clean," she said urgently. "But the question is, are you?" She was breathing as hard as he was.

His pulse skyrocketed. "Yes. I wouldn't have let you put your mouth on me if I wasn't."

All his blood rushed south as he lifted her into his arms, unable to wait another second to make love to her. Water ran like a river between her breasts as her legs wound around his waist. He loved the feel of her warm thighs against him and her hands on his cheeks as her tight heat swallowed his shaft. Their mouths came together in a smoldering, greedy kiss. She clutched at his shoulders, moving with him in a mind-numbing rhythm. Lust and love pulsed through his veins as they quickened their efforts. *More,* his body demanded, thrusting harder, kissing rougher, almost violently, needing to be even closer. Her back met the wall as he drove into her. He broke away from the kiss to make sure she was okay, but she crashed her mouth to his, giving him the green light he needed. He sped through that sucker, eating at her mouth, slamming into her time and time again, driven by the heat pooling at the base of his spine. Pressure mounted with every sweet moan. Her head tipped back, and he took her breast into his mouth, sucking and teasing the peak.

"Z—harder. So good—"

Hearing her desires took him right up to the edge of sanity. He sucked harder, and she cried out, gasping for breath. Her inner muscles pulsed around him, and his release crashed over him, pulling him under, drowning him in ecstasy.

Her body shuddered with aftershocks, and he moved her beneath the warm water.

"Z," she whispered.

"Yeah, sweetheart. Did I hurt your back?"

She lifted her head from his shoulder. "No. I just want you to know, I love that it took us so long to finally come together."

He pressed his lips to hers and lowered her feet to the floor, holding her close as they rinsed off. "Why? I wish we had all those years together."

"Because you've had time to become the man you are, and I've had time to become the person I am. And those feelings are *still* here, only stronger. And now you've written a story about us, straight from your heart. Nothing could be more perfect than that."

"You're wrong, baby. As cheesy as it sounds, every day we're together will be more perfect than the last, because every day I'm learning how to be a better man for you."

"You're the king of cheesy," she teased.

"I love you, too. Now finish up so I can take you home and devour you properly." He smacked her ass.

She squealed and spun out of his arms. Her gaze turned sinfully seductive as she cupped his balls and said, "Why wait?"

# CHAPTER TWENTY

PATCH LOADED UP a plate with gluten-free pancakes, breakfast pizza, and fruit Friday morning as he pleaded with Payton to put in a good word and get Willow hired to cater all the future set breakfasts. He looked like a rebellious teenager with his black jeans, shock of brown hair sticking up in all directions, and strands of leather and silver wrapped around his wrist. Willow knew he and Piper had met for drinks, and when Piper came by that morning, she'd claimed that was all they'd had. Willow tried to picture Zane's chilled-out assistant in a relationship with her high-strung sister, but no matter how hard she tried, she just couldn't see it. She had a feeling they were both barking up the wrong tree. Then again, until she and Zane had come together with this zany plan and cleared the air, she might never have visualized the two of them in a lasting relationship, either.

"Come on, Payton. Can't you pull some strings?" He took a big bite of the pizza and closed his eyes. "*Mm.* Willow Dalton, you are amazing."

"Thank you, but I have a bakery to run, remember?" Willow had picked up a new wedding cake job last night, and she'd spent half the night coming up with ideas. Her love for baking had only increased since she'd started her business, but the truth was, she loved spending the mornings on set, too. The cast and crew were friendly, funny, and appreciative of every little thing she did, which made her want to branch out and do more, like adding pancakes and pizza for restricted diets to the menu. She'd never considered herself much of a cook beyond baking, but their praise had her considering expanding the bakery menu in addition to her other ideas. She could hardly believe the week of filming had passed so fast. Tonight she and Zane, along with Bridgette and Ben, were having dinner with Remi and her brother, and tomorrow morning they were heading back to LA. This weekend she would see Zane on his turf, in his *home*. She was nervous and excited to see how the man she'd come to love more than she'd ever thought possible fit into a world she had such conflicting feelings about.

"Details, details," Patch teased. He draped an arm over her shoulder and lowered his voice. "Maybe I can get Zane to convince you by some other means."

Little did he know that no matter how amazing sex with Zane was, it wasn't her motivator to do a darn thing. It was the look in Zane's eyes, the loving pitch of his voice—even when he was teasing—and the complete and utter happiness he instilled with nothing more than a smile or a shrug. It was crazy how much she loved that humble shrug.

Payton tucked her long red hair behind her ear. "Willow knows I'd happily take her on as a regular. You might be interested to know that we're going to be ordering gifts throughout the year from her, so be a good boy and maybe I'll send you something sweet."

"They're setting up for the kissing scene down by the lake. Are you going to watch?" Patch asked as they walked out of the tent.

Willow glanced at the commotion taking place down the hill. She had surprised herself this morning when she'd told Zane to "kiss the hell out of Remi," and she'd meant it. Being with Zane had opened her eyes to a lot of things, but one of her biggest realizations was that her mother had been right. Every kiss counted. Last night Willow had finally gotten up the courage to read the scenes leading up to the kiss and the actual kissing scene. She'd found herself rooting for the characters, hoping they'd get together, just like she had with Zane's screenplay.

"Of course," she answered. "This is a pivotal scene, and I definitely don't want to miss it. Keisha offered to take care of things here so I could go down and watch."

"Cool," Patch said. "I'll see you down there. Remi has nixed an audience, so once they're set up, only key people will be allowed on set. You're with me, so you're cool. If anyone gives you a hard time, just tell them to speak with me."

"Thanks, Patch." Willow watched him head down the hill and wondered about Remi's request. She really must hate kissing scenes after all.

"Ever wonder what it's like?" Payton asked as they returned to the tent.

Willow busied herself straightening up the tables. "Hm? What what's like?"

"For the actors? The kissing scenes?"

*Yes, way too much.* "Remi said she hates them."

Payton poured herself a cup of coffee. "Imagine you wake up feeling cranky, or bloated, or stressed about forgetting your lines. Then you get to the set, and the makeup artists are fussing with your face and hair, wardrobe is nipping and tucking, and across the set you see this incredibly hot guy. But he's *People*'s Most Beautiful or he's won an Oscar, or he's an actor you haven't worked with before. Other than your work on the current film together, all of which has been stressful, he's basically a *stranger*. And you can flip that around for the guys, because it's just as bad."

"Gosh, and when I see it on the big screen, it seems so easy."

"Want to know another trade secret that'll burst your bubble?" She waggled her brows with a mischievous grin that reeled Willow's curiosity right in.

"You *know* I do." She leaned in closer.

"Okay, well, in the love scenes, not only are they often in full-body makeup, but the guy puts all his goodies in this flesh-colored bag and the girl wears a vag pad, which is stuck to her skin, covering up her naughty bits. And there's often fake sweat and fifty crew members watching and the director telling them, 'Move your hand, lift your leg, don't smile.' It's awful. I'd never want to be an actress because of those scenes."

"A flesh-colored *bag*?" Willow couldn't suppress a laugh. "That sounds horrible. But it shows how good the actors and actresses are. Most love scenes look natural."

"That's why they get paid the big bucks." Payton popped a blueberry in her mouth. "You'd better get down there if you want to see the scene."

Willow walked down the hill toward the set, acutely aware of her heart ricocheting inside her chest. She'd convinced herself not to worry about this scene, but now that it was imminent, she was torn by conflicting emotions. She tried to distract herself by focusing on her surroundings.

A group of people traipsed up the hill a good distance away, and she wondered if they'd been sent away from the set. There were only a handful of people within the cordoned-off area. Zane came into focus, standing tall and handsome while one woman applied makeup and a guy fussed with his clothes. She recalled what Payton had said and wondered if all of the preparation and fussing was uncomfortable for him. Was he nervous about the kiss? If so, he'd been too cool to let her in on his anxiety, but still she had to wonder.

She knew a loving kiss and a kiss given to fulfill a work commitment were miles apart, but no matter how supportive a fiancée she wanted to be, she was still a sensitive female. Wasn't it in every woman's fiber to be possessive of her partner? To nurture and care for, yes, and to have and to hold? Nowhere was it written that a significant other had to support in the sharing of their partner's toe-curling kisses.

Patch waved Willow over, and Zane's gaze landed on her. She felt his sexual magnetism and his eager affection encircling her like a blanket. Inhaling a deep breath, she reached for her inner calm. Then she dug a little deeper, past her conflicted, jealous heart, all the way to her core, where reason rose above all else, and prepared herself to watch her man kiss another woman.

IF ZANE HEARD one more *Go get her, buddy*, he was going to lose his shit. Jesus, they'd built this scene up to epic proportions, as if there wasn't pressure to do *every* scene as perfectly as possible. He'd come to the realization that this was *it* for him. The end of the line. Changing genres hadn't given him any better sense of fulfillment than acting in action movies had. Did all actors eventually feel like they were playing with water instead of working with clay? No matter how different the set, the cast, the location, it was all still pretending to be someone another person had created. Yes, he was bringing the character to life, but it was still carrying out someone else's vision. It was time to take the next step, and after handing his script over to the director this morning, he hoped like hell luck would be on his side. If Steve liked the screenplay, anything was possible.

He took his place on the set, mentally playing over his lines and hoping Remi had pulled herself together. She'd been a nervous wreck, which was ridiculous. It wasn't like they were hijacking a plane and jumping out midair. *That* was something to be nervous about. This was a piece of cake.

Thinking of cake brought his mind to his beautiful girl. He popped an Altoid and stole a quick glance at Willow, who was talking with Patch. He should be pissed at his loose-lipped assistant for spilling his secrets about his house and what was—*and what had never been*—in it. But it was hard to be angry at the guy who'd helped bring him and

Willow together in the first place. Like a kid awaiting show-and-tell, Zane couldn't wait to show her his place.

"Quiet on the set!"

Steve's voice snapped Zane into acting mode, but as he caught sight of Remi nervously fidgeting with her hands, the part of him that should want to do whatever it took to make her comfortable sort of wanted to give her a little shake and say, *It's a kiss. Lighten up.*

It was definitely time to get out of this business before he turned into an asshole.

With everyone in place, the assistant director yelled, "Roll it," and the rest of the directions fell on deaf ears. Zane was in the zone. He'd become his character, and at the sound of the clapper, he spurred into action. Or rather, slow motion, given that action in this movie moved at a snail's pace.

Remi stood by the lake with her back to him. Her short black dress hung loosely from her thin frame. In the scene, they'd just come from the funeral of her father, who had been murdered, and Zane, the private investigator her family had hired—and her past lover—was comforting her. He'd mastered the confident yet careful gait and the tender cadence of his voice the scene called for. She turned as he approached, sunlight reflecting in her damp eyes. Her trembling lips and fidgeting, nervous hands perfectly relayed her devastation. But as he reached for her hand and she collapsed against him, he felt his body tense up and worked hard to fix it, but she felt wrong. She wasn't Willow. And now he was screwed. His mind reeled as he tried like hell to get his head back into the scene.

"I will stop at nothing to catch the people who did this, Cora. I promise you I will put them away." *Okay, cool. That was solid.*

"Bob," she said breathlessly.

He lowered his mouth to hers, and the second their lips touched, he tensed up again. *Motherfucker.*

"Cut!"

"It's not you," he said as quickly as he could, knowing Remi would think she'd somehow caused his screwup. "I mind-fucked myself. Sorry." He raked a hand through his hair, not caring that makeup would have to fix it, and waved to Steve.

"I've got this. Sorry," he called to Steve, but his insides were in a full-on battle. He'd kissed more women than he could count, and never had he freaking fucked up. He forced himself not to look at Willow, but that didn't block the heat of her gaze from boring into him. He didn't want to know what was going through her mind.

The makeup team fixed his hair and Remi's lipstick, and they went through the motions again. *Three times.*

*Holy hell.*

The easiest scene of them all, and he was acting like this was his first time filming. Steve called Patch over and said something Zane couldn't hear, but Patch's pinched look wasn't good. He stalked over to Willow with his head down, took her by the elbow, and began escorting her away.

"Oh, hell no!" Willow's voice called the attention of every person on set as she broke away from Patch and stormed past the camera crew.

*Wills, what are you doing?* His eyes darted to Steve, who rose from his chair with a pissed-off look in his eyes. Zane held up a hand in his direction and strode toward Willow.

"Baby, what are you—"

"What the hell is wrong with you?" she said through gritted teeth.

Shocked, he was at a loss for words.

She stepped closer. "I'm afraid to touch you because of makeup and wardrobe and all that, but if I could, I'd grab you by the collar and shake you." Her eyes dialed down to warm determination. "Z, if anyone knows how to kiss the hell out of a woman, it's *you.* What's going on? Do you really need me to leave the set? You're a professional, and I don't need *or* want you to be anything less."

"Wills, she's not *you*, and it's fucking with my head." He felt the eyes of the cast and crew watching their every move.

"Then *unfuck* it, because I believe in you, and don't you dare let me or anyone else down. Do you hear me?"

He chuckled, but there was no denying the mental click inside his head. She was absolutely right. "Yeah, baby. I hear you loud and clear."

"Good, now go kiss her like she's never been kissed before, and if you screw this up"—she stepped closer and whispered—"you'll never find out the dirty surprise I have in store for you." She spun on her heel and strutted away.

The whole damn peanut gallery applauded.

Steve waved a hand as if to say, *Go to it.*

And Zane did just that. This time when he took Remi into his arms, he kissed her until she went limp in his arms, and when Steve yelled, "Cut!" it was Willow's eyes he found.

She mouthed, *I'm so proud of you*, and he mouthed, *Dirty surprise*, earning the sexiest blush he'd ever seen.

# CHAPTER TWENTY-ONE

LATER THAT NIGHT Zane locked the door to Willow's apartment and followed her down the back steps. He was relieved that filming was over, at least for now. Most of the cast and crew had taken off as soon as filming had wrapped for the day, but they were meeting Remi and her brother, Aiden, along with Bridgette and Ben—who Willow insisted *had* to meet them—for dinner at Tasker's Chance, an upscale restaurant on the edge of town. They were running a little late because Willow had gotten stuck at the bakery taking care of loose ends before leaving town tomorrow morning.

"Can we take Chloe?" Willow dangled her keys from her finger, looking hot in her skimpy black dress and sky-high heels. Her lips were painted an enticing shade of red, and her eyes were smoky and alluring.

"You sure you don't want to take my rental? You might be more comfortable."

She shook her head. "Nope. Chloe's perfectly comfortable."

He opened the passenger door, and she settled into her seat. Her dress crept up her gorgeous thighs, and she primly leaned both knees to the side and smiled up at him.

"You look stunning in that little number, but I thought you hate wearing heels."

She pulled him down by the collar until they were eye to eye. "I wanted to dress up for my man." She put her finger in the center of his chin and dragged it lightly down his throat to the space between the open buttons on his collared shirt.

"You don't like it?" she asked with all the innocence of a schoolgirl and the seduction of a vixen.

"I love it, and I can't wait to see it on the floor later. I just want you to be comfortable." He leaned in for a kiss, and she pressed her hand to his chest.

"Lipstick," she whispered.

"I hate lipstick," he grumbled.

It took only a few minutes to reach the restaurant, and during that time Willow was unusually quiet.

"Nervous?" He reached for her hand.

"A little." She slicked her tongue over her perfectly painted lips, leaving them glistening and inviting.

"Baby, I could do you a favor and . . ." He lowered his hand to her thigh, giving it a tight squeeze. "Relax you in a *very* pleasurable way."

Her eyes said yes, but she pushed his hand from her leg. "My body turns to butter after you have your way with me. I'd never be able to sit up straight afterward."

"Good to know."

He pulled into the parking lot and navigated to a dark spot beneath the trees. "Sweetheart, you know Remi is just a person like you and me. There's nothing to be worried about."

"Oh, I'm not worried about Remi. We drank together. I've seen the *real* her."

"Then what could you possibly have to be nervous about? The dirty promise you made? Because you don't have to do anything extra on my account. I love you just the way you are."

She lifted one shoulder with a mysterious smile and pushed open her door. "Let's not pick it apart."

That didn't sound good. He came around the car and helped her to her feet. "That's one way to make me worry, babe."

She touched his cheek, which paled in comparison to the kiss he so desperately wanted. "I promise you don't need to worry."

*Right.*

From the outside Tasker's Chance looked more like a lodge decorated for the holidays than a high-end restaurant. Greenery and white lighting followed the roofline and wound down the side of the cedar building to the trees illuminating the outdoor dining area that stretched from the side of the building all the way around back. On the weekends they offered live music on the patio. The rear of the restaurant was primarily made of glass, and from its vantage point on the hill, nearly every seat offered a glorious view of the lake and the lights of the town.

"We should go right out to the patio. I reserved a table there so we could dance." Willow took a few steps ahead and cast a sexy glance over her shoulder. Her hand swept over the hem of her dress. "Can you see my panty lines?"

After a not-so-quick visual inspection, he said, "No, babe. You look perfect."

"Oops!" Her eyes widened, and she lifted her hand in front of her mouth. "I forgot," she whispered. "I'm not wearing any."

He stopped in his tracks. How was he supposed to make it through dinner knowing *that*?

She wiggled her fingers with a glint of wickedness in her eyes. "Coming?"

"Not yet," he said under his breath. "But if the tablecloth is long enough, you will be soon."

Willow's eyes filled with heat.

Zane pulled Willow closer as they stepped onto the patio and whispered, "That was totally unfair."

"What was?" She blinked with feigned innocence.

"Oh, is that the game we're playing?" He slid his hand around her ribs and brushed his thumb over the outside of her breast, loving the instant peaks that rose to greet him.

Her mouth twitched like she was going to trap her lower lip between her teeth. He leaned closer and said, "Remember your lipstick, baby. Keep it on so we can see how hot it looks circling a certain part of me later."

He guided her, and her slack jaw, toward their table. "Might want to close your mouth, because I've got something itching to fill it." She snapped her mouth shut, and he whispered, "In case I forget when we're *busy* later, I truly love everything about you, Wills. Naughty or not, it wouldn't change a thing."

"No?" she whispered. "What if I promise to swallow? That doesn't amp it up even a little bit?"

*Holy. Hell.*

Right before they reached the table, she pressed her palms flat against his chest, causing heat to streak straight to his core.

"I'll tell you what," she said quickly. "If they say the word *hard* fifteen times during dinner, I'll leave red streaks, not just rings, everywhere you want."

She turned toward the table with a wide grin as Remi and the others rose to greet them, leaving Zane's mind to quickly sift through everything he could possibly ask to evoke the right word. *Fifteen times.*

Zane tried to concentrate on the dead ringer for David Beckham standing before him, but his mind was firmly entrenched on the image of Willow on her knees, swallowing everything he had to give.

"Aiden Aldridge." The guy with chiseled features and serious eyes offered a hand in greeting.

"So nice to meet you." Willow took his hand and nudged Zane from his fantasy. "Isn't it, Z?"

"Yes, very." Zane shook Aiden's hand, itching to sit down beside his beautiful Willow and get his hand between her silky thighs.

Aiden sat between Remi and Bridgette, who was fidgeting nervously with something in her lap and stealing glances at her handsome tablemate. Ben greeted Zane with a manly pat on the back and sat beside Remi. Zane wondered how long it would take before Ben made a play for her.

"Remi tells me congratulations are in order." Aiden lifted his wineglass.

Zane sat beside Willow and filled their glasses from the open bottle of wine on the table. "Yes, that's right." Or at least he hoped it would be. He and Willow had officially become a couple, but that was a long way from being engaged.

"Are you married, Aiden?" Zane asked. He slid his hand beneath the table and squeezed Willow's thigh, noting the hitch in her breathing.

"No," Aiden answered. "Ben and I were just discussing the woes of owning or investing in multiple businesses. It makes it hard to form lasting relationships when you're traveling so often."

Zane shifted his gaze to Willow. "*Hard*, you say?" He pressed one finger into her thigh. "Yes, I know about how difficult it can be to maintain a relationship when you're traveling. Willow's coming with me to LA for the weekend before we begin shooting again." He inched his fingers up Willow's thigh.

"I think it's important to be flexible like that, Willow," Remi said. "You're lucky your business allows it."

Willow shifted in her seat, covering his hand with hers. "To be honest, I'm pretty nervous about it. I mean, it's really only a twenty-four-hour visit. We're leaving tomorrow morning and I have to come back Sunday, but before the other night, I'd never even been on a plane."

Willow and Bridgette exchanged a glance that told Zane they'd discussed the trip in private, and Willow was more nervous than she'd let on.

Remi flipped her hair over her shoulder and leaned forward. "I'll give you lessons in LA life. It's not that hard to figure it out."

Willow smiled at Zane and moved her hand to his thigh, grazing her fingertips along the outline of his rising erection. "Hear that? It's not that *hard*."

Hell yes, he'd heard it. He spread two fingers out on her thigh, keeping track, and lifted his hips to show her just how *hard* she was making him. "Don't worry, babe. I'll do everything within my power to make you comfortable, no matter how hard things get."

Bridgette sighed. "I love how well you take care of her, Zane. But LA is really different. She might be a little overwhelmed."

The waitress came to take their orders, and they tabled their conversation while they looked over the menu. The tablecloth masked their naughty activities, but while Willow stopped stroking him, he brushed his fingers over her sex. She squeezed her thighs together, glaring at him, but he simply leaned closer and kissed her cheek.

He kept up his relentless tease as they ordered, though Willow's order came out in breathless spurts.

After ordering, Remi said, "Back to the lessons. First of all, if you see a woman smile and her face moves, she's not a native. Everyone uses Botox. Guys and girls. I swear, it's the land of eternal youth."

Everyone laughed except Zane. Willow had gotten in on the challenge again, bringing him to a full salute beneath the table. In an effort to keep from groaning aloud, he stopped teasing her long enough to trap her hand against his thigh and pull himself together. She giggled and sipped her wine with a gratified expression.

"It's not that bad," Aiden interjected. "My sister likes to exaggerate because she prefers the quiet life of Cape Cod and holing up in her cabin outside New York City. But you should probably get used to juicing instead of eating your vegetables."

"Willow, remember when we tried that juicing diet?" Bridgette said animatedly. "After, I swear, no more than two hours, Willow said it was torture. Just too *hard*. That nobody in their right mind should ever give up sweets, and then she made, and consumed, a tub of custard."

Zane pressed a third finger to Willow's thigh, earning a challenging, sexy smile from his girl.

"I readily admit it." Willow eyed Zane. "I have a thing for *creamy* treats."

He was going to be sporting wood all night if she kept this up.

"Are we going to tell tales?" Aiden shifted a mischievous look to Remi. "Because I know a certain girl who once snuck downstairs at midnight and ate half the birthday cake I had special ordered for her seventh birthday taking place the next day."

Remi waved her hand. "Guilty as charged." She laughed and pointed at Aiden. "But how about the first time we went house hunting in Los Angeles? You found that coffee shop, the one that's no longer there, and every flipping day we had to go there. *Three* times a day, regardless of how far it was from wherever we were. He was obsessed."

Aiden winked at Bridgette. "No shame in obsessing over fine coffee or beautiful things."

"I love good coffee," Bridgette said a little breathlessly.

"I think Aiden drank it all, and that's why they had to close. Of course, when it came to *him* wanting coffee, we drove across town to get it, but when I was alone, he insisted on hiring a driver for me because it would be too hard for me to get through the crazy traffic." She sighed and patted Aiden's shoulder. "He was right. I *hate* driving in LA."

Willow arched a brow, and Zane tallied up another finger.

"I guess we're spoiled because Sweetwater is so small and we can walk almost everywhere," Bridgette added. "Where do you live, Aiden? In LA?"

"I own several homes, but there's no place I'd call *home*. For me, wherever family is becomes home for however long I can make it work with my schedule. Which means when Remi's filming, I try to show up wherever she is. And if she's between films, I try to spend time wherever she is."

"I love that you two are so close." Bridgette's gaze warmed. "But you don't have any extended family?"

"No," Aiden said, shifting a supportive smile to Remi. "We lost our parents a long time ago. There's just us."

The serious turn of the conversation brought Zane's mind out of the gutter. The family he counted on, the one he cherished and would do anything for, wasn't bound to him by blood. He turned his hand over beneath the table, lacing it with Willow's, and exchanged a thoughtful glance with Ben. He was thankful for their years of friendship and the family Ben had brought into his life. He leaned over and kissed Willow's cheek, thankful for her most of all.

"I'm sorry," Bridgette said to Aiden and Remi. "I know how hard loss can be."

Zane felt bad counting that particular *hard* toward his tally, but Willow leaned in closer and whispered, "Ten more."

*Game. On.*

DINNER WAS DELICIOUS and conversation came easily, or at least the parts of the conversation Willow could concentrate on. Zane's fingers had wreaked havoc with her mind. He'd teased her with a featherlight touch, just enough to make her greedy for more. She'd been so focused on him, she'd barely eaten a thing. But she'd heard every single *hard* that came out of anyone's mouth. She couldn't believe how many times the word had come up in normal conversation. Of course, Zane had practically made it a mandatory topic of conversation. *Aiden, do you prefer hard or soft cheese? Soft serve or hard? I'm a soft-serve guy. Nothing beats licking the creamy goodness from, well, just about anything.* By the time they finished dinner, the word *hard* had been said eleven times. *Eleven!* Not that keeping her promise was a hardship, but still, she'd thought it would be more difficult to reach fifteen than he'd made it seem. Then again, she should know better than to underestimate Zane when sex was on the line. The man was insatiable. And she frigging loved it.

Ben rose beside Remi and held out his hand. "Care to show me how to dance?"

"Careful, Remi," Bridgette warned. "He has two left feet."

"And I'm not afraid to use them," Ben said as Remi accepted his offer.

"I haven't danced in ages," Aiden said. "Bridgette? What do you say?"

Bridgette glanced nervously at Willow.

Willow knew her sister wanted to be saved from having to dance, but she *really* wanted Bridgette to break out of her shell, and Aiden was not only hot, but he'd been flirting with Bridgette all night. Surely any man who'd raised his sister wouldn't have issues with Bridgette being a single parent. But Willow knew there was a problem, and she had to wonder if Bridgette saw it, too. Aiden was *too* good. Too perfect and proper. He'd stifle the side of Bridgette that Willow, and everyone who knew her sister, wanted to revive. But Willow still thought a dance would do her sister some good. Maybe even make her want to do it more often.

She'd catch hell for it later, but instead of saving Bridgette, she said, "She hasn't danced in a long time. But she was one of the best dancers around before she had Louie. Nothing could keep her off the dance floor."

Willow quickly turned away from Bridgette's glare and said, "Dance with me, Z?"

He rose to his feet and guided her to the dance floor, whispering in a voice as hot as liquid fire, "I'd say I'm *up* for anything."

When he drew her into his arms, dancing slowly despite the quickening beat, her pulse was as erratic as a summer storm. His hand slid to the base of her spine, and he touched his cheek to hers. Every time he did that, it stole a little of her anxiety but amped up her anticipation. She loved when he whispered dirty things to her at the most unexpected times as much as she loved his tender and loving side. Now his warm breath slid over her skin, but no words came. She ached for his words as much as she longed for his touch. Was that crazy? Was she hopelessly in love with him or *hopefully* in love? She closed her eyes, fighting her overthinking mind, and settled in against him.

"Sweet girl," he finally whispered, bringing her eyes open. "That was a cruel thing to make me think of you bare beneath this dress." He kissed the tender skin beside her ear. "Now all I can think about is slipping my fingers inside you and teasing you nice and slow until you're so swollen and wet you can't sit still."

"Z," she said breathlessly, feeling herself go damp.

He moved his fingers along the dip at the base of her spine, holding her tight against his arousal. "Feel what you do to me, baby. I'm enjoying our dinner, but I can think of something else I'd rather feast on. So how about we change the rules?"

She opened her mouth to answer, but he trailed kisses down her neck, and everything other than his hot, sensual mouth faded to black.

He brushed his lips over hers and said, "If they say *hard* four more times, I'll be your sex slave, baby. Anything you want, for as long as you want, any*where* that you want."

Desire sizzled low in her belly. She lifted her gaze, riveted by the mix of hunger and love in his. Tightening her hold on his shirt to combat her weakening knees, she said, "Hard, hard, hard, *hard*."

# CHAPTER TWENTY-TWO

PASSION POUNDED THROUGH Zane's veins as he took Willow's hand, apologized to the others about suddenly feeling ill, and quickly paid the bill—leaving an exorbitant tip, along with an extra two hundred bucks in case they wanted dessert and more drinks. Hell, he'd have paid thousands to get out of there without any questions. He was pretty sure Ben didn't buy his too-ill-to-stick-around act, but he didn't care. He had tunnel vision. Willow had taunted him all evening with seductive looks and tempting brushes of her leg, her fingers, her gaze, until he felt imprisoned by a web of arousal.

Every step toward her car was a test of control. When they reached the dark, deserted corner of the lot where he'd parked, he took her in his arms and finally—*finally*—kissed her as he'd been dying to do all evening. His mouth moved over hers, devouring its softness with urgency. He tried to throttle the dizzying current racing through him, but when his hand touched her thigh and she rocked against him, he couldn't hold back. He'd waited all night to feel her, and he pushed both hands beneath her dress, filling his palms with her exquisite ass. His breath sailed from his lungs in a sigh of sweet relief, like a drowning man getting a foothold on dry land.

He kissed her again, stumbling to the far side of the car without breaking their connection and trapping her between the cold metal and his hard body. He ground against her, pushing his fingers between her legs from behind, teasing her slick heat. She moaned into the kiss, moving her hips and widening her stance to allow him better access.

"Need you, baby," he said between kisses.

"Take me."

Keeping hold of her with one hand, he moved his other to the front, thrusting into her velvety heat and earning a sweet, sexy sound. She palmed him through his pants, stroking him to the same rhythm as he moved over the secret spot that drew a delicious whimper from her lips. He swallowed the sinful sound as she continued stroking him and driving him out of his mind with every tight stroke of her hand.

"I need more," she pleaded.

A quick sweep of the lot assured him they were out of eyesight, and he dropped to his knees and ran his hands up her thighs, kissing them as she tangled her fingers in his hair. She spread her legs wider, the scent of her arousal drawing him in, but even though they were alone, shielded from anyone who might come or go from the restaurant, he loved her too much to take her here. He touched his lips to the tender skin below her belly button and rose to his feet, lowering her dress.

"Not here, baby. I don't want to chance anyone seeing us."

"Take me to the bridge," she whispered.

"The bridge?" The covered bridge was about a mile from Tasker's Chance and had been known as Make-Out Point when they were in high school.

"Yeah." She pointed to his mouth. "You have lipstick all over your face."

He wiped his face on his sleeve, and she took his face in her hands and kissed him.

"Come on, big boy."

Ten minutes later they parked just beyond the covered bridge, which offered an even more majestic view of the town than the restaurant had. He reached over and brought her hand to his lips, pressing a kiss to it.

"Why are we here, baby?"

"Because I've never been here with a guy, and you were my first, so I wanted to experience this with you as my first, too. Nobody comes here anymore. It's all ours." She took off her heels, opened the glove box, and popped the hood. With a coy smile, she stepped out of the car.

He followed her to the front of the car. She lifted the hood, and he was astounded to see the blue-and-green blanket they'd made love on all those years ago. She rubbed her shoulder against his before grabbing it and closing the hood.

"You've kept it all this time?" As he helped her spread out the blanket, memories rushed in—the scratch of the blanket on his knees rivaling the softness of Willow's nubile body. The worry about the abrasions it might leave on her back. The fear of coming too soon, or too hard, or saying the wrong thing.

"I took it with me when I went away to college," Willow answered. "It's been with me ever since."

"Baby . . ." He grasped for words, but how could he put into words emotions that felt like they were expanding too big for his body? "We were so young. Everything was new and bigger than life. And it still feels that way." He reached for her hand. "You planned all of this? The dress, the tease, the blanket. Wills . . ."

She shook her head, and her hair tumbled forward, framing her beautiful face. "Not the *hard* part at the restaurant," she said shyly. "But I had hoped to drive you crazy enough that you'd want me by the time we came here."

He laughed. "That I'd *want* you? Was there even a question?"

"Well, you're not very sexual, so . . ." She hooked her finger into the waist of his pants and tugged open the button, slowly working his zipper. "Sometimes a girl has to . . ." She struggled to tug his pants down his hips. "Go the"—*tug, tug*—"extra mile."

"Is that so? I only want you every minute of every day." He gathered her against him. "Baby, the minute you said you'd help me with this crazy scheme, you went the extra mile. And in doing so, you unlocked my heart and claimed the part of me you've always owned."

The emotions in her eyes rivaled those in his heart. She crossed her arms, gathering the hem of her dress in either hand, and drew it over her head. It floated down to the blanket like a whisper. They didn't speak, didn't reach for each other, as they undressed. Their love transcended words, and space, and time. Moonlight shimmered off her skin as they came together, and he lowered her to the blanket. He crushed his mouth to hers, driven by memories of the past and hopes of the future. There was no elegance to their lovemaking, no finesse or careful, tender moments. Raw, unbridled passion propelled them into fierce thrusts, clawing fingers, and moans of pleasure. And still it wasn't enough. He needed to see her, to be claimed *by* her.

Holding her tight, he rolled them over, giving her the reins. With the moon at her back, blond tendrils cascading over her flawless breasts and her sexy, full hips moving in time to his thrusts, she rode him hard, looking every bit a goddess. But to Zane, while she was stunning, her hair and physical attributes were like makeup for an actor. They were what everyone else saw, not what made her the woman he loved.

He saw her generous heart, which nearly bubbled out with every smile. He felt her tender and carnal touches, which burned him to his core. He saw treasured memories he'd held for so many years, he knew he'd take them to his grave and follow them up to heaven. When he saw her with Louie, he saw the mother she'd become, and one day, the old and gray doting grandmother she was destined to be.

She flattened her hands on his chest, moving along his shaft with a blissful look in her eyes—the deep pools of emotions that tore at him when they were apart, and drowned him when they were together.

He pulled her down on top of him, kissing her over and over again in a series of chaste, needy kisses, and rolled them over again.

She smiled up at him as he slowed them down.

"You love me," she said with such confidence it filled him with joy.

"Always have. You're my best friend, Wills. My frosting queen." He laced their hands together and lowered himself over her.

"I know. I mean, I really believe it all the way to my bones." She drew in a ragged breath and turned her face, pressing her lips to their joined hands before meeting his gaze again. "This is our new moment, Z. Our *forever* moment."

# CHAPTER TWENTY-THREE

THE FLIGHT TO California in Zane's private plane was long but enjoyable and made even more pleasurable when they joined the mile-high club. Unfortunately, as exciting as it was, it was hardly something Willow could brag about. Which was a shame, because it was hilarious, exhilarating, and naughty. A driver picked them up from the airport in a black sedan, and she snuggled up to Zane in the backseat. A long while later, the driver pulled through a private gate and onto a long, bamboo-shielded driveway. Tall trees and wide bushes lined the pavement all the way up to the house, which was completely secluded from the road. The first thing Willow noticed was how unremarkable the ranch-style bungalow was. It looked like the kind of house the Brady Bunch might have lived in if their family had been smaller.

"Welcome to my world, sweetheart." Zane helped her from the car and kissed her cheek.

While the driver brought their bags to the door, she took a good look around his cozy little oasis. Even after Patch had told her Zane lived modestly, she'd still envisioned something more glamorous than the small, single-story home nestled among a veritable forest. And now that she was taking a closer look at the two-car garage and slate walkway leading to an arched front door, it reminded her of something else. *Sweetwater.* The foliage was different, with leafy palms and bamboo instead of the indigenous trees of Upstate New York, but it definitely felt familiar.

Zane took her hand, and a flicker of nervousness danced in his eyes. She found it endearing, like everything else about him.

"It's not very exciting."

"Actually, I really like it," she said as he pushed open the door.

Honey-toned wood floors spilled into an open living room with three sets of glass doors leading out to a deck and a pool. The walls were white with stained wood trim, giving the moderate-size room a spacious feel. A fireplace was built into the far wall, and its bricks were also painted white. A quaint kitchen was tucked into a nook to their left, with butcher-block and stainless-steel countertops. *Perfect for baking.* The vintage stove was reminiscent of her own.

Zane carried their bags in and closed the door behind them. "Go on, Wills. Take a look around."

It felt strange to walk into his house after they'd spent so much time in her apartment, which felt like his home as much as hers. She stopped walking, struck by the distance that would soon divide them. *What will it feel like going home without you? Sleeping without you? Waking up without you?*

A knot rose in her throat, and she worked hard to swallow past it. They had less than twenty-four hours together, and she wasn't about to waste any of it being sad. There would be enough time for that on the long plane trip home tomorrow. *And in the coming weeks.*

She ran her fingers along the back of the deep-cushioned sofa, wanting to flop down on it with Zane, wrap herself up in his arms, and not think about this time tomorrow, when they'd be apart. Her eyes were drawn to pictures hanging on the wall. Five pictures from their childhood. She moved closer, and the knot returned to her throat. The first picture had been taken on the island. She and Bridgette lay on beach towels in the sand, Bridgette in a pink bikini, Willow in a blue one-piece bathing suit. Willow lay on her stomach, her hands folded beneath her chin, smiling and watching Talia and Ben splashing in the water. Bridgette lay on her back sunbathing, her eyes closed. Piper's backpack sat discarded on a towel. She was probably in the woods. Willow remembered that summer. She'd been sixteen, and she'd had a major crush on Zane.

She glanced at him now, and he lifted a shoulder, crossing the room toward her as she looked over the next picture. Zane sat beside Ben on the top of the picnic table in her parents' backyard. He was gazing across the lawn at Willow with a faraway look in his eyes. She sat cross-legged, reading on a blanket in the grass. Her hair was a tangled mess, with leaves sticking out of it. She remembered that afternoon. Ben and Zane had raked the yard for her parents, and she'd jumped into every leaf pile, which had started a leaf war. She laughed softly at the memory.

"Who took this picture?" she asked.

"I took the first one, but I don't know who took the rest. When I came back one Christmas a few years ago, your mom was going through pictures, and I asked her for a few of them."

"She never told me." She glanced up at the third picture, of Zane and her father on her father's boat. Her father had a prideful look in his eyes, his arm draped around Zane's shoulder. Zane's head was tipped back, caught laughing. "I love this one."

She moved to the next picture, of him and Ben wearing their football uniforms. They were arm in arm, grinning like fools. The lights of the football field lit up like diamonds against the night sky behind them. Zane's face still held the softness of youth, not yet blessed with ever-present scruff or sharp edges, but his eyes were as focused and determined as ever.

"No wonder I chose you." She slipped her finger into his pocket. "You were hot."

He laughed. "I weighed, like, a buck thirty. I was a wiry kid."

"Hardly." She took a step up to look at the last picture, and her heart tumbled in her chest. The two of them were studying at her parents' kitchen table. Willow was pointing to something in the text-book, and he was leaning over, cheek to palm, gazing up at her with a vacant look in his eyes.

"Told you so," he said. "I have no idea how I passed math, because I was totally into you."

"Osmosis?" she teased.

He retrieved the suitcases, and she followed him into the master bedroom, taking in the king-size bed with a masculine, navy-blue comforter, a leather recliner beneath a lamp in the corner, and a single long dresser.

He set their bags beside the bed and picked up a photograph from the nightstand, running his fingers over the picture as he came to her side. "This is my favorite picture. The one Patch told you about."

She took it from his hands and sank down to the mattress, the significance of the image clinging to her like a second skin. Her back was to the camera, her head bent forward, the red rose he'd given her that night—*their night*—barely visible in her hand. She sat on the green-and-blue blanket.

Zane sat beside her on the bed, their shoulders touching, his familiar scent lulling her toward him.

"You took this that night?" She met his eyes and was bowled over by the emotions in them.

"Yes. Are you mad?"

"I might have been back then, but not now. I . . . That's a nice memory."

"Thank God. I wasn't sure if you'd be pissed off." He put his arm around her. "I followed you home that night."

"You did? After I told you to let me be so I could process what we'd done? That was rude." She smiled and added, "And pretty romantic."

"What did you expect? You don't have sex for the first time and just walk away, no matter what rules you thought up. I'd broken your other rules. I *felt* even though you said no feelings. Who am I kidding? I *fell*.

*Hard.* I looked at you differently even though you said not to. You can't control everything, sweet girl." He took the picture from her hands and set it back on the nightstand.

"I followed you home to make sure you got there safely and because I still couldn't believe you'd chosen me. Of all the guys in Sweetwater, I was the lucky one. That night, as I followed you home, all I could think about was that one day you'd realize your rules were stupid and that we should be together. And you did, so let's enjoy it."

He pushed to his feet, and she happily took his hand, following him into the living room.

"So you moved all this way, but you kept Sweetwater alive. It's in the pictures, in this *house.* I had the complete wrong impression of you."

"No, Wills. You didn't. I wasn't a saint just because I didn't bring women here. I had my fair share of meaningless hookups."

She rolled her eyes. "I didn't mean that, but thanks for that visual. Geez, Z. Just what I needed."

He hugged her. "No lies, remember? Yes, I couldn't wait to leave Sweetwater. I didn't want to end up like my parents, living an unful-filling life, paycheck to paycheck. But I didn't want to leave *all* of Sweetwater behind. That's where you were. That's where Ben was. It's where my *life* was." He kissed her softly. "I left a piece of my heart by the creek all those years ago. Did you really think I'd never come back to get it?"

"Yes," she said honestly. "But I'm glad we both finally came to our senses."

ZANE AND WILLOW decided to forgo the crowded tourist hot spots and hit the Hollywood Hills for a late-afternoon hike. A few fans stopped for selfies with Zane, and he dragged Willow into them, which embarrassed her but thrilled him to no end. At least this way when they ended up on Instagram or Twitter, none of the fans could say they were out with him and make up nonsense stories. Being back in Sweetwater had reminded him what it was like to have a normal life, and even after being interrupted by only a few well-meaning fans today, he missed it. *Terribly.*

They made spaghetti for dinner, wanting to savor every minute they had together instead of wasting time waiting for a table in a restaurant only to be interrupted by more fans. After dinner they lay by the pool cuddled up on a lounge chair, making wishes on stars. *I hope you don't blow your scenes as you finish filming. I hope you don't burn your next wedding cake.* They were careful not to mention their upcoming time apart. But now, as he lay with Willow sleeping soundly in his arms, in a room that no longer felt like home, as dawn crept over the hills, their time apart was *all* he could think about.

He'd arranged a surprise for her back in Sweetwater, and he wished he could be there to see her face when she saw it. She'd be pissed at first, because in her eyes the things he did were too big, but his girl deserved everything she ever wanted. And he was going to be the man to give it to her.

Willow stirred. "Hi," she said groggily. Her hair was a tangled mess from his greedy hands, she had sheet prints on her cheek and a little razor burn beside her mouth from their fervent kisses, and she was *still* the most beautiful woman he'd ever seen.

"Did I wake you?"

"Mm-mm." She stretched and glanced at the clock. "Do I really have to leave in three hours?"

He moved over her, kissing her neck and shoulder. Her skin was warm and inviting. "You can stay with me."

She wound her arms around his neck, cradling his hips between her thighs. "I wish I could, but I have a bridal shower to cater Wednesday, and I have to go back and fight with my distributor about getting a new oven."

"What about a man to take care of?"

"I thought you'd be upset if I had a man in Sweetwater and you here."

"You wicked little vamp." He kissed her as she laughed.

"Two weeks ago we thought we'd be staging a breakup." She grabbed his face, grinning from ear to ear. "Now you're stuck with me."

"Just the way I like it."

He slid his hands beneath her butt, angling her hips up as their bodies came together. Fire radiated from his core, thrummed through his limbs.

"Love me, Z—"

He covered her mouth with his and loved her until sunlight snuck in through the curtains, warming their tangled legs. And then he loved her again—in bed, in the shower, and he tried to tackle her for a quickie while she dressed, but she threatened his manhood.

On the way to the airport they stopped at Claude's Café, located around the corner from Zane's house. It was just about the only place he could go without being hassled by tourists. It was more of a dive than a café, with concrete walls and hand-painted signs. Refurbished stools, large black-and-white floor tiles, and an old-fashioned Formica countertop with metal edging rounded out the eclectic café.

"Dude." Claude Bouche lifted his chin in greeting. His beanie hung halfway off his head, and sprigs of thick dark curls peeked out from beneath the edges. "Good to see you again." He gave Willow a blatant, and approving, once-over. "How's it goin', beautiful?"

"Watch it, Claude." Zane wrapped his arms around Willow from behind. "I'm going to marry this girl one day." His phone vibrated, and she wiggled out of his arms and ordered her coffee.

He read the text from his public relations rep with confusion and navigated to the links she'd sent. Anger burned in his gut as pictures of Willow sprawled out on a bed flashed before his eyes on one gossip site after another. It had to be a hoax. He was going to slaughter whoever was responsible for this shit.

"Wills," he said, mentally gearing up to fight the attack head-on. "You've never had nearly naked pictures of yourself taken, have you?" He showed her the phone. "Some asshole's trying to pretend they've got racy pictures of you."

The blood drained from her face.

"Wills?"

She stormed out of the café and headed straight for the car. *"Oh my God, oh my God, oh my God."*

"Talk to me, Willow. What's going on? Did you have these taken?"

"Yes! I had them taken for *you.*"

He froze. "For me?"

She climbed into the car and stared out the window, refusing to speak another word.

He wished he'd called his driver. The goddamn traffic was relentless, and he needed to hold her and get to the bottom of this mess. He'd been giving her time to calm down, but as they neared the airport, he couldn't take the silence any longer.

"I don't understand. You had these pictures taken for *me?*"

"Yes! What don't you understand?" Tears tumbled down her cheeks. "I was eighteen and beyond stupid. I thought I could win you over by sending you sexy pictures, and then you stopped texting and I never went to pick them up. That seems like a hundred years ago. I don't know why they're all over the Internet now or how they got there. All I know is that every time I leave Sweetwater my life falls apart."

The knowledge annihilated him. Between the hurt in her eyes, in her voice, her words, and the anger in his gut, he could barely breathe. His sweet, trusting girl, who had always hated people looking at her breasts, had taken boudoir pictures for *him?* He ground his teeth against the stream of curses vying for release and reached for her hand.

She swatted it away, turning her whole body toward the door.

"Wills, I . . . *Jesus.*" No apology was big enough for what had happened all those years ago, so he focused on the only thing he could do. "The goddamn photographer must have leaked the pictures. I'll tear him apart limb by limb. I'll sue the bastard until he hasn't got a penny to his name."

"Ohmygod," she said under her breath. "You can't fix this with money."

"Like hell I can't."

She gave him a tearful, disbelieving stare. "People can't *unsee* those pictures, Zane. Maybe you're used to this kind of thing, but I'm not, and I don't want it in my life. I can't take it."

"Baby, this will blow over. You'll see. As soon as another story hits, this will be—"

"*Blow over?*" She scoffed, staring out the window again, arms crossed, as painful as a barbed-wire barrier between them that he wanted to tear the fuck down. "*Everyone* will see those pictures if they haven't already. My parents, my customers . . ." Her jaw clenched. "I can't. I just can't."

"Willow—"

"Don't. Just . . . *don't.*"

He bit his tongue but didn't silence his mind. He was going to fix this, no matter what the cost.

When they finally reached the airport, he navigated to the private parking area by the airstrip, and Willow strode from the car before he even cut the engine. He grabbed her bags, flagged the pilot to load them onto the plane, and caught up to her.

"Willow, stop. Please, baby." He was not going to lose her over this. No frigging way.

She turned, eyes red and damp, her lower lip trembling, slicing even deeper as she continued storming across the tarmac toward the plane. "Don't, Zane. This is *my* fault." Her voice escalated again, and every word struck him like a bullet. "I made a horrible decision, and it's biting me in the ass. Now I have to go home and clean up my mess."

"This is *not* your fault. It's *mine*." He didn't mean to shout, but rage tore through him. "You took those pictures for *me*, remember? If you were dating some normal guy, you wouldn't be the target of every asshole that wants to make a buck. I'm going to fix this, Willow. I promise you I will. And I'm coming home with you."

"No. You're *not*." She stepped forward, fresh tears streaming down her cheeks, and astonishingly, a small smile lifted her lips and a tender tone followed. "I love you, and I know you want to swoop in and make those pictures disappear, but you *can't*. They're out there. *Forever.* You start filming at six tomorrow morning here in LA, and I am not going to let you screw that up because of something I did."

She wrapped her arms around his neck, and he held her tighter than he ever had, wishing he could wrap her up in a protective bubble and whisk her away from all of this. The press, the hurt, the embarrassment.

"Our lives are a world apart, and right now I have to go back to mine and you need to go back to yours. I love you," she whispered, and it caused his anger to swell and dampen his own damn eyes. "I'll call you when I've got things under control."

"Willow, I'm not letting you go."

She took a step away. "I know. You never will."

# CHAPTER TWENTY-FOUR

FOR THE SECOND time in as many weeks, entering Sweetwater failed to bring warmth and comfort to Willow. Only this time it wasn't just because she'd been lying to her family, which was weighing heavily on her, or because of the stupid pictures that would embarrass the people she loved most. No. This time was worse, because the leak of those racy pictures drove home what it really meant to be with Zane.

During the long plane trip, she'd come up with a plan to go straight to her parents' house and explain everything: the fake engagement, the pictures, and why she'd taken them. She was an adult. It wasn't like they'd shame her for what she'd done as a teenager. Her father would be disappointed, though, and her mother? Willow had no idea how her mother would react, but she was pretty sure she'd feel like she'd failed Willow in some way by not making it clear that she could have talked to her. Even though she had made it abundantly clear. As conservative as her father was, her mother had always been as open about sex and emotions as Willow and her sisters would allow her to be. But as an insecure teenager taking a bold step, Willow hadn't trusted anyone with her secret. Not even Bridgette.

Except Zane.

*I've always trusted you.*

Now, as she parked behind the bakery, she couldn't do it. She couldn't face her parents. Her heart was too broken, her emotions too raw. She went up to her apartment. Only the place where she and Zane had been so happy made her feel even emptier inside, and the tears she'd held in for more than seven hours came crashing down. She staggered to the bedroom and sank down to the bed. Her family would have to wait for an explanation until she wrapped her mind around the situation, and at the moment she wasn't even close. She grabbed the pillow Zane had slept with and curled up. This situation would *not* beat her. She would not let it change the confident woman she'd worked so hard to become. She would rise above this the same way she'd risen above her heartbreak all those years ago. This time she wasn't in it alone, though it was her choice to handle it by herself.

But the rest?

Trying to figure out how to navigate this new world with Zane?

That was like making what should be a perfect cake and taking it out of the oven too early—over and over again. For that she needed strength, and she was too emotionally drained and pissed off to think straight. She closed her eyes, clutching the pillow to her chest. His scent suffused with her tears, and the next thing she knew she was waking up and it was dark outside.

She sat up, disoriented, and checked the time on her phone. It was after seven o'clock, and she'd missed three calls from Zane and two from her mother. She needed to call them both, but first she needed sustenance. After washing her face, she went down to the bakery, moving robotically through the dark kitchen, and made a beeline for the freezer. She was pretty good at baking only what would sell each day, but Friday she'd had three leftover cupcakes, and now she wondered if the cupcake gods had been in on this cruel joke.

She set them on the counter, but even the thought of eating turned her stomach. There were too many lies rotting inside her. She hopped up on the counter beside the box of cupcakes, remembering when Zane had lifted her onto the counter.

*How can I do it, Z? Your life is too exposed for me.*

She couldn't bring herself to let him go. She didn't want to, no matter how hard things got.

She called her mother, closing her eyes in preparation.

"Willow? Honey, are you okay?"

She opened her eyes, noticing for the first time the shiny new oven across the room. She pushed from the counter, dumbfounded.

"Honey. Where are you?" her mother asked. "I'm coming to get you."

"No," she said quickly, kneeling to touch the pristine oven. "I'm okay, but . . ." *I'm not okay.* Zane had the oven put in. He had to. But how?

"Honey, we saw the pictures, and I know you're not okay. I hear it in your voice. Talk to me, sweetie."

*You saw the pictures?* Somewhere in the back of her mind, she'd hoped they hadn't seen them. Snapping out of her shock, she turned away from the oven and focused on the more important issue. "I'm sorry for embarrassing you and Dad." She told her mother why she'd had the pictures taken. Her mother listened in silence, allowing her to confess how hard she'd fallen for Zane that long-ago summer and how the guy she'd brought home from college that Christmas was just to make it *appear* as if she'd moved on, when in reality it had taken more than a decade. The only cure for true love was more of the person she loved.

"I'm sorry for lying to you, Mom, but I'm not sorry for what I did. I'm glad Zane was my first."

"You don't need to be sorry for any of it. Your body, your decision. I've always told you that. But I'm sad that you thought you had to go through it alone. You're not the only Dalton child to have their heart broken or to do something embarrassing. It's like a rite of passage in our family."

Willow didn't believe that. She couldn't even imagine Talia doing anything embarrassing, much less getting her heart broken. "Thanks for understanding, but I am sorry about the pictures. Daddy must be livid."

"No, honey. He's confused, as is the entire family. But once you explain it to them, you know they'll be there for you. But you might want to leave out the part about Zane being your first. Maybe you can just tell them you had a major crush on him."

Tears of relief for her mother's unconditional love slid down her cheeks.

"There's more, Mom, and I'm not sure anyone will forgive me for this part." Willow drew in another deep breath, chasing the calm she wondered if she'd ever catch up to again. "I've been lying to you about the engagement. It was a hoax to help Zane with his reputation, but then we fell in love. I'm sorry. But there is no engagement."

Her mother was silent for so long Willow worried she'd lost the connection. She grabbed the box of cupcakes and headed out back. "Mom?" She locked the bakery door and headed for Chloe.

"We know."

Willow stopped in her tracks. "You *know*?"

"Zane came over to talk to us Wednesday evening, and he explained the whole situation. That lie, Willow? That lie hurt. You're not a kid anymore. You should be able to trust family above all else."

Willow leaned against Chloe, feeling dizzy. *He told you everything. To protect me.* "I know. I'm sorry."

"We understand why you both did it, and Zane took all the blame. But you and I both know we make our own choices, and I hope in the future you'll know that we'd never betray you in any way." Her mother paused, and it was all Willow could do to remain erect on buckling knees. "And, honey, that man loves you to the ends of the earth. He said that even if we never forgave him, he couldn't bear it if he'd hurt your relationship with us. He's a good man, Willow, and I know you're devastated about these pictures. But your eighteen-year-old heart knew what it wanted, and that girl would stop at nothing to get it."

That wasn't true, but now wasn't the time to go into that with her mother. She'd never picked up the pictures, which meant she'd stopped at her broken heart. But her broken heart hadn't been too shattered to continue loving Zane. She had just buried that love deep enough to survive without him.

*But there is no burying a love too big to contain.*

"And now the photographer has sold them, or leaked them, and everyone I know and love will see them if they haven't already." Willow gripped the phone tighter.

"That's true, sweetheart, and as embarrassing as that is for you," her mother said empathetically, "just remember why you had them taken in the first place, baby girl. I think that's where your strength will come from."

IT WAS AFTER eleven o'clock when Zane finally pulled into Sweetwater. It had been hell not following Willow onto the plane, and refraining from calling her family had been equally difficult. He'd have given anything to know she was okay, but she'd wanted to talk with them herself, and he knew she'd slaughter him if he got in her way. He drove through the dark, deserted streets straight to her apartment, but Chloe wasn't parked out back. Mentally ticking off the places she might be, he drove to each of her siblings' houses and down to Dutch's Pub, but Chloe was nowhere in sight. He headed for her parents' house, and as he approached their street, he knew . . .

He parked on the side of the road and made his way through the woods, which reminded him of the last time he'd taken that walk. His pulse raced as hard as it had back then. Leaves crunched beneath his feet. The scents of pine and damp earth infiltrated his lungs as he neared the creek. He stopped at the edge of the forest, his heart swelling at the sight of Willow sitting on the green-and-blue blanket down by the water. He remembered afterward, how his hands had sweated at the thought that he'd have to act like they'd never made love. He could still recall her trusting green eyes blinking up at him and her sweet voice, pleading and commanding at once. *Zane. I need you to do me a favor. It has to be you.*

Pushing those memories aside was difficult, because he wanted to revel in them, to relive every second of their pre-sex discussion, and every breath they took until the moment he'd stood in this very same spot. But now wasn't the time to reminisce. He needed to have her in his arms again, or his heart might leap from his chest and scurry across the ground all by itself.

He pulled his phone from his pocket and stepped into the clearing. She turned with a worried look in her eyes, and relief swept over her features. Her lips curved up, and just as quickly, she pressed them together as he knelt beside her.

"Hi." His emotions were so raw it was hard to push the words out. Her hair hung loose, blocking his view of her eyes.

"Hey. Sorry I haven't called," she said softly. "I couldn't. I . . ." She looked out over the creek, and he couldn't resist tucking her hair behind her ear so he could see her face.

"I know, babe. It's okay." He pushed the "Home" button on his phone, navigated to TMZ's website, and handed her the phone. "Have you seen this?"

She pushed it away. "I don't want to see any more of those pictures. Wait. Why are you here? You're supposed to start filming in a few hours."

"I made a deal with Steve. He gave me forty-eight hours to win you back, and in exchange I gave him the rights to direct my screenplay."

Tears spilled down her cheeks. "You . . ."

"I'll produce it, but I wouldn't care if I didn't. I'd have come if he fired me. Wills. Do you trust me?"

Her eyes dampened as she nodded.

He placed the phone in her hand, curling her fingers around it. "Then look, please."

Her gaze dropped to the phone, and she opened her fingers, leaning closer to get a better look. "What have you done?" She scrolled through the Austin Powers–slash–boudoir-style pictures of Zane sprawled across a bed, leaning against a pole, and a handful of other ridiculous shots.

He shrugged. "Pulled a few strings."

Her smile reached her eyes as she took in a picture of Zane lying on his stomach on red silk sheets. His chin was propped up with one hand, his other hand resting on his hip. His knees were bent, red stiletto–clad feet pointed upward, and his eyes were heavily lined, giving the camera a sultry look. "Zane, you look ridiculous and surprisingly *hot*. But pink panties? High heels? The caption says you've secretly been cross-dressing for years. You're insane. Why would you do this?"

Wasn't it obvious? "Nobody's talking about your pictures anymore. Mine have taken over the spotlight."

"But your reputation? A *cross-dresser*?"

"How do you know I don't secretly love high heels?"

She laughed. "This is crazy, and thoughtful, but it doesn't change the fact that millions of people have seen my body in risqué pictures that were meant only for you."

"I can't change that, but you weren't naked. Panties and a bra cover a lot." He reached over and scrolled to a picture of him wearing panties and a bra, leaning on a light post. "See?"

She laughed again. "You're ridiculous. I can't believe you did this."

"Then be ridiculous with me, baby. I love you. I'm sorry this happened, but it really *will* blow over."

She sighed heavily, and he set the phone on the blanket and took her hand in his.

"Z, your reputation? The movie?"

"I don't care about my rep or if anyone buys me as a romantic hero, because the only person who needs to believe in me is *you*. I love you, Wills. You love me. A few embarrassing pictures can never change that. Nothing can."

"But I can't live like this. I can't be worried that my every move will be captured on film, or that skeletons will come out of my closet."

He arched a brow. "Are there more I should know about?"

She rolled her eyes, and he had no intention of telling her how much he'd secretly come to love her eye rolls. They were very *Willow*.

"No," she answered. "But you know what I mean."

"I do. You don't want to be in the spotlight. I get that. I'm sick of it, too. But even if I get out of acting, there will always be some adoring fans who want an autograph or a photographer who catches us sunbathing and snaps a shot. I can't make it all go away, but I can try to protect you from it."

Her eyes warmed. "I know you'll try."

"Then marry me, baby. Be ridiculous with me and loving and sexy and happy and sad and angry. Let me try to protect you from the craziness of it all. We've come so far. Don't let anyone or anything steal our future. I don't want to take another step without you."

"Z," she whispered, and the struggle in her eyes told him how much she loved him regardless of whatever words followed. "Our lives are so far apart."

"No, baby. They *were* so far apart. I'm done in front of the camera. I'm over action movies, and I can't pretend to be a romantic hero when the only person I want to romance is you. I love you with every ounce of my soul, Wills. You're my other half. My best friend. You're my everything, baby."

"I love you, too." A tear slid down her cheek. "But I'm not as strong as you. I can't live in LA. I can't leave everyone I know and love."

"I know. That's why I told your parents I'd buy the Grand Lady as soon as they find a place to live."

Her hand flew to her mouth. "You . . ." More tears tumbled down her cheeks.

"You're *home* to me, Wills. If you can't live in LA, neither can I."

"But your career?"

"We'll figure it all out together. But I promise you I will never ask you to move away from Sweetwater." He took her left hand in his. "What do you say, Wills? You and me forever, and maybe someday we'll have little sugar-addicted babies with cocky attitudes and stubborn streaks."

Nodding emphatically, she threw herself into his arms. "Yes. Yes, Z. I want all of that. Life with you, stubborn babies . . . but I can't be this selfish. If you need to be in LA, we'll figure out a way."

"Be selfish, sweetheart. Be as selfish as you'd like." In that moment, he knew that Willow's happiness had become his purpose.

He drew back and took her left hand in his, taking off the rented ring.

She tried to pull her hand free, but he held tight. "I said yes."

"You hate this ring. It's all wrong for you." He withdrew a blue velvet bag from his pocket and turned her hand palm up.

"The rented ring is for napoleons. It's overdone and gaudy. You're a *sticky bun*, baby. Sweet, savory, and so filling I only need one. You need a ring that's just as perfect for your busy flour-and-frosting-laden days as you are for me. I've spent this week trying to figure out what type of ring to give you."

"Week? You knew you were going to propose for a *week*?"

He nodded. "Since the night at the lake, when you knocked down my walls, jumped inside, and locked the gate behind you, then got scared and hid in the tower, leaving me to nearly lose my mind."

That earned him the sweetest, most genuine smile he'd ever seen.

"But every design I came up with paled in comparison to the one I had made for you with the money from my first acting job. The ring I had planned on giving you the Christmas after we'd first come together when we were mere babes in the woods."

"You were going to give me a ring?" Her breathing went shallow as she watched him empty the bag, and the braided white-gold ring with inlaid round-cut diamonds landed in her palm. "*Oh my goodness.* Z . . ."

"Read the inscription. The inscription is new."

She picked it up with trembling fingers, and he aimed the flashlight on his phone so she could read it, hearing the words in his head as she silently read them.

### WILLS, YOU ARE MY MOMENT. Z

She lifted damp and excruciatingly beautiful eyes to his. "You've always been my moment."

He slipped the ring on her finger. "No rules this time, baby, and no expectations beyond a loving future void of trickery."

Willow smiled. "And whipped cream. Don't forget the whipped cream. And frosting. I love frosting."

"Frosting." He pressed his lips to hers, feeling as though he could finally breathe.

"And dirty talk," she said as they lay down on the blanket. "I like when you talk dirty to me."

"I'll do anything you want me to. Now can I please kiss you?"

She pressed her hand to his chest. "Wait. You had a new oven installed at my bakery. I can't accept that, Zane. You can't keep doing *big* things like that."

He touched his forehead to hers, smiling at his stubborn beauty. "Wills, you know how you'll always love sweets?"

"Yes."

"I'll always do things big, baby. Especially for you. So if you can't live with that, please tell me now." He rocked his hips against her, and her eyes widened.

"Mm. I was wrong," she said as he kissed her neck. "I do like it when you do things *big*. In fact, I *love* big."

There beneath the summer moon, in the place where they had first come together, on the blanket that once held their young, nubile bodies, they made love until the dawn of the new day.

The dawn of their future.

# CHAPTER TWENTY-FIVE

"I DON'T NEED a party," Willow insisted as she closed out the register. "I know you guys want to do this, but an engagement party seems silly since we're getting married in three months. How about if we have joint bachelor and bachelorette parties?" It had been ten weeks since Willow and Zane had gotten engaged, and eight glorious weeks since Zane had come back to Sweetwater. Willow had never felt so complete in all her life, and she didn't need a party as confirmation. She thought her mother was going to hound her about it, but her mother had understood. It was her sisters who had arrived at the bakery fifteen minutes before closing time to hassle her for the umpteenth time.

Piper groaned. "Joint? Really?"

"I like that idea," Talia said. "It shows you're a strong, committed couple."

"I agree." Bridgette grabbed a rag and began wiping down the tables.

Piper set her hands on her hips. "The old Bridgette would have given you hell for not taking advantage of your one last opportunity to be a wild, crazy single woman."

"Actually," Bridgette said, "Willow *did* make me dance with Aiden, who was a magnificent specimen of a man. Perfect for *Talia*. So maybe we should have separate parties. With a *stripper*."

Willow laughed. "A stripper? You do know who I'm marrying, don't you? Zane would tear apart any man who tried to strip in front of me. But I do love that you're thinking along those lines. Maybe our risky sister isn't gone after all."

"Payback, baby," Bridgette said with a smirk.

"Hell no, she's not gone," Piper said. "She just needs the right man to bring her back to life."

"I still don't know what you didn't like about Aiden," Talia said. "Willow said he was gorgeous and successful, seemed well educated, and he was a proper gentleman."

"As she said, he was perfect for you, T," Piper said. "We like our men a little naughtier."

Talia closed her notebook and raised her brows. "It's the quiet ones who are usually the naughtiest."

Willow giggled. "Is that firsthand knowledge?"

"Um . . ." Talia's eyes darted away. "*No.* That's what everyone says, though."

"She's holding out on us, but she'll never give up details, so . . ." Piper peered into the bakery box on the counter. "Whose delicious-looking pastries are these? They should be mine."

"A customer called in the order." Willow organized the accoutrements behind the counter. "I didn't recognize the name. Booker, I think. They were supposed to be here half an hour ago. You guys, is it crazy that I'm nervous about signing the papers on Mom and Dad's house?" Their parents had received final approval on a smaller house, and tonight she and Zane were having dinner with them to sign the contract for the Grand Lady. Willow couldn't believe the house she had grown up in and adored was really going to be theirs.

"Perfectly normal, sis," Talia assured her.

"It's no different from when you bought this space for the bakery." Bridgette finished wiping down the tables and went to rinse out the sponge as Zane came through the door. "Except now you have a hunky *almost* husband to buy it with."

"I hope you're talking about me. There's my beautiful fiancée." Zane wrapped his arms around Willow and kissed her.

Piper tapped her chin with a teasing smile. "How does it feel to know you're not lying when you call her your fiancée?"

Willow's sisters and parents had been annoyed with them for lying about the engagement, but it had blown over quickly. In the end, they understood why she and Zane had done it, but that didn't stop Piper from razzing Zane every time she saw him.

Zane kissed Willow again. "It feels fantastic. How does it feel to know you're going to have a brother-in-law you can give shit to anytime you want?"

"Better than fantastic," Piper quipped.

"How did the call with Steve go?" Zane and Steve were working out the final details of their contract so they could move forward with funding and finding talent for his screenplay. She'd never seen Zane happier than he'd been these last few weeks. She'd like to believe it was one hundred percent due to their relationship, but she knew the movement on his script played an enormous part in his feeling of fulfillment.

"Great. We're Skyping tomorrow to nail down the last of the loose ends. Are you almost done here? Want me to help with anything? We're supposed to meet your parents in twenty minutes."

Zane was always willing to pitch in and help. He'd come down with her in the mornings and help her bake or work on his screenplay while she baked, but they'd end up making out and throw her entire morning off schedule so often she'd had to ask him to come down *after* customers began arriving. *Most of the time, anyway.*

"I've got the bakery under control."

"Speaking of the bakery." Piper pointed at the ceiling. "What are you going to do with your apartment after you move?"

"Aurelia is ninety-nine percent sure she wants to go in on combining the bakery and bookstore. If she agrees, and if we can swing it financially—"

"Which we can," Zane interrupted.

Willow poked him in the chest. "Stop. No *bigness* from you. Aurelia and I want to do this on our own."

Zane rolled his eyes, and Willow kissed him. "But I love your generosity."

He smacked her butt. "I'll keep my bigness to the bedroom."

"Hey! Sexpots!" Piper laughed. "Renovations?"

"Oh, right. Sorry. We're talking about building stairs that lead up to the second floor and making that into the bookstore, but lofting the ceiling so it doesn't feel like a separate store."

Piper looking up at the ceiling, her eyes narrow. "Hand me some paper and a pencil."

"Here she goes." Talia tore a piece of paper out of the notebook she was writing in and handed it to Piper, along with her pen. "I don't have a pencil."

"It's all good." Piper bent over the table and began sketching the renovations.

"Piper, we have to go meet Mom and Dad," Willow said. "Can we do this another time? We don't even know if it's happening yet."

"Sure." Piper hugged her. "Talia? Want to grab a bite at the café?"

Talia gathered her things. "Definitely. I'm starved. See you guys later."

"What about the party planning?" Bridgette asked.

"How about something small, Bridge?" Willow suggested. "Just family? At the house? Or maybe down at Harley's?"

"Okay. Let me think on it," Bridgette answered.

"What about Remi? You guys text all the time. And if it weren't for Patch, you wouldn't have come to the resort to meet me," Zane pointed out.

"And Aurelia," Piper added. "She'd be pissed if she wasn't invited. But you guys can figure that out. I'll see you tomorrow morning. Can you make whatever you made for that customer who didn't pick up their stuff? Those look amazing." She followed Talia out the door.

"Oh, shoot. Z, give me five minutes to wrap this up?" She picked up the bakery box as a tall, dark, handsome stranger walked into the shop, and Bridgette's jaw dropped open.

"Hi. I'm Bodhi Booker. I called in an order. Sorry I'm late. I got lost."

"Hi. I'm Willow. I'm glad you made it in."

Bridgette grabbed the box from Willow's hands. "I've got this. You can go."

"Thanks, Bridgette." Zane pulled Willow toward the door.

Bridgette waved her off and approached Bodhi with a wide smile. "Hi. Are you new in town?"

Willow glanced over her shoulder at the fire in her sister's eyes. Fire she hadn't seen in years. "Call me later," she called over her shoulder as they left the bakery. Once outside, Zane tucked her against his side. "Did you see what I just saw?"

"If you mean Bridgette drooling, yes. More importantly, are you ready to sign on the dotted line on our new home?"

"Yes." She looked at her gorgeous and oh-so-perfect engagement ring as they walked the few blocks to her parents' house. It was late summer. The air was warm and the sky clear. *Just like my heart.*

When they reached her parents' house, Zane wrapped her in his arms before they went inside. He'd changed in the past few months. His eyes were clearer, his smiles more genuine, and his touch—his sensual, loving touch—had the tenderness, and the roughness, of a man who knew his woman was really *his* and still treasured every second of their closeness as if it were a gift.

"I love you, Wills. And I can't wait to make our own memories, and raise our own family, in this house with you."

"I think we need to add extra locks to the windows and doors to keep our stubborn, sugar-addicted children from sneaking out to do dirty things."

He brushed his lips over hers and whispered, "And ruin all their fun?"

"You'd be okay with your teenage daughter sneaking out and having sex with a guy who can't wait to leave town?"

Zane's brows knitted. "Double locks. And a shotgun."

"Locks, yes. Gun?"

"How about we line the yard with those net traps that hang from trees? We can catch the bastard before he touches our little girl."

"What if it's a little girl coming to meet our son?"

"Well . . ." He smirked.

She swatted his arm, laughing. "You're impossible."

"And I'm all yours." He pressed his lips to hers. "What does that make you?"

"The luckiest girl in the world."

# A NOTE FROM MELISSA

I had so much fun watching Willow and Zane learn and grow and inevitably fall in love; they've climbed right to the top of my favorite couples list. I hope you love them as much as I do!

Each of Willow's siblings will be featured in their own books. Sign up for my newsletter to keep up-to-date with new Sugar Lake releases and to receive an exclusive short story (www.MelissaFoster.com/News).

If this is your first Melissa Foster book, you might enjoy my big-family romance collection Love in Bloom. Characters from each series make appearances in future books so you never miss an engagement, wedding, or birth. A complete list of all series titles is included at the start of this book.

Happy reading!

*Melissa Foster*

# ACKNOWLEDGMENTS

Writing a book is not a solo endeavor, and I am indebted to my fans, friends, and family, who inspire and support me on a daily basis. Please continue to keep in touch. You never know when you'll end up in one of my books, as several members of my fan club have already discovered (www.Facebook.com/groups/MelissaFosterFans).

If this is your first Melissa Foster book, you have many wickedly sexy and fiercely loyal heroes and sassy, empowered heroines to catch up on in my Love in Bloom big-family romance collection.

If you don't yet follow me on Facebook, please do! We have such fun chatting about our lovable heroes and sassy heroines, and I always try to keep fans abreast of what's going on in our fictional boyfriends' worlds (www.Facebook.com/MelissaFosterAuthor).

Remember to sign up for my newsletter to keep up-to-date with new releases and special promotions and events and to receive an exclusive short story (www.MelissaFoster.com/Newsletter).

For publication schedules, series checklists, and more, please visit the special reader goodies page that I've set up for you at www.MelissaFoster.com/Reader-Goodies.

A special thank-you to editor Maria Gomez and the incredible Montlake team for bringing Zane and Willow's story to life. As always, heaps of gratitude to my editorial team and, of course, to my main heartthrob, Les.

# ABOUT THE AUTHOR

*Photo © 2013 Melanie Anderson*

Melissa Foster is a *New York Times* and *USA Today* bestselling and award-winning author of more than sixty-five books. Her novels have been recommended by *USA Today*'s book blog, *Hagerstown* magazine, the *Patriot*, and more. She has also painted and donated several murals to the Hospital for Sick Children in Washington, DC.

She enjoys discussing her books with book clubs and reader groups, and she welcomes an invitation to your event. Visit Melissa on her website, www.MelissaFoster.com, or chat with her on Twitter @melissa_foster and on Facebook at www.facebook.com/MelissaFosterAuthor.